A PLUME BOOK

# JULIA'S CHILD

Michael Lake

SARAH PINNEO worked in finance for more than a decade before making the transition from breadwinner to bread baker. Her first book, *The Ski House Cookbook*, was published in 2007. Sarah writes about food and sustainability for lifestyle publications including the *Boston Globe Magazine* and *Edible Communities*.

# Julia's Child

*A Novel*

SARAH PINNEO

A PLUME BOOK

PLUME
Published by Penguin Group
Penguin Group (USA) Inc., 375 Hudson Street, New York, New York 10014, U.S.A. • Penguin Group (Canada), 90 Eglinton Avenue East, Suite 700, Toronto, Ontario, Canada M4P 2Y3 (a division of Pearson Penguin Canada Inc.) • Penguin Books Ltd., 80 Strand, London WC2R 0RL, England • Penguin Ireland, 25 St. Stephen's Green, Dublin 2, Ireland (a division of Penguin Books Ltd.) • Penguin Group (Australia), 250 Camberwell Road, Camberwell, Victoria 3124, Australia (a division of Pearson Australia Group Pty. Ltd.) • Penguin Books India Pvt. Ltd., 11 Community Centre, Panchsheel Park, New Delhi – 110 017, India • Penguin Books (NZ), 67 Apollo Drive, Rosedale, Auckland 0632, New Zealand (a division of Pearson New Zealand Ltd.) • Penguin Books (South Africa) (Pty.) Ltd., 24 Sturdee Avenue, Rosebank, Johannesburg 2196, South Africa

Penguin Books Ltd., Registered Offices: 80 Strand, London WC2R 0RL, England

First published by Plume, a member of Penguin Group (USA) Inc.

First Printing, February 2012
10 9 8 7 6 5 4 3 2 1



REGISTERED TRADEMARK—MARCA REGISTRADA

LIBRARY OF CONGRESS CATALOGING-IN-PUBLICATION DATA

Pinneo, Sarah.
Julia's child : a novel / Sarah Pinneo.
p. cm.
ISBN 978-0-452-29731-9
1. Businesswomen—Fiction. 2. Natural foods—Fiction. 3. Motherhood—Fiction. I. Title.

PS3616.I577J85 2012
813'.6—dc22

2011014815

Printed in the United States of America
Set in Horley Old Style



PUBLISHER'S NOTE
This is a work of fiction. Names, characters, places, and incidents are either the product of the author's imagination or are used fictitiously, and any resemblance to actual persons, living or dead, business establishments, events, or locales is entirely coincidental.

For Mike, who was there at its inception.
For Rosemary, who yelled "push,"
and for Mollie and Denise,
who helped to feed and change it.

# Julia's Child

# Chapter 1

Though I wasn't familiar with the neighborhood, St. Agatha's was easily found in the middle of a leafy Brooklyn street. With only a little hesitation, I grasped the ancient-looking brass knob and opened the door.

A half flight of stairs led downward, but on the third step my grip tightened on the banister. When I'd cold-called the chairwoman of the Park Slope Parenting Association to ask for the honor of addressing one of her Thursday coffee hours, I'd imagined a cozy handful of women chatting in the basement of the church.

Through the open doors I could see an impossibly large number of women and children. They knelt in groups on the carpet, baby blankets stretched between them, toddlers orbiting each cluster. An entire cavalcade of strollers was double- and triple-parked against one wall. It wasn't a coffee circle. It was a toddlerpalooza.

I turned and beat a hasty retreat to the safety of the sidewalk, groping with a clammy hand for the phone in my purse.

My only employee answered on the first ring. "Julia's Child makes the best toddler food in the world! This is Marta speaking. How may I assist you?"

"Marta? It's Julia."

"Julia, it's five minutes to four! Are you lost?"

"No, I found the church all right. I just . . ." I cleared my throat. It didn't seem possible that all those people had come to hear me speak. "Could you double-check the date and time?"

"Why? Isn't there anybody there?"

The sound of Marta's sensible voice made me feel more than a little ridiculous. "Well, sure, but . . ." I could hear her rustling around on my desk, looking for the note. Our office is so small that our two little metal desks practically touch each other.

"Four o'clock, September 5. So go in there, *chica*, and knock 'em dead. But listen, I'm going to have to turn on the voice mail and leave too."

"Why? Do you have to pick up Carlos?" One of Marta's very few flaws was her shaky access to reliable childcare. She occasionally ran short of help to watch her nine-year-old son after school.

"No. The Mobster called. Apparently there was a power outage sometime today, and when he got there this afternoon, the freezers were off. Everything's back on now, but I thought you'd want me to go look at the product."

"Oh," I said quietly. That was very bad news. Our entire inventory was in those freezers. We needed that food for our small Brooklyn retailers and for a marketing blitz. I pictured all our hard work melting into a puddle.

"I'm going over there now to check things out."

"Oh, Marta." The full weight of the news continued to sink in, and the timing couldn't be worse. "We need that food for the trade show!"

"Hmm," Marta said with unmistakable hesitation. "We'll see . . ."

"Marta? What do you mean, 'We'll see?' "

"Julia, they're waiting for you. Go and do the coffee hour, and we'll talk about it afterward."

"Talk about what?"

She sighed. "I opened the mail after you left. The trade show returned your check. There's a letter that says our company doesn't meet the show's . . . Hang on." There were more sounds of paper rustling. " 'Annualized gross revenue' cutoff."

"Those *bast—*" I swallowed that last syllable just as two young mothers pushed their strollers past me toward the church door. I moved a few paces up the street and lowered my voice. "No kidding we're small. That's *why* we need the trade show!" It was the only way to meet the national grocery buyers who would not take my calls.

"Chin up, Julia. We'll get through this. Not everything is going wrong."

"It isn't?"

"Well, for one thing, this call has lasted at least two minutes without your phone dropping me. And more important, you are about to preach the gospel of Julia's Child to a bunch of hippies just like you. *Right now.* So go inside and tell the über-boobers of Brooklyn just how terrific we are."

"Okay," I whispered.

Marta hung up, and I wearily turned to face the church once more, but my confidence was sapped. It had now been a year—a year!—since I'd hatched Julia's Child, with the crazy idea that I had something the rest of the world needed. But I was still nowhere near breaking even. The wheels of commerce were stuck deep in tiny orders, misbehaving appliances, and brand-new opportunities for public humiliation.

Beside the church door stood a statue of St. Agatha. Her head was tipped gently to the side, stone palms open in a gesture at once calm and forthright. "Patron Saint of Fertility, Families, and Peace" was inscribed at her feet. What I needed was the patron saint of stage fright and poorly funded business ventures.

Just then another mom came jogging toward me, red hair

flying. Good manners prevailed over cowardliness, and I opened the door for her and stepped inside.

"Thank you!" she gasped. "I hope I'm not late."

As she passed by, I observed an infant napping in a carrier on her front *and* a toddler slung in a pack on her back. I'd had no idea that combination was physically possible. The rear of the backpack was plastered over with bumper stickers. "Eat More Kale" suggested one of them. "Make Dinner, Not War" commanded another.

In spite of my grim mood, I smiled. A friendly audience was the reason I'd come to Park Slope. Although I hadn't managed to sell any of my products to the big Manhattan stores, the little Brooklyn shops I'd approached had been more receptive.

And of all the Brooklyn neighborhoods, Park Slope is known as the most left-leaning, granola-eating, tree-hugging one. It's populated by mothers who nurse topless everywhere and grind their own millet at the food co-op.

In Park Slope, even the playdough is whole grain.

Steeled by the possibility of a receptive audience, I finally descended the short flight of stairs into a many-windowed room. A frizzy-haired woman sat just inside the doorway, behind a folding table. She had a coffee can and a little sign: "Suggested contribution is $3."

I approached her. "I'm, um, Julia Bailey." She wore a black crinkle skirt, enormous beaded jewelry, and an infant in a sling.

"Julia!" she said, jumping to her feet. "I'm Nadja. We're so happy you could come today!"

"Thank you. The pleasure is all mine." I held out a hand, but she leaned across the table and grabbed my shoulders in a tight embrace. I reciprocated carefully, mindful of the little person strapped to her chest.

"Listen," she said, rubbing her hands together. "My two-year-old *loves* your Apple and Cheddar Muffets! I bought out Luigi's on Fifth. Will there be any more soon?"

I sucked in my breath with the pleasure that an actress must feel the first time she's recognized on the street. "Of *course* there will be! We deliver to Luigi's on Friday. The day after tomorrow."

"Terrific!" she exclaimed. "River will be so happy. Won't you, River?" She beamed at someone on the floor behind her.

I peered over the table to see a little boy with long curly hair busily yanking on the wheels of a toy truck. He ignored us.

"So this is . . . the group?" I asked carefully. There was still a chance that the hundred or so people in the room were there for something else.

"Of course!" My hostess smiled.

"Okay," I said, attempting to swallow my fear. "Where would you like me?"

"I set up the computer over *there*." She indicated a podium and a screen against one wall. "When you're ready, give me a wave, and I'll introduce you."

"Perfect," I said with more nonchalance than I felt.

Aiming for the front of the room, I stepped carefully between the sociable clusters. Coffee and cookies were spread out on a table near the podium. Hoping to stave off nervous dry mouth, I stopped for a drink. One urn was labeled "Fair-Trade, Shade-Grown, Locally Roasted Organic Coffee" and another contained "All-Natural Decaf." I poured myself a chai.

A precociously tall preschool girl stood on tiptoes, her fingers just brushing the edge of the carefully labeled cookie stand ("Organic! Nut Free! Seed Free!"). There were crumbs on her pinafore. "What's the magic word?" she asked.

The toddler beside her had cheeks so round that when he smiled up at her, his eyes nearly disappeared. "Pease!" he chimed.

The hand he extended toward his sister had the same pads of baby fat as Wylie, my own toddler. It was all I could do not to pluck him up and give him a squeeze.

My little burst of longing reminded me that if it weren't for Julia's Child, I would be having a quiet afternoon at home, curled up with my two boys in our own undersize living room. My eyes flicked again toward the door, measuring the distance to the only escape route.

I took a deep breath. It was just the stage fright talking.

I made my way over to the podium and booted up the presentation I'd brought. "Chickens Don't Have Fingers," my title slide read. "Whole Foods for the Whole Family." Marta had found a graphic of a chicken wearing gloves. A day ago I'd found it funny. But now the sight of it made me queasy.

Ms. Aranjo—Nadja—came bounding over, her jewelry and her infant bouncing against her. She checked her watch. "It's four o'clock on the nose," she said. "Shall we?"

I nodded, trying not to tremble.

She grabbed a little microphone off the podium and flicked it on. "Welcome, parents!" she said brightly. "First off, a couple of housekeeping notes. There will be a chicken pox party at Norah Jorgensen's home tomorrow afternoon. Her infected son, Franz, will be happy to play with your unvaccinated children ages three and above from two until four. And next week at this time, we'll be hearing from Kira at Cobble Hill Midwifery on the topic of Saying No to Circumcision."

"And now I'd like to turn our attention to today's guest. Ms. Julia Bailey is someone who tackles the age-old question of 'what's for dinner?' on a professional scale. Her children's foods, labeled Julia's Child, are for sale in our very own neighborhood. But don't go looking for the Apple and Cheddar Muffets at Luigi's because River has eaten them all! Heh heh. Please welcome Ms. Julia Bailey to the Slope!"

A small amount of polite applause could be heard over the toddlers' din. Nadja handed me the microphone, and I was on.

"Uh, thank you, Nadja," I heard myself say. Thank you indeed! She'd just promoted my product so warmly and well that I questioned whether I had anything satisfactory to add. I hadn't faced an audience since my last dance recital in the seventh grade. And as mortifying as I'd found it then to prance around in spandex, at least I hadn't been expected to say anything intelligent.

The microphone felt slippery in my hand. I couldn't remember how I'd planned to begin my remarks.

A couple of yards in front of me, a toddler began to shriek. His mother reached into her diaper bag. Her hand emerged a moment later with a baggie full of green grapes, each presliced against the risk of choking. She handed him half a grape, and an instant later the child plunged his hand into his mouth and was quiet.

I raised the microphone.

"I have always found extreme pleasure in watching my own children eat," I began. "It starts right at the very beginning. You bring home this new baby, this loud little stranger, and for those first few weeks you have only one job. When the baby is nursing happily or attacking his bottle—as long as he's sucking down calories—everything is right with the world. Good mom! You win!"

I scanned the audience for signs of agreement. But it was wiggly and noisy out there. A moist spot formed between my shoulder blades. It seemed impossible to compete with all the babies and toddlers in the room for their mothers' attention.

Having no alternative, I soldiered on. "We are rewarded for our loving attention when the little screamers begin to get fat. There's nothing sweeter than finding several chins hiding under the baby bonnet or—my favorite—knees that resemble the folds on a sharpei puppy."

A woman sitting on a blanket in front of me chuckled, and I felt immediate gratitude. At least someone could hear me.

"The joy continues into toddlerhood. One-year-olds are hungry creatures, and now they can eat nearly anything, as long as you cut it small enough. I actually believe that we're *wired* to feel pleasure and accomplishment when they do. Endorphins must be released when you watch those chubby hands shovel in the food. You could actually hook up sensors to a mother's brain and then show her a video of her child eating broccoli and giggling. Her synapses would start firing like she'd just won the lottery. I guarantee it.

"But then your toddler turns two. Now that the little darling has a full set of teeth and can chew anything at all, suddenly he won't. At two the appetite slows down. Suddenly, every mom has a picky eater on her hands, a child who will eat only on alternate Tuesdays and only foods that are beige."

At this there was a little swell of laughter. And with it I felt something akin to the acceleration of an engine on the open road. Because it wasn't just the size of the crowd that scared me but the possibility that they wouldn't understand why I spend much of my week in a closet-size office, trying to placate the picky eaters of America. Even on days when my business didn't hover near the brink of collapse, I sometimes worried that I was the only inmate in the asylum.

I smiled at the crowd. "So now Mom gets edgy. Toddlerhood can feel like a personal failure. I'm sure you all know what happens next." I made my voice shrill. " 'Two more bites of chicken, Maddox! Then you can have the cookie!' "

This won me another chuckle of recognition.

"Or worse—who here among us has ever resorted to chasing a two-year-old with forkfuls of food?" I raised my own hand guiltily and saw a smattering of others rise too.

"Eventually, we seek a solution in the grocery store aisles. We troll with our shopping carts, searching for an easy fix. But there, on the shelves, some interesting products await."

I hit the space bar on Nadja's laptop, and the advertisement I'd torn from a magazine lit the screen. It was a photograph of a pod-shaped, sandwichlike item bursting with shiny peanut butter and dripping grape jelly. Marta and I had blown up the glossy image so dramatically that it became pixelated. The effect was garish—just like those backlit magnifying mirrors in hotel bathrooms that show every pore on your face in agonizing detail.

"This is an advertisement for the Zamwich," I told the room. "You can buy them, frozen, at chain supermarkets. They come four to a box, but each Zamwich weighs just two ounces—about half the size of a real sandwich. And here's the really strange thing."

I stared into the audience and saw a few faces turned my way, but also a couple dozen milling toddlers who hadn't noticed that I was speaking.

"People actually pay"—I did my best impression of Bob Barker—"*three dollars and sixty-nine cents* for these frozen peanut butter and jelly sandwiches." I paused to let the horror sink in. "Now, maybe you're thinking, What's the harm? Why is this poor woman getting all lathered up about a PB and J?

"Let's start with the practical aspects. I made a peanut butter sandwich the other day, and I timed myself. It took exactly two and a half minutes—three if you count washing the knife. But *this* product needs to be defrosted for sixty minutes before you"—I made my fingers into little quotation marks—" 'serve it.'

"But the *real* problem, as I see it, is that Zamwiches teach your child that sandwiches come from the store. That they spring, fully formed, from the box—complete with the crusts removed! If this product takes off, we might be faced with an entire generation of kids who won't ever learn how to make a peanut butter sandwich."

There was more laughter, and now I began to relax even more.

"Now, all of us here are young enough to have lived our entire lives surrounded by advertising. So we are hardened to it, aren't we, ladies? *We are savvy*. It's been decades, for example, since I realized that the dollies shown on TV are never as beautiful and fun once they come out of the pink package."

There was more laughter when I flipped to the next slide, and I made a mental note to thank Marta for making it. A row of boxed Barbies stared out at the audience, their faces partly obscured by the glare of their plastic wrappers.

"Her name is *Barbara*!" one mother hollered, in a faux heckle, which then got its own ripple of laughter.

"And yet," I said, waiting another moment for the laughter to die down. "And yet when it comes to our children, we are uniquely vulnerable. Tell me I'm not the only one."

The room had grown quieter.

"I find the Zamwich to be a bit ridiculous. It makes me laugh. But there's another trend that is much worse than overreaching in the marketing department. The latest products in the grocery store all claim a *technological* advantage over ordinary homemade foods. Let me show you what I mean."

I flipped to the next slide. The screen was filled with taglines torn from several different advertisements.

**Sunny Grahams—now a good source of calcium!**

**Only Yoyo adds GGL for digestive health!**

**Omega-3 DHA helps support brain development!**

"I tore these three ads from a single parenting magazine. It should come as no surprise that every one of these products is expensive and high in sugar. But that's not even what offends me. What I don't like is the implication that I need their miracle ingredient to safeguard my children's health. A guy in a lab coat adds that special something, and a healthy food is born. As if mothers haven't done a good job—for *centuries*—making healthy foods at home in the kitchen. Then comes the fancy ad campaign designed to make you feel *guilty* about choosing the ordinary yogurt or the less-scientific cracker!"

I paused to take a breath. I was rolling along now, on my soapbox, in my zone, expounding on topics near to my heart. But a strange thing had happened while I prattled on about the grocery axis of evil. The room had actually gone quiet. The late-afternoon sun beamed straight into my line of sight. I shielded my eyes to try to discover whether my audience was rapt or perhaps sleeping.

The mothers stared back at me with an encouraging amount of interest. And it was then that I noticed how all that silence was possible. Perhaps it was the topic, or just that time of day, but every woman in the room had one breast exposed. I could see big cantaloupe boobs and also little lemon ones—breasts of every conceivable color. And perched on each one was an infant or toddler, all nursing at once. Dozens of little busy mouths. It was just about the strangest thing I'd ever seen. Strange, but tranquil.

I nearly lost track of what I was saying.

"So I . . . uh . . ." Right. I flipped to the last slide in my presentation. "I found these five words in another advertisement, and they're the ones that scare me the most." On the screen, in enormous type, the ad screamed: "They'll Never Know It's Healthy!"

"What a horrible idea," I said sadly. "To never know what's healthy."

There was a collective sigh in the room. They were still with me. "Prepared foods have become a cultural necessity in our busy lives. I've read that, compared with the workweek in the 1970s, managers now spend an extra *month* at their desks each year. Prepared foods are here to stay. But before you spend your hard-earned dollars on foods of convenience, I hope you'll ask yourself just two questions: Is it *truly* convenient? And is it truly *food*?" I exhaled. "And now, I'd be happy to take your questions and comments."

A voice came immediately from somewhere on my left. "So, what does *your* advertising say, then?"

I squinted to locate my inquisitor, finding her beneath a head of fabulously curly blonde hair.

"You're looking at it." My floundering business couldn't afford to advertise, but there was no need to admit it. "I prefer to talk to customers face-to-face. You can even come and watch me cook the food if you want to. Thursday nights, right here in Brooklyn. Bring a hairnet. No nibbling allowed."

It was easy enough to laugh off the question, but she'd put her finger on one of my biggest problems. "It's hard for me," I admitted, "to picture a glossy ad campaign for Julia's Child. My foods are all about having a short and recognizable ingredient list. So it's difficult to imagine where I'd put the exclamation marks, right? Because 'fresh broccoli!' is never new and improved. It's never reformulated."

"Ahem," interjected the voice from the left.

I nodded toward her.

"If you're so disgusted with the processed food business, then why would you start one?"

At that moment the adrenaline coursing through my veins turned on me, souring my confidence. On the face of it, the question wasn't a tough one. The canned answer was obvious enough: I started Julia's Child to feed my dear children. And surely that had once been true. But lately my skills in the kitchen had done nothing but threaten their college fund and keep them sequestered with the sitter.

The audience was waiting for my answer.

"Well," I began tentatively, "I started Julia's Child because it turns out that I have a knack for . . . for creating recipes that toddlers will eat. Out on the playground with my son, I'd listen to mothers obsess about kids who would eat only plain pasta. They didn't believe me when I told them that Jasper ate chili or lentil salad. Sometimes I'd offer it to their kids. 'Ari will *never* try that,' they'd say. And then Ari would scarf it down too. And in the grocery stores . . . I didn't like what I found." That was an understatement. Some of the foods marketed to children were so abominable that I could scarcely believe they were legal.

Those were heady days, at the beginning, when I was filled with optimism. It seemed like the market was just waiting for me. The idea for Julia's Child had honestly begun as a mission of love. But reluctant grocers, five-hundred-page health department manuals, and expensive packaging had quickly intervened.

Forgetting that I held a microphone, I sighed, which made a sound like a hurricane. This I followed with another of my uncomfortable silences. Standing there in the church basement, it seemed impossible to answer the question without spilling my innermost conflicts to the audience.

"I'm just . . . a girl with an idea," I said finally. "The idea that kids' food should be healthy, tasty, and natural. If you read the list of ingredients on one of my packages, you'll see organic whole grains, vegetables, and fruits. That's all. No binders or fillers, but also no tricks. And no hype. But I really had no idea what I'd be up against. I had no idea that 'pure and simple' was the hardest thing in the world to sell."

My throat seemed to be closing up. "Thank you very much," I croaked. "It's been such a pleasure to talk to all of you today."

And then I heard something that we're all secretly hoping to hear at some moment in our lives. It started slowly in the back and then swelled to a roar. I heard applause.

# Chapter 2

I'd always suspected that every mother on the planet had a special well of angst in her heart just for nutrition. Sure enough, after I set down the microphone, their mealtime obsessions bubbled out.

"I have a question for you," one woman had said, touching my elbow as I drained my chai.

I turned to face her. She wore a fashionably blousy white tunic and bright green sunglasses. A cute toddler wearing matching shades was perched on her hip.

"Shoot," I invited.

"I always cook a balanced dinner, but then my daughter eats only the rice. Maybe she'll eat one bite of the meat. That's when I feel like running to the freezer for some chicken fingers, you know? Because rice . . . It's just not dinner."

"I hear you," I said. "If you really *need* her to have a little variety, you could try my rice dish. It's just a little more nutritious than the plain white stuff. It's called Rome Wasn't Built in a Day Rice and Lentil Salad."

She laughed. "What does that mean?"

"It's a stepping-stone to more adventurous things. It has rice, which makes the dish look safe and familiar. But it also has a few lentils, for protein, and carrots minced down to the size of the rice. I flavor it with a hint of citrus."

"I'll try it!" she said.

"But then," I cautioned her, "if she eats it and ignores the other food on the table, don't panic. Just enjoy the meat yourself, or the other vegetables, and smile. How old is your daughter?"

"She turns two next month."

"Ah," I said. "Don't sweat it. She imitates everything else you do, right?"

She laughed, tossing her hair around. "Yes! She wants my sunglasses. She wants my lip gloss. She wants my keys."

"She'll want your food, eventually. And rice won't kill her. My pediatrician says that's what they eat at that age—carbs. Toddlers usually get plenty of protein from milk. Just serve real food, and she'll learn to eat it. Hang in there!"

The mommy exhaled dramatically, as if I'd lifted the weight of the world off her shoulders. "Thank you," she said.

I found myself dispensing advice faster than "Dear Abby."

"If pasta is her thing, you could try my couscous—it has minced yellow squash and shallots for flavor . . .

"It sounds like he doesn't like the *texture* of vegetables. It might not be the flavor that's putting him off. Have you tried serving them raw? Some children take to raw vegetables, even things *you'd* never eat uncooked. Or you could try my It's Not Easy Being Green Beans. They're sautéed but still crunchy."

The last question was from Ms. Nadja Aranjo herself. "I'm just beside myself," she sang, shaking her pendulous earrings, "because River has decided he doesn't want to drink milk anymore. All that calcium and protein . . . I don't know what to do."

I nodded seriously. "I think a lot of kids go off milk for a while. It's tempting to offer to dump chocolate into it, isn't it?"

"Yes!" she shrieked. "But I don't want to go there. He doesn't eat yogurt either. What else is there?"

"How about mac and cheese?" I asked. "Will he eat that?"

"Yes." She was tentative. "But I just don't know how much actual cheese is in there." We both looked down at River, who was attempting to scale her leg like a tree. His T-shirt read "I do all my own stunts."

I laid a hand on her arm. "I've got the perfect recipe for you. It's for high-protein macaroni and cheese. It actually solves two problems at once because it's a snap to make. Five minutes of prep time and tons of milk and cheese in it. I'll e-mail it to you tomorrow."

"Really?" she squealed. "I would so appreciate that, Julia. It's a pleasure to meet you." She grabbed me for another one of her bracing hugs.

By the time my feet hit the streets of Brooklyn again, it was five thirty and I was still jumpy with adrenaline. The ring of my phone startled me, and then a glance at the caller sent my heart skittering with fear. "Hello, Marta!"

"Buenas tardes, chica." Marta had been trying to teach me Spanish.

"Buenas tardes." But *was* it? For at least an hour I'd managed to forget Marta's dire errand, checking our freezers.

"Todo sigue congelada," Marta said.

"What? *Todo* . . ." I swallowed. "All is lost?"

"No, *chica*," Marta laughed. "I said 'everything is still frozen!' When I got there, the temp on the thermometer read thirty degrees. I ripped open ten packages—five from each freezer. But there were no signs of defrosting."

"Oh, Marta, are you sure? Were the peas still loose?" These are the things that the brain trust at Julia's Child thinks about all day. Vegetables that have been flash-frozen properly stay loose and pebbly inside the package. Peas that have defrosted and refrozen will clump together like a rock.

"The peas were *definitely* still loose," she said. "Shakin' better than a nice pair of maracas."

"I'm so relieved."

"Me too. Night, *chica*."

Now I was finally headed home to Manhattan. Though I wouldn't get there before six fifteen, my steps toward the subway had a new spring in them. Now I knew that the asylum for the food obsessed was larger than my office. It was as least as large as an entire Brooklyn neighborhood.

Brooklyn provided proof that not every part of the country had been paved into a homogeneous mall. I ducked into a tiny store on Seventh Avenue with a promising name—Russo's Old World Mozzarella. Even I—who made things from scratch that others bought at the store—didn't make my own cheese. At least not that often.

A bell hanging from the door jingled as I walked in. The air was tinged with the scent of spicy salami, and big sides of prosciutti hung from the ceiling. A man in a white apron stood behind the counter. "Hello there," he called out. "Can I help ya?"

"Hi! You have fresh mozzarella?"

"I make it every day," he said. "Salted or unsalted?"

"Salted, please." I steered around a pyramid of imported olive oil tins. "And one of these," I added, grabbing a crusty baguette from a local bakery out of a basket.

"That will be eight dollars," he said. It was a bargain, I thought, for two foods made just hours before, right here in this neighborhood. Priceless, really.

"Have a good 'un!" he said, handing me my change.

"You too," I said over my shoulder, running now for the F train. As the subway doors slid closed, I hatched my dinner plan. I would heat up the rotisserie chicken I'd bought that morning at Whole Foods. To go with it, I'd throw together a quick Caprese salad of tomatoes and fresh mozzarella.

Pushing open the door to our building, I gave a nod to the so-called doorman lounging in the chair behind the desk. I pictured my hungry family five floors up, milling about the apartment wondering where I'd gone. The last obstacle between me and a hastily prepared family meal was a trip up my building's plodding elevator.

As if summoned by my darkest insecurities, the door flew open again behind me to reveal the slender rear end of our neighbor Emily, pulling her double jogging stroller into the lobby.

As if his chair had received a high-voltage shock, the doorman leaped up to hold the door wide open. "Good evening, Mrs. Nordsen," he said.

"Evening, Mario," came Emily's aristocratic drawl. "Hello, Julia."

"Hi," I managed, peering at the elevator for signs of life. I turned to face my neighbor. "Hi, Sadie," I said to her one-year-old daughter, occupying one side of the enormous lime green carriage.

"We were just out for a jog, weren't we, Sadie?" Emily crooned. "The marathon is still five weeks away, so we only did twelve."

"Twelve . . . miles?" A quick comparison between Emily and myself furthered my discomfort. It wasn't obvious which of us had just run a half marathon. My strange mission to Brooklyn had left me rumpled and sweat stained, whereas Emily's stylish running outfit was pristine, her blond ponytail sleek. The only telltale sign of exertion was a towel—the same citrus shade as her stroller—draped around her neck.

"It always puts Sadie to sleep. If Wylie has trouble going down for a nap, you should try it. Oh—but I suppose you're at work! How's the food business?"

I gritted my teeth. "Great. I'm, um, working on a new product. With chickpeas, eggplant, and figs. And a kiss of ginger. It's all organic," I prattled on. "And flash frozen for optimal nutrition."

Mercifully, the old elevator car finally appeared through the window of the antique door.

"Well bless your heart, Julia," chirped my neighbor. "You're . . . you're saving the world one bite at a time."

Unsure whether she was mocking me, I fell silent.

The doorman had hovered, waiting for this moment. Emily's husband was president of our co-op board, with Emily as his eyes and ears. Behind our closed apartment door, we referred to her as the First Lady. Now Mario swept the door open for her with a flourish—and right into my waiting shin.

"So where can I shop for your products?" Emily asked as I limped into the only corner of the elevator unoccupied by her double-wide.

"Uh," I said, wincing in pain. "Right now we're only in a few specialty stores. In Brooklyn. But we'd like to roll out Manhattan really soon," I told her, as if it were up to me.

"Elllllllll!" Sadie shrieked from the stroller. "Ell!" She strained against her harness, reaching for the buttons on the control panel.

Emily gasped. "Wow, Sadie! Good girl! That's exactly right! *L* is for 'lobby'! We know a song about the letter *L*, don't we?"

My neck got very hot as I realized that Emily was about to break into song.

"*La-la-la-la lobby!*" she trilled in a surprisingly robust soprano.

But little Sadie had lost interest and was now chewing the edge of a book titled *Baby Brain Builders*. Emily stopped singing and grabbed it from her. "Oh! Sadie, books are not for chewing." The picture on the cover showed an infant wearing a diaper and a mortarboard.

The elevator continued its glacial ascent away from the la-la-la-la-lobby.

"Listen, Julia." Emily turned to me. "I saw your nanny feeding Jasper and Wylie in the playroom again yesterday."

My heart sank. The common playroom in the basement, its cleanliness and wholesomeness, was the First Lady's cause célèbre.

Unfortunately, our babysitter had already proven herself to be less than fastidious, but I thought I'd sorted it out. "What, uh, what was Bonnie feeding them?" I asked reluctantly, fearing the worst.

"Grapes," Emily answered with a frown.

"Oh!" I said, relieved. "But grapes . . . There probably weren't any crumbs, then?" With my luck she was about to say that my children were doing their own version of the Italian wine-making ritual: crushing them into the playroom rug with their bare feet while singing bacchanalian songs.

"No crumbs," she said. "But rules are rules. And if *other* babysitters see *one* child eating, then . . ." She trailed off, as if the horrors were too graphic to voice aloud. "The sign clearly says 'No Eating,' and I'd like to avoid another chicken and rice incident." She nodded gravely at me.

Mercifully, the elevator doors parted, and Emily began to steer her enormous stroller out of the cab.

"I'll, uh, speak to Bonnie," I muttered.

"Wonderful! See you soon," she sang, and then she trotted off down the hall, leaving me in front of my own apartment door. I could hear pleasant voices and music inside. That was good—better than shrieks of hunger. I turned my key in the lock and pushed open the door, to the sound of laughter. Still carrying my shopping bag, I walked into the dining room to find everyone sitting at the table. My husband, Luke, looked up at me, his face tan and handsome in . . . Was that candlelight?

"There she is," he said. "C'mon in, sweetie. Take a seat."

I hesitated on the threshold, feeling inexplicably like a gate crasher. The tableau before me was startling. They were already the perfect picture of a family at table. There was Luke in his usual spot at the head. But Bonnie, our Scottish au pair, sat in my place, her back to me. Bonnie, who had the voice of Mary Poppins but the looks of a willowy African model, wore a nice sweater instead of her usual T-shirt. It fit rather more tightly over her slim frame than usual.

On either side were the fair heads of Jasper, my kindergartner, and Wylie, age two. Their dinner was in progress—no, it was practically over. Their plates held just remnants. They didn't even look up at my arrival, because Bonnie was telling them a story.

"And to this *day* people still say"—she paused dramatically—"that a mermaid can be heard crying there, by the rocks." Bonnie picked up her wineglass, from the exact spot on the table where mine usually sat, and drained it. "Hullo, Julia!" she said, swiveling around gaily. "I have made a Scottish delicacy to go with the chicken."

"Pancakes!" hollered Wylie. "But Bonnie say no syrup."

"*Potato* cakes, luv, don't need syrup. And it hasn't slowed you down even a wee bit." Smiling, she wiped Wylie's mouth with her own napkin.

"Can we have these every night?" Jasper asked.

Whether or not he sensed my discomfort, Luke beckoned to me. Then he reached for another dining chair, from where it stood against the wall of our tiny dining room, and made space for me between himself and Jasper. "Sit right here," he said. "I'll get you a wineglass." He started to get up.

"I'll get it," I told him. "I have to put this away." I held up my shopping bag.

At the door to the kitchen, I stopped. Every surface was trashed. Two mixing bowls were piled on the counter, bits of potato and some kind of batter dripping down the side of one. A greasy frying pan sat on the stove. The cooking oil stood open with no sign of its cap anywhere.

I squeezed my eyes shut, trying hard not to get upset.

From the cabinet, I pulled a wooden cutting board. On its worn surface I balanced a wineglass and my ingredients from Russo's. I carried everything carefully back to the table and kissed Jasper's blond brush cut as I sat down.

The chicken had already been thoroughly enjoyed. Rather than pick at its carcass, I turned my attention to slicing the crusty baguette. For the boys, I always bought whole wheat sandwich bread. But in my heart I loved a crusty artisanal loaf like this one. Whole grains be damned.

Luke's face was flushed from laughing at some joke of Bonnie's that I had just missed. He put one hand on my knee. "So tell me," he said quietly. "How was your day?"

I sliced the ball of fresh cheese into milky discs as I considered the question. "It's actually quite hard to say."

"Meaning?" he asked, tossing a shred of the cheese into his mouth. "Good stuff you got here."

"Is it? Made today in Brooklyn. Let's see . . . On the positive side of today's balance sheet, I gave a talk to a big parenting group in Park Slope. And I *killed*, as they say. But on the other hand, ANKST returned my check."

"Who?"

"ANKST. It stands for All-Natural Kid Stuff Tradeshow. The one on which I'd pinned all my hopes for bagging Whole Foods as a buyer."

"Oh, the trade show," Luke said, sipping his wine. He was quiet for a moment. "I guess there's always next year?" he suggested.

I looked into Luke's blue eyes. He never panicked, and I loved him for that. But as a consequence, it was difficult to tell when he was really worried. And we couldn't discuss it at the dinner table, in front of God and everybody.

I took a sip of my wine. Luke and I both knew it was a stretch to pretend that I could go another whole year bleeding the family's nest egg for the ego trip of my so-called business. What's worse,

Luke's bank had just been acquired by an even larger one. Though Luke had always been a valued employee, there was talk that up to a hundred people in the technology department would get pink slips.

I laid a white slab of mozzarella onto a slice of baguette. I sprinkled it with a quick turn of the pepper grinder. "Who would like one of these?" I offered.

"Me!" Jasper said at once. I completed the open-faced sandwich with just a drizzle of olive oil and handed it to him. "Yum," he said obligingly. Jasper had always been a great eater—a boy after my own heart.

"Me!" screamed Wylie, who unfailingly followed his brother, with varying results.

I made the same again for Wylie, even though he wasn't yet a fan of cheese.

A study I once read concluded that a child had to be offered a new food *ten times* before it was clear whether or not he liked it. Ten! Who could blame a mother for giving up on brussels sprouts after two or three attempts? I had a good laugh, trying to imagine the study in progress. I pictured scientists in white lab coats, steaming broccoli for the seventh time while making notes. "Subject threw plate off table after sixteen seconds." And I thought *my* job was weird.

Predictably, Wylie had some trouble with his open-face hors d'oeuvre. I'd hoped that the softness of the mozzarella might win him over. But it was not to be.

"Too crunchy!" he moaned, and I realized he meant the bread.

"You just need a way in," I told him calmly. "Bite the edge hard, just once, and you'll get to the soft stuff inside."

But it was almost bedtime, and Wylie was tired. I could see it coming, the evening meltdown. Big tears squeezed from his eyes and headed down his chubby cheeks. "Toooooo crunchyyyy!" he wailed, dropping his head. Then the slab of mozzarella began to slide off the bread. "Fall off!" he screamed. "It fall off!"

At that moment my entire day came full circle. Surely Zamwiches never caused a mother so much angst.

"Oh, honey," I said. I caught Wylie's kicking, sausagelike feet in my hands and rubbed them. He was still wearing his favorite pair of striped socks, which I'd put on him that morning. It seemed like ages ago. "I think it's time for pajamas now," I said, giving the bedtime cue. I had not yet eaten a bite.

Luke stood up, putting a hand on my shoulder. "I got it," he offered. "You eat." He scooped Wylie off his seat, despite loud protests, and headed for the bedroom.

"He's tired," I said, as if it weren't obvious to the three of us left at the table.

"Surely," Bonnie agreed. "He skipped his nap today to play with Sadie in the playroom."

I winced. "Actually, Bonnie, I saw Emily in the elevator." I should have stopped there. But unfortunately I went on. "She said something about food in the playroom again."

"That *b*—" she caught herself. But her eyes flashed at me from across the table. "That is just unfair! Did you know that she had a *security camera* installed in the playroom? She just wants me to feel uncomfortable, you know. It isn't *food* she's against, it's . . ."

I was terrified that Bonnie was about to utter a racial slur.

"Babysitters!" she spat. Then she took her plate, and Wylie's, and strode into the kitchen, where she deposited them in the sink with a loud crash. Her door slammed shut, and I could hear her dialing the first of many expensive, long-distance calls to Scotland.

I closed my eyes. I never should have brought it up. Instead, I should have thanked Bonnie for making dinner, which is not part of her usual duties. But now it was too late.

So Jasper and I were left alone at the table. He was polishing off his bread and mozzarella, seemingly oblivious to the fireworks. I watched him scrape his plate with the crust, trying to catch any drops of olive oil, and I smiled. If only those nervous mothers of toddlers could see how an active school-aged boy eats.

If you serve it, they will come.

"So," I whispered to my sweet kindergartner, "Bonnie's potato cakes? Pretty cool, huh?"

"Not cool like *Batman* is cool," he said, his mouth full of bread. "But good. Put salt on it."

With my fingers, I pinched the last potato cake from the greasy platter. It was cold—surely they'd been more appetizing right out of the frying pan. I salted and peppered it. I chewed.

"Not bad," I said. Then again, that was the minimum flavor yield from frying a potato in any kind of grease.

"Wylie!" came Luke's shout from the direction of the bathroom. Then we heard a crash and the sound of little feet escaping justice.

A moment later Luke poked his head into the dining room. "He's not in here, is he?"

"Maybe in my closet?" suggested Jasper helpfully. "What did he do this time?" There was a hint of glee in the question.

"He squeezed toothpaste into a big pile in the sink."

"Again?" I failed to keep the sound of exasperation out of my voice.

"I only turned my back for a split second," Luke said, shaking his head. He disappeared toward the bedrooms. "Wylie, we're going to clean up the sink and then you're going to bed. *Without* a story."

I winced, knowing more wailing would follow.

"Read story!" shouted Wylie from his hiding place somewhere toward the back of the apartment.

"No!"

"*Dadddddyyy!*" It was a shriek. "I throw you in the barbage!" he threatened.

Jasper giggled.

I put my hand on his back. "Come on, sweetie. Let's go put on your pj's. If you're quick about it, I'll have time to read you the knight book."

An hour later I stood scraping plates. I plucked a bit of chicken Jasper had left behind and popped it into my mouth. On particularly frantic nights, those stolen leftovers made up a pathetic portion of my meal. I surveyed the ruined kitchen. The potato cake batter had hardened into a starchy substance resembling brick mortar. As I worked, Luke placed his warm hands on my shoulders and began to massage them. I dropped the sponge in the sink and closed my eyes.

"Will you have a gin and tonic with me?" Luke asked. "Or do I have to throw you in the barbage?"

"I choose number one," I said.

"Excellent choice!" From the high cabinet he took the gin bottle and then began to dig around in the refrigerator for a lime.

This part of the day had long been my favorite. When we'd hired Bonnie, I'd been worried that a strange adult in the apartment would strain my already limited time alone with my husband. The couple of hours after the boys were asleep, and before I collapsed with exhaustion, were the only time Luke and I got to talk. We liked to put our feet on the coffee table and have a drink—alone. I had feared that having a twenty-year-old Scottish lassie in the room would torpedo our casual intimacy.

I shouldn't have worried. Within weeks, Bonnie had discovered the Williamsburg music scene. Most evenings, as the rest of us sat down to dinner, Bonnie would kiss the boys and then vanish on to the subway.

I resumed wiping down the counters. "So you caved in and read him a story after all?"

"Of course," he admitted. "And his eyes were rolling back in his head by the time Sam-I-Am ate the green eggs. Then he went down without a peep."

"Nice work, honey," I said as I sprayed hot sudsy water all over the pasty substance in the mixing bowl. "But Sam-I-Am is the other guy. The pusher."

"Oh. Whatever."

I shut the water off suddenly. "You know, that should *never* have worked," I said forcefully.

"What shouldn't?"

"*Green Eggs and Ham*! What a loopy, drug-induced story. It's genius, of course, but just think of the marketing pitch: 'Buy my book about a lumpy guy trying to feed unnaturally colored food to another weirdo, in rhyme!' I mean—really! 'Could you, would you, with a goat?' Oh—and it's for *children*." I scrubbed the bowl rather more violently than was necessary. "Gosh! Let's go ahead and print ten million copies! I'll bet even Whole Foods carries it."

Luke gave me a worried frown. "Honey, I think you need to unwind. How about we go to Vermont for the weekend?"

I sighed. "That sounds like a great idea."

To: nadja@parkslopeparents.org
From: juliaschild@gmail.com
Re: Mac and cheese for River

Dear Nadja,

Thanks so much for the opportunity to speak yesterday. It was a pleasure to discuss some of my favorite topics with the lovely mothers of Park Slope.

Here's the recipe I promised you. It is a real time-saver—you don't boil the pasta first! You simply bake the uncooked pasta in the milk and cheeses, and it works like a charm. The milk provides the liquid *and* the protein and calcium, which I think is pretty neat. One thing, though—it's better if you don't do the math on how many fat grams are in here. Because you're going to want to eat this yourself, and because that way lies the abyss.

Enjoy,
Julia

### Mac and Cheese with Plenty of Dairy

*Cooking Time: 70 minutes (10 minutes prep, 60 minutes unattended—giddyap!)*

***Ingredients***

**1 cup organic cottage cheese (not low fat)**
**2 cups organic whole milk**
**1 tablespoon Dijon mustard**
**Pinch Hungarian paprika**
**16 ounces shredded cheddar cheese (about four cups)**
**8 ounces dry pasta**

***Instructions***

Preheat your oven to 375°F. Coat the inside of a 2-quart covered casserole with cooking spray.

In a blender, combine cottage cheese, milk, mustard, and paprika. Allow your toddler to blend until smooth. (I've never met a toddler who didn't have five minutes to operate heavy machinery.)

In a large mixing bowl, combine dry pasta and the shredded cheese. Pour the milk mixture over it. Allow your toddler to stir the mixture gently.

Clean up from the toddler's stirring.

Pour the mixture into the casserole. Cover and bake for 30 minutes.

Uncover and bake for another 20 or 30 minutes until brown and bubbly.

Cool for 15 minutes and enjoy!

# Chapter 3

My mother was a harried, indifferent cook who looked upon dinnertime as a chore. We ate plenty of tuna casserole at our house—the sort that's made from cream of mushroom soup. And vegetables always came out of a can.

But my father's aunt Odile was French. She taught me to clean leeks when I was four, standing at her sink on a wooden crate. She taught me to make polenta at five. I stirred the coq au vin when I was six. We made duck à l'orange when I was seven. By eight, we were blowtorching the tops of crèmes brûlées in ramekins. It was the seventies, when women were supposed to eschew cooking for liberation. But to me cooking *was* liberation. And I cooked, in my bell bottoms, singing along with Gloria Gaynor on the radio, which Aunt Odile called "the wireless." Those were my fondest memories of childhood. Great Aunt Odile died when I was fifteen. But I can still picture her beautiful kitchen with its enormous farmhouse table and rustic apron sink.

Lately, I did my cooking in a far less charming room. The next night found me surrounded by the linoleum and stainless surfaces of our production facility, La Cucina. I unwrapped blocks of cheese, while Marta washed organic apples in the giant steel sink.

Marta shut off the water and looked around. "*She's* not here, is she?"

I shrugged. "I haven't seen her." Things were decidedly more peaceful when the Cucina's ironfisted matriarch was not on the premises.

The scuttlebutt around the kitchen was that the government paid "Auntie" Maria to teach employable skills to welfare mothers who were losing their benefits. With one hand, Uncle Sam had slashed aid to poor mothers. With the other, he paid Zia Maria to educate them.

Zia, ever enterprising, had then hit on the idea of renting out the kitchens at night and on weekends to earn even more money. To fill these off-hours slots, she turned to another vulnerable population—hopeful entrepreneurs. There were now ten struggling businesses like mine renting time during the graveyard shift at the Cucina.

Zia's frugality was legendary. To force one enterprise to support the other, she required her welfare mothers to work several shifts a month for the entrepreneurs, at less than minimum wage.

And that's how I'd met Marta. By the time I arrived on the scene, she was nearly a graduate of Zia's program. She could peel ten cloves of garlic in ten seconds flat and mince onions without shedding a tear. More important, Marta knew how Zia's kitchen worked—which burners on the overused stove lit evenly and how to run the clanking flash freezer.

Marta's many talents announced themselves to me immediately. I could see that she was her own gum-cracking variety of superwoman, able to leap tall egos in a single bound. As soon as I was able, I hired her—full time. We were a tiny company, so Marta's job was to be my gal Friday. I paid her a salary of forty thousand dollars, which was a hell of a lot less than she was worth but more than I could afford.

Marta was not without her quirks. She was full of old wives' tales. She thought cold water from the tap would come to a boil faster than warm water, in spite of the obvious physical impossibility. She also thought that too much stirring drove the vitamins out of food. But I hadn't hired her for her scientific insight. I was after her skills with both kitchenware and diplomacy.

Into Zia's industrial food processor I fed great hunks of organic cheddar. The machine was deafening but quickly produced five pounds of cheesy smithereens.

"Did you get a nap?" I asked Marta.

"No. I got coffee instead. You?"

I smiled. "Same. Who's sitting with Carlos?" On our production Thursdays, Marta bribed a rotating collection of little old-lady neighbors to spend half the night on her living room sofa, keeping an eye on her son.

"Señora Díaz tonight. Carlos likes her well enough. She lets him pick all the TV shows."

"Groovy."

I dropped the cheese into a mixing bowl the size of a Roman tub and looked around for a paddle. I didn't mind our late nights in the kitchen. Making the actual food was for me the part that made all the bureaucratic nonsense bearable. Still, there was no time to waste when your workday ended in the wee hours.

"I made the flyers," Marta announced. She wiped her hands dry on her apron and then pulled a colorful page from a Kinko's envelope. "Julia's Child Sold Here!" There was a pretty photo of our packaging. But I also saw a small inset photograph of me cuddling Wylie against the leafy backdrop of the playground.

I blinked. "My picture? Where'd you get that?"

"Luke," she said breezily. "The colors work—don't you think?" She admired her work. "Green words, green trees, green product. Green mommy. Save the world. Get it?" She pulled on a hairnet.

"Subtle," I said. I wasn't sure about having my picture pasted up in store windows, but I had to admit that it was a punchy document.

Marta cracked her gum at me. "Where's *your* flyer, then?"

"It looks great, Marta. It's perfect. Do you think any of the stores will object to putting our signs in their windows?"

"I don't plan to ask permission," Marta answered, pulling on her latex gloves. "I'm going to tell them you're sending a hundred new customers their way."

From across the room, we heard a shriek. "Ay! You no can put in there! You stink up my churros with your stinky pickles!" Lila, of Lila's Churros, was hollering at Bob, of Bob's Old-Fashioned Garlicky Dills.

More than three hundred years into its history, the Brooklyn melting pot was still going strong. Most of the entrepreneurs who used the Cucina made ethnic specialty foods, selling the flavors of home to their countrymen. Aside from Lila and Bob, we'd worked alongside producers of Brazilian empanadas, Polish pierogi, and Indian chutneys.

Marta and I were the only ones cooking for the toddler nation. We always got along well with the others. But tonight's skirmish was repeated often enough—a familiar UN standoff over refrigerator space.

Lila looked in our direction for support. "You *see* he do this? Put garlic pickles in with churros?"

"I'll *move* 'em!" Bob roared. "Just quit yer hollerin'." He poked around in a neighboring refrigerator, rearranging things.

"But I have to make all over again! Churros taste like garlic now!" Lila looked ready to weep.

I trotted to their end of the kitchen. "Let me taste one, Lila. I'll bet they weren't in there together long enough to cause a problem." She handed me one of the delicate cinnamon-flavored donuts, and it melted in my mouth. "Fine," I told her. "Not a whiff."

"I'd better taste it to be sure," Marta said from the other end of the room.

I broke off a piece of my churro and walked back toward Marta. "Lila," I said. "Watch this." I tossed the piece toward Marta, who caught it in her mouth like a trained seal, all without breaking her rhythm with the apple peeler.

Lila's eyebrows went up in surprise. She forgot her anger and smiled.

"¡Muy bien! Delicioso," Marta declared. "Toss me another bite," she demanded. I turned my back to her and tossed it over my head. I heard Lila gasp with surprise when Marta caught it. It was just one of my assistant's strange skills. Once, I'd nearly choked to death on a grape while trying to imitate her.

"Nice light touch with the cinnamon," Marta complimented the chef.

"Gracias," said Lila happily.

"See, I ain't such a bad guy," hollered Bob from his corner of the kitchen. We ignored him.

"So all this cheese is for muffets?" Marta asked me, getting back to business.

"Double batch," I explained. "Ms. Aranjo mentioned them specifically in my introduction at Park Slope Parenting. Her son loves them."

"Let's hope he's hungry," Marta grumbled.

"Ha. After these, we're going to make the Carrot and Black Bean Muffets, and if there's time, we'll do a batch of Gentle Lentil."

The muffet—a savory baked good made from unexpectedly healthy things—was our most popular and innovative product. No child could resist a baked good, even one containing protein or vegetables.

We made hundreds of muffets. While Marta stirred batches of batter, I filled the muffet tins, placed them into the commercial oven, removed them after exactly eighteen minutes, and then started all over again. After four hours, my motions began to feel robotic. The muffets cooled on racks. When the first ten batches were cool, Marta cranked up the flash freezer and began zapping them into frozen little muffetsicles. I stood at the other end, mechanically placing them with gloved hands into our packaging, until the packaging and the product began to blur together.

"That's the last of them," Marta finally said.

If there had been a chair in the kitchen, I would have collapsed into it, but Zia Maria allowed no chairs in the kitchen as she was generally opposed to rest and comfort. So instead I leaned heavily against the stainless steel countertop. I took a moment to eat a broken muffet. "I'll get the coolers," I announced, heading sleepily toward my car. Outdoors the air was refreshingly chilly, a genuine fall evening. Perking up, I dragged the coolers out of the hatchback while droning cars rushed past on the Brooklyn-Queens Expressway, which ran practically overhead.

Back inside, Marta and I packed the frozen muffets among ice packs. Each shiny package, clean and perfect, was the result of our labor. Even with heavy eyelids, I admired their beauty. I had never once, in my years as an accountant, felt this way about my work. Holding the packages in my hands, it barely made a difference whether or not Julia's Child would turn a profit. Moms would buy these very packets, tear them open, and hand the contents to their children. What could be more important than that?

With a satisfied sigh, I zipped everything up. I grabbed the handles of the rolling coolers and took a few steps toward the door. "You could make the delivery if you'd rather." I made my usual offer to Marta. It was a quicker job than the cleanup. But she never took me up on it.

She waved a hand at me. "You go. I'm fine finishing up here."

I winked at her. "I'll give Mr. Pastucci a kiss for you."

Marta made a face. She and I didn't agree about Mr. Pastucci, or the Sons of Sicily Social Club. I found them to be harmless relics of Brooklyn's storied past, while Marta said she found old Mr. Pastucci and his establishment creepy.

"I don't know what they're up to at these social clubs, but it isn't good," she'd said, the first time we visited the space. "Old men, sitting around together in the dark."

It was only a three-minute drive with my cargo over to his low-slung Court Street storefront. Mr. Pastucci's was the last of the Italian men's clubs that used to line the street, or so I was told. That was back when the Italians ruled Brooklyn, before four-dollar lattes and pricy bistros came to the neighborhood. As far as I could tell, the Sons of Sicily Social Club was nothing more than a dim box of a room with a little old bar, a smattering of folding chairs, and a pool table. I pulled my Subaru into the dark alleyway between the club and a dry cleaner. The back door was in reach, but as per my arrangement with the proprietor, I went around to the front door, a scraped-up metal model with a peephole. I banged the knocker against the door four times, as Mr. Pastucci requested. And then I waited.

After a few moments, the old man opened the door a couple of inches. Behind him I could see the dim lighting and wisps of smoke from the members' cigars. Piano music played softly on tinny speakers.

I smiled at him. "Open . . . saddle soap?" I asked. We always did a bit of a shtick from an old Bugs Bunny cartoon before he let me in the back door with my goods. "Open sarsaparilla?"

Mr. Pastucci's glance floated over my head, as he checked the spaces behind me, like a movie mobster. Then he nodded.

If any of his paranoia was genuine, I assumed it was because he operated the little place without a liquor license. I pulled my coolers containing "da merchandise," as Mr. Pastucci called it, into his small back room. There was nothing there save for a utility sink, a mop bucket, and two enormous chest freezers that I rented for a hundred dollars a month.

Zia Maria's rates were usurious by comparison. And the location was perfect, since we produced the food in Brooklyn and our only retailers were in Brooklyn.

It took me just a few minutes to fit all the muffets into the two freezers while Mr. Pastucci watched.

"How's business?" he asked.

"Okay," I answered as cheerfully as I could at so late an hour. "I met some potential customers in Park Slope yesterday, and it went really well. So I made a lot of product tonight. Sales might pick up this week. Speaking of which . . ." I closed the top of the freezer and reached for my purse. I fished out two fifties, still crisp from the ATM machine, and handed them to him.

He smiled. For another month, I was helping him keep the light on over the pool table and beer in the cooler.

"Any of the stores give you trouble?" he asked. I bit back a smile. He sounded like the Godfather checking up on his *famiglia*.

"Only the stores I'm *not* in are trouble," I said with a smile. "That makes approximately eighty thousand grocery stores around the country that give me trouble!"

"But Brooklyn has been good to you," he said, his voice low and gravely. Mr. Pastucci loved Brooklyn. I wondered if he'd ever been anyplace else.

"Of course!" I said quickly. "Brooklyn is my savior. I wish Julia's Child was stocked at Entrefina in the Heights, but really I can't complain." It was time for me to leave. "Take care of yourself, Mr. Pastucci." Then, happy to have the night finally reach its exhausting conclusion, I gave him a quick peck on the cheek and went for the door.

"Good night, sweetie," he said.

# Chapter 4

"Get this. The new toothpaste I bought you has a childproof top."

"Groovy," Luke answered. He hit the car's turn signal and steered us toward the exit off the interstate.

"I also bought you a different shampoo," I told Luke. "This one is organic and not tested on animals."

"I'm fine with that," Luke said. "Just as long as you don't make me smell like a woman."

"I promise if anyone at work asks to borrow your perfume, you can switch back to your old one."

"But seriously—just don't switch the toilet paper," he warned. "First of all, I don't like the idea of recycled toilet paper."

"They don't mean recycled *from* toilet paper."

He just shook his head. "Even so. I try to be 'green' too, Julia. I'll plant some extra trees in Vermont if you want. But I'm not using sandpaper in the bathroom."

I shifted in my seat. It was such a puzzle. Why were men, who by all accounts were less frequent users of toilet paper, so much more opinionated about it? Could their skin really be that much more sensitive?

We'd been in the car too long, all four of us. But the Green

Mountains were finally coming into view, and I felt my spirits lift. Very shortly we'd be there. "Back on the farm," I said. "Back on the farm."

"Who is?"

"Me! I've always wanted to say that. Now that I have a farm, I can say it whenever I want to."

Luke smiled. "Okay, honey. But you don't exactly have a farm. You have a very nice barn, a pretty meadow, and a patch of dirt, where you hope that two college dropouts will figure out how to grow some better vegetables."

He had a point. Our neighbor's grown children had produced for me a crop of organic eggplant and zucchini that wasn't exactly worthy of photography, let alone praise. But it had only been their first try.

"I *still* think the great vegetable venture might work out." I hoped it would. Otherwise the project would become yet another entry in the list of things that cost me more money than they made. But we'd come to Vermont to relax, and so I would try not to worry about it. "Don't rain on my parade."

"I couldn't, even if I wanted to," he said. "Look at that sky! Not a cloud in sight."

Dutifully, I lifted my eyes to the impossibly blue sky, where it met the rounded peaks of the Green Mountains. We'd been coming here together, to our little house, since before the boys were born. Luke and I were in perfect agreement that Vermont was the most beautiful place on earth. And my farming project amused him, even if he didn't really understand why I wanted to try producing some of the ingredients for Julia's Child.

A shriek from the backseat broke through my reverie.

"*Where Elmo go?*" Wylie was showing the strain of three hours strapped into his car seat. At the moment he was watching a video.

"I'm sure he'll be right back, honey," I sighed. At home we had a strict no-TV policy for the boys. I hated the zombie faces they wore while staring at the screen. But in the car, I'd made an uneasy truce with Elmo. For the last third of the trip, when I'd run out of stories and songs and snacks, I always put in some *Sesame Street* videos to keep the kids entertained.

Videos in the car were something that belonged on my list of Things I Thought I'd Never Do.

I wanted my boys to have the experience of coming to the country—not just a suburban stand-in, but the real thing. Vermont was the genuine article. I was thrilled to share with them the hilly terrain, the unspoiled farmland, and the only state capital in the union without a McDonald's.

But it was more than three hours from New York.

So Wylie had taken to Elmo like an addict. As many times as I'd thought I might kill myself if I ever heard the Elmo theme again, I needed the little red menace with the squeaky voice more than I dared admit.

"Where Elmo *go*?" he yelled again.

"Mama, the screen really is black," Jasper explained.

I craned my neck uncomfortably to retrieve the DVD player from where it hung between the seats. The battery was dead. And the car charger we had for it wasn't very reliable.

"Sorry buddy," I said to Wylie. "Elmo is taking a break."

"Where him *go*?"

"Him is . . ." I shook my head to clear it. "Is anybody hungry? How about a muffet? I have Apple and Cheddar." I swiveled uncomfortably around again just in time to see Jasper shaking his head violently. "Jasper! A simple 'no thank you,' will do."

"*No thank you.*"

Lately, Jasper won't eat muffets. If I put them in his lunchbox, they come home untouched. I understand that the poor kid is probably just sick of them. All the same, I was trying not to let it bother me. If I couldn't even please my own child, it didn't bode well for me as a businessperson.

"*Where Elmo?*"

"Oh, Wylie. Let's sing a song, okay?" With Elmo on break, I was back on duty. "How about the ABCs?" I suggested. "You start."

"We do dat already. *Want Elmo!*"

"I know—I'll sing the ABCs backwards." I'd once tried this, on another car trip, and found it spectacularly difficult. But that was fine, because I'd also discovered that making a fool of myself was something for which Wylie and Jasper had a boundless appetite. In order to enter the town of Gannett with both eardrums still intact, I was willing to take one for the team.

I sang. "*Z, Y, X* . . . uh, *W, V, T!*" I took a breath. "*U* . . . Crap!"

Wylie giggled.

"No, Mama. Like this." Jasper took a deep breath and began to sing. "*Z, Y, X, W, V, U, Teeeeee.*" He took another breath. "*S, R, Q, P, O, N, M, L, Kayyyy.*" Not only was he in tune, but he didn't seem to have to think about the letters.

"Jasper!" I gasped. "That's amazing."

He beamed.

"Jasper," Luke asked, taking a quick peek over his shoulder into the backseat, "where did you learn that?"

I thumped Luke's leg. "He's a *prodigy.*" I'd always known it.

Jasper gave me a funny look. "I learned it in the playroom. With Sadie and Bryan."

Our neighbors' names made me frown. "Emily's kids? But Sadie is just a baby."

Jasper shrugged. "She can mostly sing it. Forward and backward. Also in Spanish. Only, she thinks its all one word."

Luke burst out laughing so violently that I checked to make

sure that the road wasn't about to make any hairpin turns. "Really? Sadie and Bryan can do the alphabet forward and backward? In Spanish?"

Jasper had already lost interest in the subject. He looked out the window. "It isn't that hard. Sadie's mama has these cards she holds up if you get stuck. And then Sadie and Bryan get fruit punch if they do it right."

"It's because Sadie has an *extra-special* mommy," Luke snickered.

"Luke!"

He was still laughing. I felt a prick of irritation. "Hey—fruit punch? In the playroom? Isn't that against the rules?"

"Bonnie said so," Jasper replied. "But Emily said the rule is no *eating*. And fruit punch is a drink."

Luke's phone rang just then. He took it out of his shirt pocket and flicked his eyes at its digital display. "Speaking of mommies," he said, flipping open the phone. "Hi, Gayle! You've caught us in the car on the way to the house."

"Why's she calling *you*?" I whispered. It was bad enough that my mother left messages on my own phone every other day.

"You say she's avoiding you?" Luke snuck a glance at me.

I shook my head vigorously. I wasn't in the mood to be quizzed by my mother.

"Oh, I'm sure she isn't. But her phone doesn't always ring when it's supposed to. Would you like to ask her yourself?"

I took the phone from my husband. At least my own quirky phone knew not to throw me under the bus with my mother. "Mom, I'm not avoiding you. I've been busy."

"Honey, busy is your permanent condition. That's no reason not to call your mother."

I let it slide by. I would not become ensnared in our usual pointless discussions. This time I would try to be very Zen and hold my tongue and get off the phone as quickly as possible. "What's going on?"

Before she could answer, Wylie howled again for Elmo.

"One second, Mom." I fished in the glove compartment for the car charger. I handed the DVD player back to Jasper and plugged it in. It worked as long as I remained leaning forward, jamming the plug into the car's lighter socket.

"Your father and I have decided to accept your invitation to come up for Thanksgiving," my mother said. "And I'd better make those airplane reservations now. It's almost October."

"Oh . . ." My mind whirled like a disc drive as I attempted to recall any previous conversation about the holiday. It took me a minute to realize that the invitation was just one more of my mother's machinations. I opened my mouth to argue but managed just in time to bite back the words "but I didn't invite you."

During the pause, my mother added, "Unless you'd like to bring the family here instead."

I hesitated again, sensing a trap. But there was my own distaste for the South Carolina golf community where my parents had retired. And flying with Wylie was still a bit like dog years—the flight segment seemed to last approximately seven times longer than it should. "No," I said through gritted teeth. "You should come here."

"That's what I thought you'd say. I'll call the airline next week. I should probably get going now—the potluck is in an hour, and I'm not ready."

A snarky question leapt onto the tip of my tongue, and this time I didn't hold back. "What are you *bringing* to the potluck?" I'd seen her contributions before, and it wasn't pretty. She made "pizza" out of refrigerator crescent rolls with cream cheese spread on top. She also made a casserole with canned beans, canned cream of mushroom soup, and freeze-dried onion rings on top.

My mother is the only person I know who wears out her electric can opener every year or so. But today she surprised me.

"I'm bringing the most darling spinach and feta turnovers, and a fresh leek tart."

I tried to imagine my mother crimping the edges of phyllo dough or fanning the layers of a leek at her kitchen sink. "You're making all that? You might need more than an hour."

"No—Olga next door made it for me, and I'm heading over there to give her a French manicure beforehand. We have a deal."

"Oh." It made so much more sense now. The Earth's rotation had not, indeed, reversed course. "Is that a fair trade, Mother? Leek tarts are quite a project."

She sniffed. "Olga's hands could really use the help."

I'll bet they could, after all that effort in the kitchen. I looked down at my own. My nails looked like I'd hacked them off with a bread knife. "Well, Mom, the phone service gets pretty choppy up here. I should say good-bye."

"But you didn't tell me—how are my boys?"

"They're great. They're . . ." I craned my neck. In the backseat, I saw two slack faces, two sets of eyes focused on a tiny DVD player slung into the opening between the front seats. "The boys are anesthetized. By *Sesame Street.*"

"Ooh! I can't wait to pinch their cheeks."

She could pinch them all she wanted to while they were staring at that screen. I doubted they would even feel it. "You'll get your chance in November. Talk to you later, Mom."

"Bye, honey."

I handed Luke's phone back with a sigh. "My parents are coming to New York for Thanksgiving."

"Then I'll have to whip up a batch of martinis." Luke chuckled.

"Luke! You wouldn't." My mother doesn't handle hard alcohol

very well. We'd learned one Easter that martinis seemed to encourage her to criticize me even more freely than usual.

"Sweetie, the martinis will be for *you*. We'll keep her on weak white-wine spritzers."

With a sigh, I straightened up, letting go of the DVD cord to save my back.

"Elmo!" Wylie yelled.

I was suddenly depleted. "Oh, Wylie. Let's look out the window. We're almost there." It was just a few more miles up the little two-lane highway running west toward Gannett. Then one more mile up a dirt road to our house.

Wylie shifted tactics. "*Pease* Elmo," he begged.

I reached my arm behind Luke's headrest and into the backseat to take his hand. "Wylie, we're getting out soon. I promise. At the house."

He took my hand in his two small ones. "Where house go?"

"Just up the road. See? There's the farm stand. Hey! It's pumpkin season! And look! There's a horse. On Jasper's side of the car."

And on the other side, there's the ugly new subdivision, I could have added. A local developer by the name of Randy Biden had been busy building McCabins around Gannett. Ever since our local ski mountain expanded three years ago, Randy had been raking in the cash selling faux-rustic four-bedroom log homes with Sub-Zero refrigerators.

Luke turned the car onto our dirt road, leaving the subdivision behind. The trees arching overhead were just showing the first tinge of yellow. He rolled down the window as the car climbed the hill. "I love that smell," he said. When he reached our road, Luke always rolled down the window—no matter what the weather—and declared his love for the smell of Vermont. I inhaled. It was especially lovely today. The September air was still rich with the perfume of flowers, with just a tinge of decay, as summer began to give up the fight.

"Where smell go?" Wylie asked.

I turned to him and took a long, exaggerated breath. "Smell it, Wylie? The trees and the flowers and the cool Vermont air?"

He began to breathe in and out, very fast. I listened with growing concern, hoping he wouldn't pass out from hyperventilation.

At the top of the hill the road made a lazy curve to the left. Our petite little house, in the style of honest-to-God rustic, sat on the left. Behind it rose ten wooded acres beside a little pond, which an entire community of frogs called home.

On the other side of the road was the Barker Farm—or rather, the farmhouse, where the widow Barker still lived with her two grown children. Behind their old white house, forty acres of farmland rolled along the hilltop.

And twenty of those acres were now mine.

When Mr. Barker died, about a year and a half ago, his widow sold off their little herd of dairy cows. Jasper and Wylie missed seeing their tawny forms grazing across the road, but, aside from the loss of our pastoral view, we hadn't thought much about it.

Then last summer I'd opened a piece of registered mail from the Town of Gannett. The letter informed me that in one month's time the town's Development Review Board would hold a hearing on whether to allow the subdivision of the parcel for a forty-unit condominium to be built. Abutting property holders were to consider themselves notified.

"Oh, shit!" had been my reaction.

The developer, Randy Biden, had offered the widow Barker fifty thousand dollars for her back acreage. "If I can get the town to approve a condo subdivision, that is," he'd hedged.

It was to be called Lincoln Lodge, with log construction for the condo units and post-and-beam carports in the parking area. I was horrified that our quiet gravel road might become a superhighway.

Luke had stroked his whiskers thoughtfully. "I suppose we could fight it," he said. "It's within our rights to object to forty new condos across the street. But Mrs. Barker probably needs the money."

I was sure that was true. I had another idea, but I hesitated to make such an expensive suggestion. At the time, I had just borrowed the first ten thousand dollars from our brokerage account to start Julia's Child. "Luke," I said carefully, "what if *we* bought the farmland instead?"

His eyes opened wide. "I was *just* thinking you'd look cute in a milkmaid dress. And then we could roll in the hay."

I swatted him with the envelope. "This is your chance to become a redneck."

He caught the envelope and pulled me close. "I love our Vermont place too, just the way it is. Let's talk to Ida Barker when we go up there next weekend."

As it turned out, we weren't the only people who objected to the Lincoln Lodge Condos. "It's Junior and Kate," Mrs. Barker said from across the fence. "My kids are upset. They don't want to see their father's farm become a rich people's playground." She sighed. "They have it in their heads to farm some organic pumpkins instead. Maybe open a U-pick operation. But them kids . . ." She shook her head, declining to finish the sentence. Junior and Kate were twentysomething twins who still lived at home.

"And that Randy Biden!" she added. "He's such a slick fellow, I feel like washing up right after I shake hands with him. But if I don't sell now, he might go find himself another twenty acres. That kind of money could do a lot for us. New roof on the house . . ."

That was our cue. "Mrs. Barker," Luke said casually. "What if Julia and I bought the land instead? And *didn't* develop it."

"And," I jumped in, "your kids could still try their hand at vegetable farming. I need organic produce for my new business. I'd be willing to lease the land back to the kids for a song, so they could give it a go. If it doesn't work out, I'd find somebody else to grow vegetables there."

At first Mrs. Barker looked at us in disbelief. Her mouth actually fell open, revealing a lot of what Luke called "summer teeth."

"Because some are teeth and some are not," he'd once explained.

When Ida Barker regained the ability to speak, she climbed with her slippered feet onto the lowest rung of the cow fence to throw her arms around me. I stepped forward to accept the embrace, praying that they'd turned off the electric current since selling off the herd.

Everybody lived. The next day we called a lawyer in town to handle the sale of the property. And I'd felt a swell of satisfaction just looking at that shaggy hilltop ever since.

I was thrilled when Luke swung into our gravel driveway and cut the engine. The sudden silence was beautiful. My window still down, the chorus of the birds was the first sound I heard. I spun around in my seat to unclip the kids from their car seats. "Who will race me to the barn?" I asked.

"Me!" was the enthusiastic answer from both. After the long ride, it was just what the doctor ordered.

We hopped out of the car and took off toward the distant red structure. The meadow grasses were waist high. Junior had mowed a path through the greenery and wildflowers to the barn, leaving a narrow canyon of meadow rising up around my boys. They barreled down the path, and I jogged behind. Grasshoppers leaped out of our way, and the breeze felt lazy in the late-afternoon sun. At that moment the three-hour trip seemed like a bargain.

As I watched my boys run up the path in front of me, I experienced a moment of absolute certainty that they were the most beautiful children in the world. Wylie trucked along in a toddler's run, as heavy as a linebacker, soft elbows thrust out to the sides. There was a zero percent chance that he could beat his brother to the barn, but he gave it his all. And he laughed as he ran.

Jasper was ahead and gaining margin, thanks to the suddenly leggy frame he'd acquired in the short time since his fifth birthday. His roly-poly toddlerhood was all but invisible now. Even though he kept looking over his shoulder to smile at us, he handily won the race. He threw up his hands in victory as his little blond head disappeared around the corner into the open barn doors.

Then he gave a bloodcurdling scream.

# Chapter 5

"Don't touch it, Mama! It's poisonous," Jasper warned as I came panting around the corner. My cautious son pointed at something black moving through the hay on the floor.

"Honey, that's only a garter snake," I wheezed. I put my hands on my knees to catch my breath. "There aren't any poisonous snakes in Vermont."

"Well," said a soft voice from the barn's other open door, "not *many* poisonous ones, anyway." I looked up to find Kate Barker standing there in a long, flowing skirt and bare feet. She tossed her head, rippling her straw-colored hair like a river. "If you hike the cliff trails, it's possible to find a rattler." She glided into the barn, the many bracelets around her wrists and ankles jingling lightly.

"Hello, Kate," I said cheerily. "Do you want to see the *little* garter snake we found?" Work with me here, would you? "It's so cute! Look, boys. When the snake sticks out his tongue, it's bright red."

"Where tongue go?" Wylie asked.

"Come here and watch," I whispered. Sure enough the snake, encouraged by our lack of motion, held still, its head in the air. It flicked its bright red tongue intermittently.

"Cool!" Jasper said at last. "Now I'm going to see the goats." He went past Kate, out the side door of the barn, into the slanting afternoon sunlight. Wylie followed him without a word. If big brother went, then so would he.

I turned to Kate, preparing to broach the sensitive matter of her vegetable production. I needed a tactful way to ask if she could do better than forty pockmarked eggplants and eighty scrawny zucchini.

"So, what are you up to now that your harvest is finished?" I began. It was something I'd long been curious about. What would a young, single woman find to do in this tiny town?

"The earth and I are resting," she explained dreamily. "Until the living soil is ready to receive the rains again."

I nodded with what I hoped was understanding. It was fine with me if Kate wanted to play the role of earth goddess, although it left the role of the shrill businesswoman to me. "Excellent," I said. "How best do you think we could . . . diversify the output next year? It seems like . . . if we planted more than two vegetables, we'd have a greater chance of . . ." I was trying to avoid the word "success."

"I believe the southern soil is asking for legumes," Kate said, tracing a pattern in the hay with her big toe. Then she stopped and stared with a squint into the rafters. "Yes, I can see green shoots, and a vine."

"Okay," I said, encouraged. "How about sweet peas? I could use those. They have a lot of natural sugar, which works well for toddlers."

Kate thought about it. I mentally begged her not to suggest lima beans. There were some foods that couldn't be sold to children in any form.

"Sweet peas. I like it," she said finally.

"Great!" I clapped my hands together. But there were other serious matters to attend to. "Now, we also need to nail down our organic certification. You haven't heard from Kevin Dunham, have you? We really need to get a hold of that guy. And quick."

Kevin was the organic inspector I'd hired to help process my certification with the USDA.

"No," Kate answered with a shrug. "I haven't seen him. But look!" She moved closer to the open barn doors.

I hurried to the door. I saw the goats in their pen and the children walking toward them. That's all I saw.

"Beautiful! I rarely find them on the property."

I followed Kate's gaze more carefully and realized she was staring at a hummingbird, doing its distinctive swooping flight.

"The ruby-throated is the only hummer in Vermont," she said dreamily. "And they're attracted to the color red."

"Ah," I said. That explained why those glass hummingbird feeders I'd seen at the hardware store were always red. "He'll figure out soon enough that the barn is not an enormous flower." Kate didn't laugh. I cleared my throat. "So . . . I'll try to call Kevin Dunham again this week. But the thing is, he hasn't returned my last couple of messages. I was hoping you'd bump into him in town."

Kate sighed petulantly, still peering out the doorway after the bird. "But it's not like we *need* the government's rubber stamp to grow the best food on earth."

At that I had to take a deep, cleansing breath through my nose, the way they teach you to do in yoga class. "That's true. But we need organic certification to sell it," I insisted gently. "You don't mind getting *paid* for the best food on earth, I assume?"

She shrugged, tipping her dreamy face to the side as her gossamer hair slid down over her shoulders. Money seemed not to weigh very heavily on her mind.

I envied her that. But I needed her help nonetheless.

Two months ago I had hustled my family to Vermont for the big organic inspection. After three and a half hours of clapping along with Elmo, I'd sprung from the car, ready for an intense afternoon proving the wholesomeness of the farm and its wares.

While Luke and the boys had headed over to the pond to catch frogs, I tiptoed over to the cultivated rows of zucchini and inhaled the sweet smell of the earth. Sinking to my knees, I admired the arching stems and tendrils before me.

The impulse to be green and clean hit me like a ton of bricks when Jasper was born. Here was this brand-new, fragile person, and the one responsible for his care was unaccountably me. The dim sum and Starbucks muffins that had sustained me during college and long hours at work would no longer do. Clearly more care and attention to foodstuffs would be necessary. I didn't want to mess up.

Later, when I began researching organic food trends I learned that the first organic purchase many women ever make is a jar of baby food. Just like me.

And now, out of the mere *dirt* right in front of me, vegetables grew. And I in turn would put those vegetables into food for children. And via another mysterious and miraculous process, their calories and vitamins and minerals would transform those children into bigger and smarter people. With more pride than I'd ever felt before, I'd sat at the edge of my field, awaiting the organic inspection team.

Forty-five minutes later, a battered VW bus finally rattled up the road. I rose as it eased to a stop beside the barn. An eternity later, the rusted door creaked open, releasing a billow of sweet-smelling smoke. Kevin Dunham stepped out, red eyed and bleary.

"Morning," he'd said.

It was a quarter to three. "Hi," I'd said weakly, wondering if there'd been some mistake.

He'd looked up at the sky for a minute, as if he'd left something up there for safekeeping. Then he stepped away from his van.

He eyed me unsteadily, saying nothing.

"Right. So . . ." I was at a loss. For support, I turned to my clipboard and the fourteen-page application I'd filled out. "Would you like to see our fertilizer sources first?"

"Lead on."

I gave him the nickel tour. First I brought him over to our goat enclosure, explaining how we composted manure for fertilizer and straw bedding for mulch. "And here is"—I riffled through the papers on my clipboard—"the receipt for the supplementary feed we bought last year. Just a small amount from an organic producer in Brattleboro."

I showed him our cultivated acres. "And those acres on the other side of the divide are fallow and will be ready for cultivation next year." I prattled on about our cover crop of buckwheat and our anti-erosion plans.

Dunham didn't ask a single question. To our rainwater-collection system and our well, he said, "Yeah."

Uneasy, I handed over the application that had taken me so many late-night hours to assemble. "It's . . . all in here." I'd slaved over that document, converting acres to hectares, explaining adjoining land use. It was difficult to hand it all over to a man who seemed not to remember my name.

I should have trusted my gut.

"Thanks," he'd said, and then headed toward his van. He put my precious paperwork on the passenger seat and then climbed in.

"Wait!" I'd said, in disbelief. It couldn't possibly be the end of my inspection. He hadn't even looked at the vegetable plants I'd dug up for him. And he hadn't gotten closer to our soil than the edge of the plot. "Aren't you going to *test* anything?" I asked. I could hear in my voice an echo of the straight-A high school student I'd once been. I was prepared for this inspection, damn it, and desperate to prove it.

"But testing's not required. Organic certification is all about *process*, ma'am." It was by far the longest statement he'd made. "The results, we don't really look at 'em."

The surprise must have shown on my face. Or maybe he woke up and realized he'd been hasty. For whatever reason, he decided that his next joint could wait a few minutes. "Actually, ma'am, I got a soil test kit in back, if you want to know how your mineral levels stack up," he said. "But it'll be extra."

"Yes, please" had been my answer. My tiny little farm was the very model of clean living, and I wanted something to show for it.

He'd spent a few minutes putting soil samples into test tubes. Then he'd climbed back into the van.

"When will I hear from you?" I whimpered.

"Soon," he'd said, backing out.

Two months had passed between that sunny July day and this lovely September afternoon. Luckily, small producers can legally sell their organic produce without certification. Since Kate and her brother had handily underperformed the five-thousand-dollar benchmark, this year we were in the clear. But a new season would soon be upon us. And I had big plans for Julia's Child. I'd need that certification to make my business legit.

Kate, I noticed, was now holding the garter snake. They were having a chat. She whispered to the snake, and it flicked its bright red tongue in response. I waited for their private conference to end. When she put it back on the floor, I made my case one more time. "Please, if you see Dunham in town, ask him to call me. If he doesn't come through soon, I'm going to have to hire another team of inspectors. And I know how you hate to have people tromping around in your fields."

Kate made a face. "You won't believe who I caught snooping out here last week."

"Who?"

"Randy Biden."

"The developer? Why?"

"I don't *know* why," Kate said with a stamp of her bare foot.

"But I put up a 'No Trespassing' sign the very next day. I think he's up to something."

I shrugged off her paranoia. "Maybe he just wants to know if we're really farming anything up here. Maybe he thinks if it doesn't work out, he can approach me again next year and try to buy the land."

She looked stricken. "You'd *never,*" she yelped. "Do you even *know* his latest scam? It's just horrible."

"Tell me," I said. "But let's step outside, where I can see the boys." I walked through the barn's open door, toward the shaggy little organic-fertilizer producers in the pasture. Wylie stood inside the split-rail fence. "Me a goat farmer," he said as I climbed up to sit on the top rail. He patted the head of a small goat, who took the opportunity to gnaw on his jeans.

Jasper crouched at the other side of the corral. With a frown of concentration he pitched pebbles at a fence post. "*Doozsh, doozsh,*" he said under his breath as he strafed an invisible enemy.

Kate perched on the fence rail next to me. "So," she began, her voice lowered conspiratorially, as if the goats were likely to repeat whatever she was about to tell me. "Randy Biden gets paid by EcoPass to plant trees!"

"Sorry?" I asked. Planting trees sounded like a good thing for a developer to do.

"Do you know what EcoPass is?"

I shook my head.

"It's a carbon-offset company. They let people pay for their sins. If you feel guilty, say, about taking a cross-country flight, you can purchase vouchers from them. Then EcoPass puts your money into projects that offset the carbon you've selfishly burned in the atmosphere."

"Okay. I've heard of that," I told her. "They try to prevent methane gasses from escaping into the atmosphere . . ."

"That's right," Kate agreed. "But in Vermont, EcoPass plants trees. And Randy Biden is one of the people they pay to do it.

We're talking about a man who uses a bulldozer to clear trees from his building sites. He builds *log homes.* And then, when the project is finished, he plants some saplings around the property so it won't look too ugly to sell. And EcoPass pays him to plant them!"

I burst out laughing, which made Kate furious. But I couldn't help myself. The man was a genius. "Holy shit!" I said. "He's getting paid to replace a few trees that he would have planted anyway?"

"Exactly." Kate sighed. "I hope he burns in hell."

"Mama! You said 'shit,' " Jasper said, without looking up from his pebble-tossing game.

Of course I understood Kate's outrage—I wasn't deaf to the irony. How many trees did the man have to cut down for each log home? Forty? Eighty? He'd have to replant the entire state of Vermont just to break even. But you had to admire the developer's pluck, not to mention his understanding of the way the world worked. Here I was, on the side of the "good guys," fighting just to keep my head above water. Hell, if Randy Biden was also a certified organic inspector, I'd hire him on the spot.

"Oh, Kate, I'm sorry. But that's why we need to get our organic act together. So we can win a round, like him."

She was silent.

I climbed over the fence into the goat's pen. "Boys," I called, "it's time to go back to the house." I patted Wylie's sun-warmed head. "Okay, pal. Let's go say hello to the frogs in the pond." I wanted to get back to the house and help Luke unload the car. I hoisted Wylie over the fence, despite his complaints, and began to lead him back down the path toward home.

"See you, Kate! Say hello to your mother for me."

"Have a blessed evening," she mumbled.

# Chapter 6

Wylie and I had already washed and torn the lettuce together. Now, standing on a chair to reach the counter, he was peeling onions. I didn't happen to need any onions, but Wylie didn't know that. His little pink lips were set in concentration as he teased the papery skin away from a bulb.

From the other room, the phone rang. "One minute, sweetie," I promised Wylie. Just so that there would be no misunderstandings, I carried my eight-inch chef's knife, the one I'd been using to slice tomatoes, into the living room with me. "Hello?" My eyes went to the clock. It was a few minutes after five.

"Julia, it's Marta!" She was out of breath.

"Hi, Marta. How were the deliveries? Did you put the flyers in the windows?"

"Yes! But there's something I called to tell you."

"Okay," I said, wondering how Wylie was doing all alone in the kitchen. Our Vermont phone was old school, with a cord. I was tethered to the living room. The kitchen was oddly quiet. "Can I . . . Just one second. I need to check on . . ."

But Marta was having none of it. "Julia! Listen. When I was making the delivery to Luigi's, I ran into Lizzie Hefflespeck!"

"Um, who?" Now from the kitchen came the sound of furniture

scraping against linoleum. I stretched the phone cord as far as it would go, and Wylie came into view, pushing his chair toward the sink.

"One second, Marta," I said, wondering how old my children would have to be before I could carry on an uninterrupted, adult conversation. "Whatcha doing, kid?" I called to him.

"I wash yettuce more!" he called back.

"*Okay!* Sorry, Marta. Now, who did you see?"

"Lizzie Hefflespeck, Julia!"

"Marta, I'm not trying to be dense. But I don't have any idea who that is."

"¡Dios mío!" Marta sighed. "She's the blonde one on *The Scene*."

Ah! So Marta was trying to tell me about a celeb sighting. But she'd picked the wrong girl to share it with. "*The Scene*?"

"You live under a rock, you know that? It's a morning show with five hostesses. The one that fired Mimi Beener last year? For fighting with her cohosts?"

That sounded vaguely familiar. The bit of gossip about the famous comedienne feuding with other TV divas had briefly penetrated the harried bubble in which I lived. "Oh! Sure. So you saw one of them in Brooklyn?"

I heard the sound of the water running hard in the kitchen. Playing in the sink was a time-honored toddler distraction. I craned my neck to see Wylie holding a tiny fragment of lettuce under a torrential shower. The waste of water pained me, but I didn't want to be rude to Marta.

"I didn't just *see* her!" she shouted in my ear. "I *met* her—her and the little daughter. Because—you'll never guess what they were shopping for!"

I perked up at that. "Don't tell me they were looking for our product."

"They were! They just didn't know it," Marta said smugly.

"Tell me!"

"It was Lizzie and the baby and the personal assistant. And Lizzie and the baby were dressed to kill. Lizzie was decked out in a dress, like Lilly Pulitzer maybe, and Ava had on a matching print but with . . ."

I bit back the urge to cut Marta's description short. I was dying to hear whether the TV star fed her daughter a muffet, but I'd blown off work and left all the legwork to Marta, so I let her tell it her way.

"They were in Brooklyn for a photo shoot."

"Both of them?"

"For a magazine—a 'famous mother and adorable infant' kind of spread. And the kid was hungry . . ."

"And you walked in with your delivery of muffets! Did they buy some? That's great, Marta!"

"*Chica,* this story ain't even half over. Lizzie was looking at the bananas, asking Luigi if they were organic . . ."

"She was *not*!" I laughed. Luigi's Convenience Store was about the size of a Volkswagen Beetle. It didn't smack of gourmet choice.

"She was! And I latched right on to that mama like white on *arroz,*" she said. " 'Here's your organic snack!' I told her. 'They're called muffets, and I'm delivering them from our company, Julia's Child, which makes healthy things for cute little girls like Ava.' And then, because I'd recognized her, she dropped Luigi like a hot potato. And here's the kicker, Julia. I had a fresh muffet in my purse. It wasn't frozen—I was gonna eat it with my *café con leche* when the delivery was done. So I gave it to little Ava. And I told Lizzie that it was black beans and carrots, all organic, and she said, 'Oh, I don't know if she'll eat it,' and you know what happened, right?"

I smiled. Because I did know what happened. "She chowed it."

"She did! And what do you think happened next?" Marta squealed.

"She bought a whole box of them?" I guessed.

"No *way* honey. I *gave* her a couple of boxes of them. And she was just so chirpy about everything. She loved the flyer with you and Wylie, 'Oh, it's so cute,' and what a neat little company, and then she said the magic words."

" 'Marry me'?"

Marta sighed. "No! She said, 'I think we should have these on our show.' "

Fresh out of wisecracks, I finally shut up and listened.

"So her personal assistant, this twenty-year-old intern or whatever, is standing outside on the phone, trying to get her a table at Per Se or something, and Lizzie, like, snaps her fingers and the girl comes rushing into the store. Lizzie throws the boxes of muffets at her and tells her to make a note that 'We want this product on the show.' So the girl is jamming that into her BlackBerry. And I make a real gushy good-bye to Lizzie, tell her how much you'd love to be on her show. *And* I get the personal assistant's name as I'm leaving. So I can follow up on Monday, right?"

"*You* are a rock star, Marta." And I meant it. I wondered if I would have had the wherewithal to throw myself at the celebrity the way she had. I probably wouldn't have even recognized her.

"Damned straight. But my story's *still* not over. I made it back to the office after the deliveries, by two thirty. Almost nothing happened all afternoon, by the way, and I was thinking of heading out a few minutes early. But at quarter to five the phone rings. It's a producer from *The Scene*. Some musical guest canceled for Tuesday, and they want to know if we can be there."

"Oh, shit! *This* Tuesday?"

"That's right. So of course I told them yes."

"Oh, shit!" sang Wylie from the kitchen.

"Jeez!" I said, still in shock. "Are we ready for national television?"

"You will be," Marta said, cutting to the chase. "Leave it to me."

"*Oh, shit!*" yelled Wylie again. "Wet!"

I dropped the phone on the sofa and ran into the kitchen. Lettuce and water were flowing in a green stream over the edge of the sink and down the front of the cabinet. Wylie had somehow wedged the salad spinner over the drain and overflowed the sink. I shut off the water, unwedged the spinner bowl, and ran back to the phone.

". . . hair and makeup. We're called for 9:00 A.M. The first segment starts at 10:00, but you're slotted for 10:45," Marta was saying. "We have all day Monday to get ready."

One whole day. "Yikes. I guess I'll be in early," I said, the enormity of the situation just starting to sink in.

"See you then!" Marta said cheerfully. "I gotta call my sister now," she said. "She's still bragging about the time she saw Justin Timberlake walking down Broadway."

# Chapter 7

"She'll be there at 2:00," Marta said, wrapping up her fifth call before 9:00 A.M. "Thank you!" She hung up the phone with a definitive click.

I didn't have the faintest idea who Marta had been speaking to or where she'd promised I'd be. She had taken over, turning our office into Mission Control, and I'd sunk into a terrified haze. After hanging up the phone, she disappeared into the bull pen outside our private closet and then reappeared a minute later rolling a piece of equipment on a cart. It wouldn't have surprised me if it were a NASA-style countdown clock. *T* minus twenty-five hours. And counting.

Instead, it was a rather ancient-looking television and VCR.

Marta folded her hands across her chest and turned to where I sat, cowering, in my chair. "Listen. Since we can't get a media expert in here to help us, we're going to have to wing it. I'm just going to tell you everything I know about the program, and then we're going to watch an episode."

"Okay," I said helplessly.

"*The Scene* airs from ten to eleven in the morning, in several segments. The first part is just a discussion among the five cohosts."

"About what?" I asked. I'd never seen the show.

"About . . . whatever," she said, as if it were obvious. "About politics. About Beyoncé. About whatever is, you know, *out there.* But they do it in a personal way. They sympathize with the victim. They tell their own stories. It's very confessional. Then, in the next segment, they do the stars, on the sofa."

"Stars?"

"There are one or two interviews of famous people. Like an actress with a new movie coming out or someone who's getting married. Whoever's hot. Then finally they have either a musical guest or someone who shows them a new product or a recipe. That's where you come in."

"Because I'm a product? Or a recipe? Will they have me cook on the show?" That didn't sound so bad.

"Yes, but only for pretend," Marta said.

"Pretend?" I thought of Wylie stirring up pancakes on his wooden play stove.

"See, we'll have the ingredients for a batch of muffets. You'll stir them together, and then the hosts will taste the finished product."

"Okay. So we have to bring those ingredients." I wrote that down in my notebook. "What else?"

"Well . . ." Marta hesitated. "They always give the studio audience a gift from each segment of the show," she said.

"A gift?"

"The guest's latest book or a copy of their CD. Since you don't have a book . . ."

"And I haven't cut a CD lately." I shivered with discomfort.

Marta ignored my sarcasm. "I told them we'd give away muffets to every audience member."

"How many . . ."

"Two hundred and fifty," Marta said, before I could finish.

"Two hundred and fifty!" I yelped. "Where are we going to get that many extra packages of muffets by tomorrow? Zia Maria is probably booked tonight."

"Calm down, Julia, because I have a plan. First of all, we're going to make up a package of two muffets for each person, not twelve."

"But still . . ."

*"And,"* she continued, one long finger in the air to shut me up, "the reason we do our cooking at La Cucina is because . . ."

"Because it's illegal to make the product at home."

"It would be illegal to *sell* it from a home kitchen. The muffets for the show are to give away, not to sell," Marta said carefully. "We can make them anywhere we want."

I blinked at her. "Oh."

"So I'm going to make them at home tonight," Marta said decisively. "And this afternoon I'm going to work on the packaging, since we don't have anything the right size. And I want to do something a little more promotional . . ."

"But what about freezer space?" I asked. I hadn't seen Marta's freezer, but I doubted it would hold five hundred muffets.

"I don't have to freeze them. They'll taste even better fresh."

"Oh." Of course they would. "But still, Marta, I can make them today in my own kitchen."

"No, you can't."

"Why not?"

"Because you're getting your hair cut and colored at two o'clock. At Frédéric Fekkai. Then after that I need you to go and get a manicure and a pedicure."

I was really out of my element now. "Did you say 'colored'?" Tree huggers like me try to avoid harsh chemicals.

*"Sí, señora.* We can't have those gray hairs glinting on high-def."

I put a self-conscious hand to the top of my head. Last time I'd checked, there were only a few gray hairs there. Let's not get crazy.

"And right before your haircut, we're going shopping."

You'd think, after the hair color, I would have seen that coming. "Oh," I said stupidly again. "Where?"

"Barneys," was her answer. "Or Bergdorf. You can choose."

"Thanks," I said, with a hint of indignation, though it had been years since I'd bought any garment that could not withstand jam-smearing and machine washing.

"So, moving on." Marta crossed a couple of things off her list. "Let's talk more about the show and about your segment. To really make it on *The Scene*, you have to be confessional," she said with an air of authority.

"But . . ." It was hard enough to picture myself cooking for a bunch of chirpy millionaire talk-show hosts. It was nearly impossible to imagine dishing dirt with them. "How? I'm not a soap opera star with a secret boyfriend. We're tasting muffets here."

She shrugged. "They sit around and dish. That's the show. So you've got to give them something to dish about. That's what we should work on now."

I took a deep, Lamaze-worthy breath. Then I capped the paper cup of coffee I'd been drinking and tossed it into the garbage can. The combination of caffeine and swelling terror was proving to be a bad one. "I don't know about 'confessional,'" I told Marta. "But I know I can romanticize the story. I'll tell them about how I started the business almost accidentally because I wanted the very best for my little boys, but also to save the world."

Marta chewed her gum thoughtfully. "You do that role well. But I'm telling you they really want to hear about how your husband left you for his secretary and how you've sold a kidney to finance the business. And how the titans at the big grocery chain stores want you to sleep with them before they'll stock your product, but you won't do it—"

"But none of that is true!" I cried. "Although I'd keep an open mind about that last part."

Marta rolled her eyes. Apparently I wasn't very credible as a slut. "Look, I'll show you what I mean."

Marta pulled a videotape out of her purse and stuck it into the VCR, which was part of the rental suite's communal hardware. "My neighbor had this, and it's only a week old."

Snowy static on the screen became an ad for allergy medication. And then, to bouncy theme music, a group of five shiny talk-show hostesses sashayed out from behind a red curtain and onto a warmly lit stage. To whoops of appreciation and massive applause from the studio audience, they took seats at a half-moon-shaped maple dining table.

Marta pointed at the skinniest, blondest hostess. "That's Lizzie Hefflespeck, our savior." The young woman had layers of silk for hair. She was blonde and as slim as an haricot vert, not at all the mommy figure I had pictured. She wore a stylish little wrap dress, size zero. Ten perfect fuchsia fingernails clutched her coffee mug.

In fact, all five hostesses clutched matching mugs, in perfectly manicured hands. It was probably as an attempt to make the whole production feel like a casual sit-down among friends. But I was not even a little bit fooled.

"My dear friend Gwyneth has a new film," Lizzie cooed on screen.

Marta muted the show. "Background information," she said. "Lizzie's married to an Olympic athlete who was her personal trainer. He's the Ken to her Barbie. Their little daughter is a year old, and it's like Lizzie's the first person to ever have a child, you know what I'm saying? When she was trying to get pregnant, they interviewed Lizzie's fertility specialist. I'm surprised she didn't have the in vitro on camera. When she was preggo, they interviewed her OBGYN. These days, she's obsessed with the health and nutrition of her miracle child. That's why you're getting your big break."

Lucky me.

"Moving on," Marta said, pointing at the next host in the coffee klatch. "That's Wanda. She's the *new* smart-assed one who spars with everyone. You want to stay on her good side. Then there's Charity, who used to be a serious journalist, but then she won a season on *Survivor* and her career really took off."

"Marta?" I gasped. "How is it you *know* all about this show? And these people? We're here at work every day when this show is on."

Marta fixed her gaze on me. The look was affectionate but also hinted at how much my failings amused her. "Because I *read*."

# Chapter 8

It is true what they say about television lights—they are surprisingly hot. I feel like I'm melting, and I haven't stepped onto the actual stage yet. Everything is happening too fast. I can't see into the studio audience, where I'd hoped to spot Marta. Then I hear my name called, and I feel short of breath. I plaster a smile onto my face and I start to move forward.

Too late, I realize that I'm still wearing flip-flops, not the stiletto heels that Marta made me buy.

Hopefully the cameraman will be kind.

Then I'm somehow standing right next to Lizzie Hefflespeck, and she's poking me in the arm. Repeatedly. I'm being poked in the arm on national television.

"Mama?"

The poking doesn't stop.

"Mama! Your radio is on. And Wylie wants to get out of his crib."

With a gasp, I sat up in bed and whirled to face the clock. It was a quarter to seven, so my alarm had only just begun broadcasting the morning news. I was sweaty. But Jasper stood calmly next to the bed, already dressed in khaki pants and a polo shirt. He stopped poking my arm.

"Mama, up now!" Wylie hollered from the other room.

"Thank you, Jasper," I gasped.

Next to me, Luke rolled over. "*Arfnargh,*" he said.

"Dada!" Wylie hollered from the crib. He had ears like a bat but apparently only one volume setting. "Where Mama go?"

"Coming, Wylie!" I croaked, hoping my heart would soon return to a more normal rate. I heaved my legs over the side of the bed. "Luke, sweetie, please get up. I've got to get ready for my . . ." The panic of my dream was still fresh, and I almost couldn't finish the sentence. "Interview."

He opened his eyes and smiled at me. "Ah! Your fifteen minutes of fame!"

"I'm told it will be more like four minutes," I corrected him. "Can you feed the kids?"

"Certainly, oh famous one." Luke slipped his legs over the other side of the bed and reached down to pull his pajama pants off the floor. My husband likes to sleep in the nude, which the children find odd.

"Daddy, I see your butt," Jasper said, predictably.

"Oatmeal!" Luke said, ignoring him. "It is time to make Daddy Bear's steel cut oatmeal for my two little cubs. *Argh!*"

"Pirates say *argh,*" Jasper argued, following Luke out of the bedroom. "Bears only roar."

"Want it Mama!" Wylie howled when the two of them walked into the boys' room to fetch him from the crib.

"Wylie," I heard Luke tell him, "Goldilocks has to go straighten up her three-hundred-dollar hairdo. But if you come with me, I'll let you stir the oatmeal."

The breakfast worked. I heard only one minor argument, over who had more raisins in his bowl, but blissfully I was left alone to shower. Marta had confirmed that hair styling and makeup would be done for me before my appearance. That left plenty of time for me to dress carefully in the cerulean blue V-neck sweater whose purchase Marta had supervised. I'd wanted to go with a simple navy blue sweater, and she'd lobbied for a plunging wrap dress. We compromised on the V-neck, which fit well and wasn't too revealing. But I wished the color were a few shades less brilliant.

I emerged from the bathroom. It was almost eight o'clock, when Luke and Jasper would leave together for school and work. Luke bent over to retrieve a folded paper that had been slipped under our door. I saw him skim the contents then slip it into his pocket.

"What's that?" I asked.

He looked over at me guiltily. "It's nothing. Just a note from the building."

"Let me see," I said, stretching out a hand.

"Later," he said dismissively.

"Luke! What the hell?" I asked.

He fished it out of his pocket and handed it to me. "It's nothing. Really. I didn't want you to get all worried about it before your big appearance."

> Dear shareholders in apartment 514:
>
> Even though the regulations for use of the basement community room are posted clearly on the wall, board members have observed your children's caregiver repeatedly violating the rules against eating and drinking.
>
> If you are unable to bring your family into compliance, the co-op board will have no alternative but to ban the occupants of your unit from using the community

room. Subsequent violations could ultimately result in the revocation of your proprietary lease.

Sincerely,

*Rothman Property Management*

"That *bi*—" I bit down on my lip. My nervousness probably had plenty to do with it, but tears pricked my eyes. The letter seemed to suggest that we could be kicked out of a co-op apartment *that we own* because of a bunch of seedless grapes. "I can't *believe* . . . ," I sputtered.

Luke gave me a sympathetic smile. "That's what they do," he said, shrugging on his suit jacket. "Last year the Randolphs told me they got a similar letter about umbrellas left to dry in the hallway. Management companies don't bother to ask nicely."

I swallowed hard, I couldn't help it. I was so insulted and embarrassed. "Have a good day at work," I managed.

"Cheer up, sweetie. And break a leg. Nice sweater, by the way. Jasper, let's go!" Luke opened the apartment door.

Jasper came tearing out of the boys' bedroom with his Spider-Man backpack. "Bye, Mommy."

I dove forward to plant a kiss on his head as he ran out the door.

I took the deepest breath I could manage after the door closed on Luke and Jasper. As I tried to think deep, cleansing thoughts, I fought the urge to confront Bonnie.

I carried the ugly letter into the kitchen and laid it on the counter where Bonnie would come across it whenever she was ready. I added a note at the bottom. "Bonnie, this is what we're up against! They're terrible, aren't they? But I'll have to live with them long after you've become a European recording star. Please make sure Jasper and Wylie eat their snacks at our dining room table."

I turned my back on the letter, but my heart would not stop racing. There were a few minutes left before I had to go, and I needed to calm down. So I went into the living room and knelt down on the rug, careful not to stretch out my skirt. Wylie was busy with his choo-choo bridge. I just wanted to be close to him. Both little round arms held a train engine, and they jockeyed for clearance. "Not your turn! Boom!" He was deep in the game, but I rubbed his back anyway. I swept my hand over his head. His hair still had the soft texture of a baby's.

While I felt that the faces on Wylie's train engines were more than a little bit creepy, he loved them. I sat still on the rug, my new stockings mindfully out of reach of the rolling stock, listening to his monologue. I had no personal recollection of that freedom—of spinning out crazy ideas without any thought to whether others were listening or found them worthy. How magical to be two—and how very different an experience from dolling yourself up for national TV and caring for all the world what others thought of you.

I took a deep, excitement-filled breath. Today would be a good day for Julia's Child. On the good days, it was a bit easier to leave Wylie with the au pair. When things went poorly, none of it seemed worth the sacrifice of those hours with him. But Wylie was the same Wylie whether business was poor or flourishing.

Before I knew it, it was eight forty-five, and the hour for primping and philosophizing was at an end. I told Wylie it was time to wake Bonnie.

"Otay!" he cried, jumping up and running for her little room off the kitchen. Waking Bonnie was a task he thoroughly enjoyed. When she first arrived from Glasgow, three months ago, I wouldn't have dreamed of allowing the children to disturb her. But by now I'd learned that it was the only way to drag her out of bed.

The TV studio was sending a car for me, which was probably already waiting downstairs. I rose carefully from the rug, checked for lint, and headed for the front hall. I took the teetery heels I'd bought the day before out of their box and slid them on. I checked my look in the mirror by the door. I forced my shoulders back and stood up straight. I could do it. I could pull it off.

I looked in the mirror and sucked in my stomach. Here stands the world-famous television personality, sucking in her stomach before the show.

"Mama?" Wylie padded back out to me. "Bonnie no home," he said simply.

"What, sweetie? Where's Bonnie?"

"I not know," he said.

"She's . . . not in her room?" As I said the words, I began to steer the stilts I wore on my feet toward the kitchen and Bonnie's door. Wylie had left it open. Bonnie's bed was made, and the schedule for Jasper's after-school soccer practice was on the comforter, right where I'd left it yesterday afternoon.

Bonnie was not home. She had gone to Brooklyn yesterday evening, as was her custom, and apparently had never returned.

I turned on my heel and grabbed the cordless phone off the kitchen counter. I dialed Bonnie's cell phone.

Immediately, I heard: "This is Bonnie's mobile phone," the Mary Poppins voice drawing out the *i* in "mobile" the long way. The British way.

Mary Poppins had her phone switched off.

"Oh, dear God," I whispered under my breath.

I ran back to the front hall and dug my own cell phone from the depths of my purse, praying to see the message indicator lit. But the display was dark.

"Happened, Mama?" Wylie looked up at me with big eyes.

"It's . . ." I leaned over and scooped him up. "Nothing happened, Wylie. I'm just not sure where Bonnie is. And I'm supposed to go to work right now."

"Wylie go with you," he said simply.

He was still wearing his rocket-ship pj's and a saggy diaper. I kicked off my scary heels and ran with him toward his room. Then I pulled his pj's over his head and replaced them with a T-shirt with a bulldozer on the front.

Wylie, sensing adventure, allowed me to dress him with unprecedented cooperation. He didn't run away or roll around on the rug while I tried to put on his diaper. There was only a minor skirmish over his socks.

"I do it b'elf," he said.

"I'm sure you could do it by yourself," I said tactfully. "But I'm just going to help you a little." I jammed those little sausage feet into the socks and shoes. Then, running to the door, I slipped into the heels once more and opened the apartment door, willing my toddler to follow me.

"I go to work with you," Wylie said smugly, as the elevator arrived.

"Kid, it's your lucky day." It was almost nine already. A stretch limousine sat at the curb. The driver, in a suit with gold buttons and a perky hat, stood waiting.

I hesitated. That rig couldn't be for me.

"Miss Bailey?" the driver asked.

"That's us," I said.

He opened the door of the gleaming black car. "Come on in," he said cheerily. "The studio wants you right away."

"Bus!" Wylie said happily. I guess there weren't many limos in his picture books.

I gave him a little push through the door, and the driver closed it after us. The interior was a cool, leather oasis. The driver wasted no time starting the engine. As it hummed to life, he floored the gas pedal.

I grabbed Wylie and belted him in. "Dis is Taxi?" he asked,

rubbing his little hands on the expanse of buttery seat on either side of him.

"Sort of," I answered. "A really nice one."

Wylie adored taxis, primarily because they didn't have car seats.

I fumbled for my cell phone. I needed to warn Marta that she would have to amuse Wylie during the interview. Then I'd call Luke at his office and brief him on the Bonnie situation. Calling the police felt a bit premature.

But I didn't get to dial a single call, because the small video screen on the partition between us and the driver blinked to life, with live programming from the network that carried *The Scene.*

"Want it Elmo," Wylie demanded nonchalantly.

"Oh, honey," I said. "Elmo is only in *our* car."

He didn't believe me. "Touch buttons," he said. He strained against the seat belt, one stubby finger outstretched. He couldn't reach the screen. "*Elmo!*"

The limo careered down Central Park West, and I reflexively held my hand in front of Wylie's chest, pinning him into his seat, which only made him angrier.

"Want it!" he yelled.

We'd made it down to Lincoln Center. But now the traffic gods frowned. Ahead of us, taillights from the traffic ahead began to flash more brightly than the Rockefeller Center Christmas tree.

"Brake lights!" I yelled. The driver slammed on his brakes. I put my hand on Wylie's forehead, to keep him from sliding. He pushed it off.

Then we were stopped completely. I looked anxiously out the front window. A block ahead I saw a mass of people. I realized they were holding up hand-lettered signs.

"It's . . . a protest march?" I said aloud.

"Oh, Lord," the driver said.

"Want touch it!" Wylie strained for the screen. Since we were currently going zero miles an hour, I let go of him.

I dialed Marta. She picked up on the first ring. "Where are you?"

"I'm stuck in traffic, behind a protest rally."

"Ay!" she said.

"Marta, I have Wylie with me. I'm really sorry. It's a long story, but Bonnie wasn't home."

"Not home! Where is that *chica*?"

"If I only knew. I'm trying not to fear for the worst. I have to call Luke now and fill him in. We'll be there as soon as we can."

"Okay. Don't panic. The prop stylist and I have got your table almost all set up for the segment. All you'll have to do is hair and makeup."

"Marta, you're the best. I mean it."

I hung up and called Luke.

"What do you mean, missing?" he asked.

"Missing. Her bed has not been slept in. Would you try her cell phone again now? And keep yours out on your desk?"

"Of course I will. But do you think . . . Should we call the police?"

I chewed on my lip. There were cars honking all around us now. Frustrated motorists, taxi drivers, delivery vans. Half of them seemed to be lying on their horns. Wylie didn't seem to notice. He was glued to a clip from a Broadway musical.

"We could," I said. "But maybe she just decided to stay out for the night and then overslept. Wherever she is, Wylie wasn't there to wake her." I found myself chuckling. "Well, maybe we should just be grateful that Wylie didn't wake up *two* people in her room this morning."

But Luke wasn't laughing. "She's not seeing anyone," he said, soberly. "I think we should call the police. I'm on it."

I sighed into the phone. "Thanks, honey."

"Talk to Dada!" Wylie demanded. I handed him the phone. "Hi, Dada," he said.

I looked out the window. We had not moved an inch. We were at Sixty-sixth and Columbus, which was twelve blocks from the TV studio. That was just over half a mile. Normally, no big deal. I walked that every day. But with Wylie and my torturous footwear, it was practically an odyssey.

"Okay, bye, Dada," Wylie said. Then he snapped the phone shut and pocketed it.

"Wylie, that's *my* phone."

"Mine," he said, eyes already glued back on the screen.

I waited, trying to stay calm. But the screen showed a teaser ad for *The Scene*. "Coming up next!" the announcer's voice promised. Time was running out, on so many levels.

The brake lights on the vehicle directly in front of us went out, and that car inched forward about six feet. My heart leapt with hope. But that was all. We'd moved six feet in about fifteen minutes. I was now almost a half hour late.

I stuck my face between the break in the glass partition. "Okay. That's it. I'm sorry, but I've got to hoof it."

"Miss! It's my job to get you there," he argued.

"Sorry, but it's not working," I said. "I'll tell them you did your best."

"C'mon Wylie." I scooped him off the seat and onto my lap. I opened the door gingerly, so as not to bump the neighboring car. I squeezed the two of us out and threaded through the stopped traffic to the sidewalk. Then I put Wylie down. "Hold Mommy's hand," I told him.

But in my terrible heels, I was three inches taller than usual. His short arm strained to reach high enough to hold on.

"No pull on me!" he complained immediately.

I dropped my shoulder as low as possible, stooping a bit. We struggled along the sidewalk. It was thick with traffic too, the picket line slowing pedestrians as well as cars.

"No working," Wylie complained. He stopped. He raised both arms over his head. "Pick up."

Wylie weighed about thirty pounds. I'd carried him far and wide but never in heels. "Oh, buddy, I don't know if I can."

"*Pease,*" he said pathetically, arms still outstretched.

I hefted him. As I'd suspected, the pain was immediate. My pinkie toes felt as if there were nails driven straight into them. My heels cried out in agony.

I made it one block, closing most of the distance to the protest march. I set Wylie down again. "I'm sorry, honey, but you'll have to walk. Mama's feet hurt."

"I kiss it?" he asked.

"Um, not now, Wylie. But that's very nice. Let's go." I was getting panicky.

"No walking, Mama," he said. "Go home now?"

"I'd love to, but we can't," I said, near to tears. There was only one thing to do. I reached down and took off the shoes, placing my stocking-clad feet on the sidewalk. I jammed my shoes under one arm and picked up Wylie in the other.

"No shoes!" Wylie laughed.

I felt oddly naked. The stockings would be shredded, but I could toss them. Just more of the day's collateral damage. At a trot, I reached the street where the march was in full swing. The police were running around, setting up sawhorses to try to contain the crowd and restart traffic.

One flustered uniformed officer waved me away from the barrier. But then he turned his back. I ducked quickly through the space between two sawhorses. I was surrounded by marchers.

"Human rights now! Human rights now! Human rights now!" they chanted.

"Them yelling," Wylie commented.

"Yes, they are," I agreed. Straight in front of us, one protestor waved a gruesome sign depicting what I assumed was a tortured prisoner covered with blood. I turned Wylie's face away and struggled forward. It hadn't been so very long since I was a student joining protests just like this one. Now, instead, I was racing through the crowd like a fullback, toward a daytime television appearance. Time flies.

Once on the other side of the fracas, I looked around for a cab. From across the street, a face brightened. It was a young male pedicab driver.

Sensing opportunity, the young man did a U-turn in the near-empty bit of Columbus Avenue and pedaled his touristy contraption toward us. "You need to go where?" he asked in an eastern European accent I couldn't quite place.

I plunked Wylie on the seat and climbed in next to him. "How much to Fifty-fifth and Ninth?" I asked.

"Thirty dollar," he answered.

"Twenty," I snapped. I was done losing time and money today.

"Okay," he said, already pedaling toward midtown.

# Chapter 9

It was showtime. I had been styled to perfection by a team of hair and makeup specialists.

And so had my vegetables.

Standing on the stage, I surveyed the ingredients spread out before me. The perfectly julienned zucchini was heaped on the cutting board. A whisk glinted like silver under the bright lights. The whole wheat flour was artfully mounded in a sparkling glass bowl. A single perfect egg perched in a glossy cup, just waiting for me to crack it into the bowl once the cameras rolled.

Thankfully, I wouldn't have to teeter onto the stage in my heels. After the commercial break, I would magically appear on the set.

As I looked up from admiring the beautiful table, Lizzie Heffespeck stepped onto the stage in the flesh. She wore another version of the pencil-size wrap dress I'd seen in the video. She walked toward me with an electric smile, reaching out to shake my hand. "So glad you could join us! Ava just loves your muffets!"

"Thank you!" I beamed at her. "What's her favorite flavor?" It was great to have a few minutes to get to know Lizzie before the segment began.

"Fifteen seconds," the producer said from the edge of the stage.

My mouth fell open with surprise. Fifteen seconds?

"Oh! Don't be scared," Lizzie smiled. "Just pretend the studio audience isn't even there."

My heart began to race, and the lights came up with such intensity that it was suddenly possible to take Lizzie's advice. I could no longer see the crowd.

"Ten seconds! Cameras one . . . three . . . four . . . and six . . ."

A young woman in an apron scurried onto the stage like a frightened chipmunk. She slid to a stop in front of Lizzie, just long enough to pat the star's nose with a powder puff, and then dashed away again.

I managed to close my mouth, just as the producer began to say, "In five . . . four . . . three . . . ," and then there was the sound of a jazzy intro tune. A red neon sign at stage left lit up with the word "Applause!" but the invisible audience needed no encouragement. They screamed like a crush of teenage girls at a pop concert.

When they quieted down, Lizzie spoke. "So there I was in Brooklyn," she said breathlessly, as if it were some exotic locale worthy of mention ("So there I was in Taipei . . ."). "Ava and I were in the middle of a photo shoot, when I realized that the poor thing was starved!"

"Ohhhhhh," the audience said.

"I went into a little store to try to find something yummy for her, and there we stumbled upon a wonderful food called a muffet, made by an outfit called Julia's Child, and Ava loved it! We called the company right away, and we're lucky to have Mrs. Julia Bailey here this morning to tell us all about her wonderful organic line of toddler foods. Welcome, Julia!"

The applause was so sudden and loud that I nearly jumped.

Marta, in her preparations for today, had tried to ease my fears about the live studio audience. "They write in for tickets," she'd said. "There's a lottery, and people wait for months to get seats. They're almost entirely women, and they clap for everything, laugh at every joke. Then they take home an enormous goody bag full of DVDs, books, and other booty. So don't worry. They're primed to love you."

"So tell us about your company, Julia," said Lizzie. "How did you come up with muffets? And the name—I love that too! So cute!"

And I was on. I said the first thing that came into my head.

"Well, my children have always loved the nursery rhyme about Little Miss Muffet!" I enthused. "But my boys think she's kind of a wimp—to be scared away by a spider!"

The audience roared, as if I'd just told the funniest joke ever. Now I understood. They loved me because Lizzie Hefflespeck's love shone—however briefly—down on me. And I wasn't immune to the glow. Suddenly, I had 250 new friends, and I was going to tell them what they wanted to hear.

But Lizzie interrupted me. "And here's a picture of *my* little miss eating her muffet."

Apparently, the big screen behind us showed something adorable, because the audience made a collective "Aw!" like they'd just spied so many bunny rabbits.

"That's right," I said. "No child can resist a baked good. Muffets are as easy to hold as a muffin, but so much healthier. Shall we stir some up right now?" I gestured toward the beautiful mixing bowl the show had provided, in a shade of robin's egg blue, and the stylishly coordinated rubber spatula.

"Oooh! Which flavor are we making?" Lizzie chirped.

"This is Autumn Harvest, our newest recipe for fall. It has all the wonderful seasonal ingredients we find at the farmers' market this time of year. We've got zucchini . . ." I tipped the prepared zucchini slices toward camera four, the way the producer had taught me. "And we mince it down to the size of a grain of rice, to get the texture just right. Here we have whole wheat flour—ours is grown and milled in Vermont—and some lentils for protein, and pureed organic pumpkin for flavor and color."

"Such wonderful veggies!" Lizzie gushed.

"They sure are!" I said, carried away, sounding for all the world like an infomercial. "I like to cook food for children that is right out in front, visible. But you know . . ." I put down my spatula and turned to face Lizzie. "I'm swimming against the tide. The current fashion is deception. And I've got to tell you, I really don't agree with those moms who hide spinach in their brownies."

Lizzie's heavily mascaraed eyes opened wide in surprise. Last year a famous singer had made the talk show rounds with her book, *Behind the Spinach Curtain*, full of deceptive recipes for hiding vegetables in cake and cookies. "Oooh!" Lizzie gasped, as if I'd just insulted her taste in shoes. "But those brownies are so good!"

"I'll bet they are," I said, returning to my mixing. I dashed the egg quickly against the bowl and dropped its contents expertly onto the minced vegetables. I knew that attacking spinach brownies would put me out on a limb, and I hoped it would work out. "But what's the end game?" I asked, picking up a whisk. "Will you still be making those spinach brownies for your thirty-year-old?"

The audience laughed then, and I was off the hook.

"Ladies," I tipped the flour into the mixing bowl. "We should be teaching children that healthy food tastes *good!* Do we really not have the courage to say that? We need to help children to make their own smart choices. And it isn't that hard!" I gave the muffet batter a final stir. Under the sparkly stage lighting, the green zucchini and the orange pumpkin shone like jewels in the bowl.

There was thunderous applause and cheering, as if I'd just solved the Middle East conflict.

"I noticed you didn't put any sugar into that," Lizzie said.

"True!" I said, in my excited commercial voice. "There's no refined sugar in this recipe."

"So your own children, they eat very little sugar?"

"*Very* little," I said. As the words came out of my mouth, I recalled watching just an hour earlier as Marta lured Wylie away from me with a chocolate chip muffin from the greenroom. It had been the size of his head. "Uh, instead of sugar, I use fresh vegetables or fruits that are naturally sweet. And every one of my recipes has a *very* short ingredient list."

"That's just so great," Lizzie sighed. "Because preservatives are usually everywhere. I have a terrible citrus allergy, and you'd never *believe* how many products have citric acid as a preservative! It's just awful!"

"That must be so scary!" I sympathized. "But I never use preservatives, which is why my products come frozen—for freshness."

"So let's taste your other recipes, Julia." She led me toward the other table on the stage, where a spread of my products had been artfully arranged on platters. "What do we have here?"

"Here you see the entire family of muffets," I cooed. The show's food stylist had outdone herself. On the first platter, one muffet sported two apple wedges poking out of the top to make a bunny shape. I tipped it toward camera number two, as I'd been instructed.

The audience did its "Awwww" thing again, just as the other four hosts of *The Scene* appeared onstage. They clustered around us at the table. "So can we eat now?" asked Wanda, the comic.

"Sure!" With a flourish I offered a plate of bite-size slices. "These are the Apple and Cheddar, and"—I gestured regally, like a game show hostess helping contestants to buy a vowel—"here we have the Carrot and Black Bean, and on the end we've got Focaccia Fiesta."

That's when I stopped cold. Because one of the ingredients in the Focaccia Fiesta was lime juice, for flavor. And Lizzie had just said she was allergic to citrus fruits.

Sweat pricked my neck. The five hosts of *The Scene* were swarming around the table, popping bites of muffets into their mouths, tasting the various flavors.

"I don't really taste the black beans in here," challenged Wanda.

But I almost didn't hear her, because I was staring at Lizzie who was within striking distance of the Focaccia Fiesta.

"It's . . . ," I stammered, weaving between silken talk-show hosts toward Lizzie. "The, uh, black beans are sweetened up by the uh . . ." I planted myself at Lizzie's elbow, body blocking her from the fated muffets. "The carrots," I finished lamely.

"Oooh! I wish I'd had these when Gabby was little," said the hostess named Charity, from the other end of the table. "She loved anything with apples. Still does. I can't believe cheddar goes so well with the apples!"

"Gross!" countered Wanda. "Cheddar and apples, *together*?"

Next to me, Lizzie pouted. "That's Ava's *favorite*. They are absolutely *not gross*."

For a minute I felt redeemed, but then I realized that praise warmer than "not gross" was usually necessary to sell TV viewers on the flavor. I opened my mouth to say something, but then became distracted again as Lizzie's hand crept toward the focaccia plate.

I grabbed the plate. Then, by reaching behind the backs of the other hosts, I set it on the opposite end of the table, in front of Wanda. "Here—I bet you'll like these."

I wondered what would happen to Lizzie if she ate citrus. Would she get hives all over her face, or would she swell up and turn red? Would she sue me if she couldn't appear on the show for the rest of the week? Would my business insurance policy even cover that?

The sweat was rolling down me now.

"I just feel so good about giving muffets to Ava," Lizzie said, nibbling a bite of Carrot and Black Bean. "Every one of them is so much better than fast food."

"I'll bet Julia's kids don't eat fast food," Charity commented as she tossed another bite of muffet in her mouth.

"You're right," I said. "But remember when it was perfectly acceptable to advertise a 'secret sauce?' Remember that?"

"Yes!" Lizzie shouted. "Nobody cared that we didn't know what was in it." She traded places with Wanda and landed in front of the dreaded focaccia once again. "Eew! We were so foolish then."

"But that was before the finger-in-the-chili days, wasn't it?" Wanda said wryly.

The audience made telltale grossed-out sounds, and Wanda grinned.

"It's a different world now," I managed, as I wove my way over toward Lizzie again, just in case she should reach for the wrong muffets. "I would like everyone to know how muffets are made, so they can feel good about giving them to their children."

Lizzie's manicured hand reached for the focaccia.

Panicked, I grabbed both her hands and squealed. I very much hoped the gesture conveyed the sort of excitement teenagers might express having discovered a big sale on designer shoes. On TV it might have looked like I made a strange pass. "I have an idea," I said desperately. "I'm going to *give* away the muffet recipes on my website. All of them. So mothers can know exactly how they are made or even bake a batch themselves if they want to."

"Oooh! You'll give them away *for free*?" Lizzie asked. "How generous!" She gracefully dropped my hands, widening her embrace to include the entire TV studio. "Julia, it's been lovely having you on the show. And for our lovely studio audience we have Ava's favorite muffets for everyone! Thank you, Julia. And thank you to all my wonderful costars! Where would I be without you? We'll see you all again tomorrow on . . . *The Scene*!"

There was a final burst of wild applause, and I clapped right along with them. The music swelled, and then finally the lights went down. The air around me magically cooled by about ten degrees. Just as I was processing this phenomenon, I felt a swish of wind to my right where Lizzie had been standing. She was gone. Without a word, she and her costars had swept off the stage, probably to the five dressing rooms with the stars on the doors that I'd glimpsed during my hurried arrival.

I looked back toward the audience, which I could finally see more clearly, now that the studio lights were off. Somehow they'd filed out with remarkable speed, as if there had been a fire drill. But then I remembered the enormous goody bags full of giveaways the ladies were rushing toward, and it all made sense.

I was suddenly perfectly alone on the stage, my two-hundred-odd new friends having vanished before my very eyes. I felt some kind of weird grief at the loss. And my feet were killing me. A lone stagehand, dressed in black and whistling, began coiling up an electrical cord a few yards away. Even he didn't look at me.

I had the sudden urge to cry.

"Mama! Mama!"

"Wylie!"

He came running toward me, chubby arms pumping. He arrived at my feet, lunged forward, and hugged both of my knees together. I scooped him up and buried my nose in his soft hair. "Were you a good boy for Marta?"

"I see Mama on TV!" he said.

"You did?" I asked.

"Like Elmo."

Marta caught up with us then. Her eyes were wide. She gave

me an enormous high five but was otherwise uncharacteristically speechless.

"What's the matter? Did I do okay?"

"Genius!" she whispered. "Giving the recipes away is genius."

"Oh, Marta, it was an impulse. It *sounds* like a no-no. But I thought that maybe three potential customers will actually cook them instead of buying them. And another three thousand might love me for it and become loyal customers."

Marta nodded, her eyes flashing. "Absolutely. Genius."

I laughed, but tears pricked my eyes. Who knew that being on TV would make me so emotional? "God, I didn't plan to say that. I was trying to keep Lizzie away from the focaccia."

Marta's eyebrows went up. "Why? Because of the lime juice? *Chica*, I left it out for this batch. Because of her allergy."

I stared at her. "You did? Oh my God, I was so panicked."

Marta waved a hand dismissively. "She did a whole segment about it last year. The poor girl has never even tasted a margarita. Isn't that sad?"

"Margaritas?" I could really use one myself. Pass the tequila and organic limes. Maybe it would bring my heart rate back into the normal range. Then I remembered. "Marta, I have something for you. Do you have my purse?"

She opened up her shoulder bag and pulled it out.

I set Wylie down on the stage and pulled the envelope out of my purse. "Marta, this TV appearance is the best shot we've had at a break. And it wouldn't have happened without your quick thinking. So I want to give you this."

I handed her the envelope. She took it with a curious frown. She unfolded the paper inside and looked with confusion upon the numeral ten.

"Marta, the lawyer won't have the documents ready for a couple of days. You are to own ten percent of Julia's Child. I had Jasper draw this for you—it's a stock certificate!"

Now understanding, Marta put one hand to her mouth, and two tears squeezed out of her eyes and rolled down her cheeks.

"Oh," I said. "Please don't cry. I want you to have it. And, hey, it's not like we've ever turned a profit, so I've really just given you ten percent of nothing."

"Oh, shut up, Julia," Marta said. "An equity stake?" She pressed her hand to her mouth. "Thank you. It's the nicest thing anyone has ever done for me. Do you think . . . Is that supposed to be Spider-Man?" She held up the stock certificate. Indeed, there was a red and blue, webbed scrawl in one corner.

"Probably," I said. That made it a high honor from Jasper too.

Marta dabbed her tears with her sleeve. "Well, check *him* out." She pointed.

Wylie had climbed up on the display table where I'd "cooked" for the show. He was kneeling there, licking the batter off the spatula.

Marta laughed. "Turn the cameras back on. That's the shot we want."

I gave the stock-in-trade mommy line: "Wylie, tables are not for climbing." He ignored me.

"Come on, honey, we're leaving," Marta called to him. "Time to bail your nanny out of jail."

My mouth fell open. "What?"

"Luke called," she said, by way of explanation.

"Where jail go?" Wylie asked.

# Chapter 10

The closest I'd ever come to a real courtroom was on television, so I wasn't prepared for Courtroom 125. It was a windowless dungeon striped by wooden pews. Fluorescent lights flickered over a rumpled judge who sat at the front on a raised dais. I scanned the sparsely populated benches, looking for a familiar face.

I spotted Luke in the middle of the room, sitting just behind a railing that divided the front section from the rear. I scurried down the aisle and slid onto the bench next to him. He looked up expectantly and then opened his arms to gather me in. When he smiled, the corners of his eyes crinkled.

"How did it go?" Luke whispered into my ear.

I gave him a thumbs-up sign, mindful of the proceedings in the front of the room. A scrawny, tattooed young man faced the bench and was standing beside a suited woman who might or might not have been his lawyer.

I turned back to my husband and cupped a hand to his ear. "What happened? Have you seen Bonnie?"

Luke shook his head. "I haven't, but . . ." He pointed.

Ricky Dean, Luke's now-balding high school buddy, approached from the opposite side of the railing—the business end of the room. Years ago he had graduated from petty arraignments to more lucrative litigation and was obviously here as a favor to Luke.

Ricky leaned over the railing to give me a quick kiss on the cheek. "Hi, gorgeous," he stage-whispered. "How are the boys?"

"Great, and yours?" We rarely saw Ricky and his family because they had decamped to the burbs several years earlier.

"Good! And, you know? We're actually expecting a *third* one early next year."

Luke grinned. "Rick, when are you going to leave that poor girl alone?"

"Docket 7-4-2-7, case 1-7-Z-42!" erupted one of the court workers at the front of the room.

My back stiffened at the announcement, but Ricky didn't even seem to hear it. "That's not us," he said without even a glance toward the judge.

"So now will someone please tell me what happened to Bonnie?" I asked in a whisper. She was nowhere in the courtroom.

"Bonnie is *fine*—pissed off, but fine," Ricky said. "On her way home last night, she fell asleep on the subway and missed her stop. A cop woke her up, told her she couldn't sleep there. Bonnie got very upset that the cop was trying to throw her off the train like a homeless person. The train had gone all the way into the Bronx then circled back around into Manhattan, and Bonnie wouldn't get off the train, because it was headed home."

"So . . . he arrested her? For falling asleep?"

"It's illegal to sleep on the train. You know, so they can keep the place from filling up with homeless people. But the cop only brought her in because she pissed him off. Apparently, she sassed him. Accused him of racial profiling. That kinda thing."

"Oh," I said, trying to make sense of it.

"As I told Luke—this will probably be over fast. I'm hoping the ADA goes for the ACD," Ricky explained.

"Um, what?"

"The assistant district attorney. He might give us an adjournment in contemplation of dismissal."

"They might throw out the case?"

"Sort of. It would stay on the books for six months. But as long as Bonnie's not arrested for anything else—no speeding tickets or fines—it will go away completely."

Luke looked at his watch. "You think that will work?"

Ricky beamed. "Sure! Look around you. The other poor slobs dragged through this room have nobody. We're going to look like the Brady Bunch in comparison. They took her to central booking, found no rap sheet at all. It will be fine. The DA even looks cheery today," he added, gesturing toward a ruddy man at the front of the room. "Maybe he got lucky last night. Hey! Is that your little man?"

I turned to see Marta carrying Wylie down the courtroom aisle. He beamed at us from Marta's hip. His was the only smiling face in the room.

"I sent them around the corner to buy some diapers. I didn't want him in here any sooner than necessary. This place is skeevy."

Ricky laughed. "You want skeevy, you should see the holding pens." He sat down on a bench on his side of the divide.

"Daddy!" Wylie exclaimed, scrambling over me to reach Luke, as if to say, "Fancy meeting you here." All the world was a party to Wylie.

Marta slid onto the bench next to me. "I should head back to the office now," she whispered.

I smiled. "The phone might be ringing off the hook! Orders rushing in."

"You never know, *chica*. Besides, we have a website to figure out."

Didn't I know it! Good thing I was married to a computer genius. "Pssst," I said to my husband. "I need a website."

He nodded. "Makes sense."

"I mean, I need one by tomorrow. It's a long story, but I announced on live television that I would publish my recipes on the Web."

"Tomorrow? I don't know many Web developers."

Luke didn't seem to understand what I was asking of him. "Sweetie, I know you're not really a Web developer, but . . ."

Luke stared. "You don't mean *me*?" he hissed. "I'd be . . ." He trailed off. "Inappropriate for that position."

"Are you saying it's like Mrs. Picasso asking her husband to paint a signpost?"

Luke chose his words carefully while allowing Wylie to yank on his necktie. "You had a big day, so you should think big. If you hire a proper Web developer, you'll get professional results."

"Are you saying you won't do it? It would take you, like, fifteen minutes!"

"If that were true, I'd be happy to help. But you need someone who is familiar with all the latest fashions. My field is systems architecture, not page design. You'd be asking me to choose things like . . ." A look of distaste crept onto his face. "Typestyles," he finished, as if I'd asked him to select a nail polish color.

Marta nudged me. "*Chica*, don't worry about it. We'll get Derrick's team."

I wasn't quite ready to let Luke off the hook, but Marta's idea had merit. Our little Manhattan office at the Chelsea Sunshine Suites was part of a small-business ghetto. Most of its other, younger denizens worked for Internet start-ups. Derrick, a hip-looking dude with a pierced lip, sat out in the bull-pen area. Even if I'd never exchanged more than polite greetings with him, it was somewhere to start. "Great idea," I agreed. "As long as he has time. They always look busy."

"We'll offer him extra," Marta said. "And if he still says no, I'll sleep with him."

I feigned surprise, mindful of Wylie. This is the kind of situation where our *español* habit comes in handy. "¡Puta sucia!" I threw one of Marta's colorful phrases at her, one I heard whenever her computer acted up. The translation was "dirty whore."

"Ladies," Ricky warned over his shoulder, "even though the baby doesn't speak Spanish, everyone else in the courtroom can. Including the judge."

"Me not a baby," Wylie pouted.

"Docket 7-4-2-7, case 1-7-Z-43!" a court officer called out.

"Here we go," said Ricky, standing. In four great strides he moved to the front of the room. A metal door on the left clanged open, and a young woman was led, head down, into the courtroom by two muscled bailiffs. I stared, unsure if it was really Bonnie up there. With her back to the room, and her sleep-flattened hair, the poor girl could have been any sad waif. The Bonnie I knew always held herself with a queen's bearing.

When her bailiff escorts stopped in front of the judge, she shrugged off their touch. She took a deep breath and improved her posture. That was the Bonnie I knew.

I wasn't the only one who saw her. "Bonnie!" Wylie shrieked from Luke's lap. As quick as a flash, he slipped off Luke's knees to duck under the railing. He slid in front of Marta and me, gunning for the center aisle. He clearly meant to rush the stage.

We dove at the same time, thrusting one arm each through the railing. I caught an arm, and Marta grasped his pants. Together we pulled him back toward our side of the courtroom.

"No take Bonnie!" He struggled.

Startled, the two bailiffs actually stood back, as if God himself had ordered them away.

I scooped Wylie back over the railing and held him up. "Shh," I told him. "Bonnie will come out in a minute, okay? Shh."

He stopped yelling, thankfully. But then he began to sob. "Want it Bonnie. Where Bonnie go?" I held him tight and whispered in his ear.

Bonnie turned around then, a look of terrible remorse on her face. The defiant posture disappeared again. She met my eyes only for a second and then turned back to face the judge, her chin drooping toward the floor.

Ricky craned his neck around toward us with a grin and a wink. Wylie's outburst pleased him. He put his arm around Bonnie, patting her back, although they hadn't even met properly. But it made for a nice tableau.

Meanwhile, an officer of the court read off the charges. "Disorderly conduct and resisting arrest," he droned.

"Your Honor, may we approach the bench?" Ricky dropped his arm from Bonnie's shoulders and took a step forward.

The ruddy DA met him in front of the bench, and they held a whispered conference.

"I hope the bail isn't thousands of dollars," Marta said under her breath.

Good Lord! I hadn't thought about bail. And I was about to spend probably several thousand dollars on a website.

The sounds of the conference drifted toward us. "With all due respect," Ricky said, "the charges amount to a verbal argument between a sleepy au pair and a police officer on a subway train. We ask that the suspect be released to her host family. The Baileys, standing right behind us, are eager to have Bonnie back at home. She has no prior record and a good job with people who love her."

The judge, the DA, Ricky, the court reporter, and the handful of other bystanders all turned to look at us. I had a moment of absolute self-consciousness, far worse than I'd experienced that morning on live TV. I smiled in what I hoped was a warm, friendly way, and Luke quickly put one arm around me and the other around Wylie.

The judge gave a slight cough and looked down at the DA.

The DA rolled his eyes for just a fraction of a second and then said, "The people are willing to consider adjournment in consideration of dismissal in this case."

Quickly, before the DA could change his mind, Ricky said, "Your Honor, we've reached an agreement of ACD."

"Granted," the judge said, giving the gavel a quick tap on the bench. He handed paperwork down to the DA. "ACD. The defendant is ROR."

"What?" I asked.

"Released on her own recognizance," Marta said. "Don't you *watch* TV?"

It was over that quickly. Ricky led Bonnie toward another door, on the opposite side of the room, which a bailiff opened for them.

"Where Bonnie go?" Wylie sniffed.

"Outside, honey. We'll go get her," I explained.

Marta bid us good-bye at the courtroom door. "I'm sure you're heading home with Bonnie. That girl needs a bath. I'm off to work."

Marta was right. Even though I was anxious to figure out how to capitalize on my big appearance, I couldn't chuck Wylie into a cab with a shaken Bonnie and bid them adieu for the rest of the day.

"Of course," I said. "I'll join you as soon as I can. The website . . ."

"I'll find Derrick. If he's on board, you can start talking about it from home." With that, Marta turned on her heel and departed.

I carried Wylie toward the exit, wondering what the fallout from Bonnie's embarrassing escapade would be. This was going to be far worse than grapes in the community room.

Luke read my mind. He put an arm on my shoulder as we headed toward the sunlight. "Let's go with, 'it could happen to anyone. Don't let it happen again.'"

I laughed. "Okay. I'll staple my lips together on the way home."

He kissed me on the cheek. "Good luck with that."

To: marta@juliaschild.com
From: juliaschild@gmail.com
Re: website contents

Good work getting Derrick to design our site! I don't need to know *all* the details of your negotiations! ;-) I'm working on the recipes while Wylie and Bonnie nap.

The first time I wrote this one, I put "organic" in front of every ingredient. But it looked overzealous and uptight. (Don't say it—kind of like me.) What do you think?

## Apple and Cheddar Muffets That Lizzie Hefflespeck Declares "Absolutely Not Gross"

*Ingredients*

**1 very large apple or 2 small ones**
**2 tablespoons butter**
**⅔ cup all-purpose flour**
**½ cup yellow cornmeal**
**2 tablespoons granulated sugar**
**1 teaspoon baking powder**
**¼ teaspoon salt**

**1 egg lightly beaten**
**⅓ cup whole milk**
**1 cup sour cream**
**1½ cups grated cheddar, divided**

*Instructions*

Preheat the oven to 400°F. Generously grease and flour 12 muffin cups.

Peel and core the apples and dice finely. If your toddler is helping, peel and slice an extra one to share. If you play your cards right, he or she will be busy eating the apple slices while you're measuring out the dry ingredients.

In a small skillet, melt the butter and sauté the apple until tender and just beginning to brown, about 7 minutes. Remove the pan from the heat and set aside to cool.

Meanwhile, combine the flour, cornmeal, sugar, baking powder, and salt in a large bowl. In a small bowl, whisk together the egg, milk, sour cream, and 1 cup of the cheese. Stir the wet ingredients into the dry ingredients, then add the apples and butter. Stir just to combine.

Spoon mixture into the prepared tin, and top with the remaining ½ cup of cheese. Bake for 20 to 25 minutes, until very brown and a toothpick inserted into the center of the muffets comes out clean. Cool for 10 minutes on a rack. Loosen muffets by rimming their edges with a plastic knife. Turn them gently out onto a plate. Serve warm or room temperature.

# Chapter 11

The day after my TV appearance, I sat at my desk, trying to choose the imagery for my new website. There were several distractions, including a very hyper Marta. She migrated repeatedly between the outer office, where Derrick, the pierced twenty-something Web developer, was attempting to bring our site to life, and our tiny cell. She would dash in, bump into my desk, and ask, "Did anyone call?" Marta was sure that our phone would be ringing off the hook with new orders for muffets.

"No, not since you asked me two minutes ago. Would you look at these?" There were pictures spread around my desk. I didn't have any idea which of them best conveyed the new face of organic baby food. "When the customer first lands on the site, what should they see?"

Marta shrugged. "A picture of our packaging and logo?"

"Of course they'll see that. But what else? A child? A vegetable? Perhaps a child *hugging* a vegetable?"

"That sounds good." Marta turned on her heel and again headed out the door toward Derrick's desk.

"Maybe," I said to the empty room. "I'm just afraid the cliché police might come and arrest me for that one."

Marketing children's foods was, relatively speaking, a new

problem. In 1927 a young mother grew tired of standing in the kitchen and straining peas for her infant. She implored her husband, who ran a food company, to make special food just for babies. The woman's name was Dorothy Gerber, and the rest—as they say—is history. The iconic Gerber baby face, with its tousled hair and apple cheeks, is one of the most recognized logos in the world. One woman's quiet request became a marketing department's dream.

Pandora's box was opened, and a new little consumer tumbled out. Babies became special customers—special enough to require their own brands of food and drink, in enough variety to fill their own aisle in the supermarket.

And the newest trend was food for toddlers, with their own distinct consumer tastes and whims. They required their crackers to be shaped like fish or bunnies and their ravioli to be no larger than a half-inch square.

And thank God. Because without consumers' willingness to go deep into their wallets for toddler-friendly food, Julia's Child would not exist. I was not completely comfortable with that. I was throwing fuel onto the fire of the very same kind of overmarketing that I hated.

Marta trotted back into the room.

"I am a parasite," I said. I pushed my chair away from the desk with disgust. It promptly smacked into the brick wall immediately behind me. "Maybe I should put an amoeba on the home page."

Marta rolled her eyes at me. "Will you just choose some pictures already? It's just like you to get all tangled up with the meaning of the universe. How hard can this be?" Then the phone rang, and Marta had to quit scolding me and dive for it.

I sifted again through the stack of shiny, glowing children's photos we'd pulled off of a stock photography website.

Marta plunked the telephone receiver back into the cradle with a little shriek, her hand resting triumphantly upon it. "An order! A big one!"

"Terrific!" I said, happy to be distracted with good news. "From whom?"

"From Entrefina, the big gourmet shop in Brooklyn Heights. You know it?"

I laughed. "That's so funny! I was *just* telling Mr. Pastucci that I hoped to get in there. They must watch *The Scene*! Terrific news, Marta."

Marta gave a curious frown. "Actually, they didn't mention the show. But I assumed that's why they called." The phone began to ring again. Marta shrugged and answered it. "Julia's Child." Her dark eyebrows rose to form two peaks. "Julia is . . . taking an order at the moment, but she would love to speak to you. Just a minute, please. *Gracias*." She placed the call on hold.

I studied her. "What are you playing at, Marta? Who is it?"

Instead of answering, she chanted, "One Mississippi, two Mississippi, three Mississippi—"

"*Who is it?*"

She winked at me. "It's Whole Foods. But let's not look too eager."

I lunged for the phone. "This is Julia Bailey."

"Good morning, Ms. Bailey. My name is Kai Travers, and my wife enjoyed your appearance on *The Scene* yesterday."

"Oh! Thank you so much. Please call me Julia."

"Okay, Julia. I'm the frozen foods buyer for the Northeast region at Whole Foods Markets."

I didn't speak right away. The man who held the keys to the freezer case next to the pizzas was finally calling for me. I let the moment wash over me, savoring the sweetness. I had been waiting for this call for a long time.

"Ms. Bailey? Julia?"

"Yes!" I came to. "Whole Foods. I've heard of it."

Kai Travers laughed. "Excellent. Listen, I was planning to sample children's products at the All-Natural Kid Stuff Tradeshow next month. Will I see you there?"

My mouth opened and closed like a fish. "We . . ." I gulped. Not the damned trade show again. "No, instead we're . . . marketing the product more *directly* to our buyers," I floundered. "It's . . . We take a really *personal* approach with our marketing, you see. I find that it helps to maintain the integrity of the product, which I understand is really the Whole Foods way of doing things . . ."

Eavesdropping from her line, Marta gave me the thumbs up from across the room.

"And that goes way beyond our marketing," I continued. "I've got my own plot of organic farmland in Vermont, and—"

"Hmm. I understand, Julia," Kai said. "So you're not on the trade show circuit yet. Very well. But can you produce your product in commercial quantities?"

"Of course!" I practically shouted into the phone. "We're delivering to a dozen independent shops in Brooklyn, and our distribution grows larger every day!"

"Hmm." Kai seemed to be mulling this over.

I held my breath.

"Well, you certainly have a head start with the national TV publicity. And that makes my job easier. So here's what I think I can do. How about this? Send me a gross of muffets. If you can deliver them immediately, we'll try them out in three of our Manhattan stores."

"Terrific!" I said. I was in! I wanted to leap over the desks with joy.

"This is just going to be a trial, okay? We'll give the muffets a shot, in those three stores, for a month. Until the trade show. Then, after I get a look at everything that's out there, I'll firm up my kiddy lineup for the Northeast region."

"Oh, okay," I said, a little less certainly. So I was on probation. Either way, my little company would live or die in the next sixty days.

"Now, let me give you some numbers. Do you have a pen handy? If we decide to take you regionwide in two months, that's fourteen stores, well, sixteen by November. The Northeast region includes Massachusetts, Connecticut, New York, and New Jersey. We need one case per SKU for the initial delivery. Then we need you to be ready to deliver a three-case follow-through per location. Who are you using as a distributor?"

I hesitated. "My, um, distributor is local to New York," I said. My distributor was me in a hatchback Subaru.

"Oh," Kai said diplomatically. "Why don't you call Bob over at Enorme? Tell him that Kai recommended him."

That particular distributor had laughed at me when I'd approached them without any orders in hand. "I'll call him, Mr. Travers."

"Kai."

"It's a pleasure working with you, Kai. You'll love the muffets. You know, we also have other lines. We make couscous with—"

"Let's just focus on muffets for now, Julia. Can't wait to try them! Oh—and is your website down? I tried to look at it this morning."

"Yes! It is down." It had had the same "Under Construction" sign since I bought the domain name a year ago. But he didn't need to know that. "We're down *temporarily,* in order to add some recipes, as I mentioned on the show."

"I'll look at it tomorrow, then. And feel free to have your people call my assistant, Janice, with any delivery questions. Talk to you soon, then."

He gave me his phone number. And he was gone.

Marta and I stared at each other for several seconds, from

opposite ends of our little room. Then, coming to our senses, we jumped out of our chairs, shrieking like schoolgirls.

"We did it!" Marta yelled, as I whooped with joy.

Our door popped open. Derrick, the Web developer, stuck his head in. "Everything okay in here?"

"Yes!" I said, offering him a high five.

He returned it expertly. "Good. I thought maybe you ladies saw a mouse or something."

I tried—as I always did—not to stare at his pierced lip. "Things are *fantastic,* Derrick. We just got an order from"—I paused for effect—"Whole Foods."

"Terrific," he said politely.

Of all the little businesses housed at Chelsea Sunshine Suites, ours was the only one that made a product you could touch with your hands or buy at a store. Every other start-up was "virtual"—websites, consulting, and viral e-marketing. We were quaint by comparison. I didn't expect Derrick to understand.

"I'd better get back to work on your website, then." He turned to disappear back to virtual land.

"Hey, Derrick?" I stopped him.

"Yeah?"

"I just promised Whole Foods that the website would be back up tomorrow. Is there any way you could . . . ?"

His mouth fell open in surprise. A ray of light from Marta's desk lamp hit the stud in his lip, and the full spectrum of colors was reflected in the glinting light. "*Tomorrow* tomorrow?" He looked at his watch. "Good thing I came in early."

"I really appreciate it. Listen, I'll buy you lunch today, in case that helps."

He winked. "Better get a whole lot of coffee too." Then he shut the door.

I took out my calculator. "Okay, Marta, let's crunch some

numbers. We can bake, say, two gross of muffets in one night at Zia Maria's. So—going forward—if Whole Foods has sixteen stores in the northeastern loop, and each sells out of its initial stock once a week, that means our production would have to increase to . . ." I stabbed at the calculator, my frown lines multiplying along with my numbers.

"What?" Marta prompted.

"We'd have to bake . . . Let's see . . . How many hours per week, and how many nights . . ." It couldn't be true.

"How many?"

"Nine," I sighed.

"Nine hours?" Marta asked hopefully.

"Nine nights."

"But last time I checked, there were only seven."

"I know." My heart raced. "We can't cook nine nights a week. Or even seven. But . . . I'm getting ahead of myself. That's a phase-two problem—only *if* we survive Kai's probation period."

"But we *will,* Julia. It's a great product, and it's going to work. We're going to need that inventory." Marta sat heavily into her chair. "It's time to find a new kitchen. One that lets us cook during daylight hours."

"Right." My mind whirled with all that needed to happen. Which problem should I tackle first? It was just like the age-old riddle: the free-range chicken or the cage-free egg?

I took a deep breath. "We need a plan." I took up a pad and a pen with a flourish. "So, first we get this website up—"

"First we bake the initial order for Kai," Marta broke in.

"Um, okay. Both of those things are first. Next, I'll have to find our new production facility. *And* we get the distributor lined up." Good Lord! I wasn't going to see my family for a month. "We'll have to work like Cinderella to do all of this."

"At least you already have the handsome prince," Marta

observed, tugging on an earring. "We're going to need some help in the kitchen," she said. "On short notice."

"Mice into footmen?" I suggested.

"I was thinking of my cousin Theresa. She just lost her baby-sitting job."

"Great!" I said, though I hadn't meant to sound so gleeful about someone losing her job. "Why don't you give her a call? There's someone else I need to call," I said, digging around on my desk for the number.

"Who?" Marta asked.

"ANKST. The trade show. Now that we've hooked up with our fairy godmother, we can restate our revenue figures. I'm going to demand that we go to the damned ball."

# Chapter 12

The voice mail message was brief, but it was just the one I'd been waiting for. "Da eagle has landed," declared a scratchy male voice.

With a grin, I snapped the phone shut. The sound drew the attention of a mother leaning over her stroller to execute a familiar maneuver. With her finger, she wiped away remnants of peanut butter and jam from her little girl's face. Then she pinched the girl's nostrils together quickly, removing a drop of unsightly nasal mucus from the little button nose. The child yelped in protest. She caught me watching her, just as she wiped her gooey fingers on her own pair of very fashionable skinny jeans. She frowned assertively at me, perhaps embarrassed to be caught in the act of on-the-go toddler hygiene.

Without my own preschoolers in tow, she probably assumed I was a tidy, childless woman who wouldn't dream of wiping snot on her own clothing. Hey! I'm on your side. I too have made the motherly decision that it is better to wear goop on your jeans than to let the world see it on your toddler's face. She marched away, pushing the stroller.

In spite of the bright fall afternoon, I yawned. The week had featured more late nights than I cared to count. Answering the message I'd just heard—though important—could wait five minutes until I got home.

Our lobby was blissfully empty, except for the drowsy doorman. As the elevator carried me upward, I charted the rest of my busy day. I could return the call from my kitchen, while I threw dinner together for the family. I would eat a little something and then rush to Brooklyn for a shift in the kitchen. And somewhere in there I'd hug the kids and call Luke. And maybe even my mother.

When I opened the door to my apartment, I heard muffled giggling. It was Wylie's voice, but somehow far away. I closed the door softly and made a quick turn from our tiny entry hall into the kitchen. I poured myself a glass of water and bolted it down.

Wylie's muffled laughter and the low sound of Bonnie's voice filtered into the kitchen. Whatever game they were playing, they were deep in it. I picked up my cell phone to call my new driver, Lugo. Last week I'd asked Mr. Pastucci if he knew anyone with a refrigerated delivery van. He'd put me in touch with Lugo, whose voice mail had just confirmed that the very first Whole Foods delivery had been made. Lugo and his beat-up truck were both antiques. But the truck chilled to thirty degrees. I'd checked it myself.

"Lugo!" I enthused when he answered my call. "You did it!"

"Of course, missy," he said. Lugo called me "missy" either out of endearment or because he'd forgotten my name. I wasn't sure which. "The deliveries went down without a hitch," he said.

"Excellent! To all three Whole Foods? Thank you so much."

"Yep. Nicest loading docks I ever seen. Snazzy outfit you must be running, missy."

"Thanks, Lugo. You'll be around next week too? We might need to deliver more. I hope."

"No problem, missy. See you soon."

I hung up, smiling through my exhaustion. So it was official.

Julia's Child was in the door at Whole Foods. On the premises! It was all I could do to keep from running down there right away to see for myself. I'd waited so long for this moment, to see those packages staring back at me from the other side of the freezer-case window.

It would have been nice to make the delivery myself. But there was no way I could maintain the illusion of professionalism if I showed up in my Subaru, weighted down with coolers chilled by those freezer packs moms carry around with bottles of breast milk.

If my business were ever to get off the ground, I would have to learn to let go, to rely on people. I would have to trust them with my proverbial baby. The alternative, I reasoned, was a schedule so manic that I'd never see my real babies.

With that in mind, I attacked a red pepper, chopping it to a quarter-inch dice in about sixty seconds flat. It would soon be sprinkled all over the homemade pizza I planned to make for my family for dinner. Cooking for them was something I felt I had to do, even if I didn't get to see them eat it.

Buoyed by the satisfaction of finally appearing at Whole Foods, I dialed my mother. Waiting for her to pick up, I scraped up the pepper remnants with one hand.

"Darling! What's happening in the Big Apple?"

"It's official. Julia's Child is for sale at Whole Foods."

"Congratulations, honey! I'll have to make a road trip to Charleston to see it."

I winced. "Better wait a few months, Mom. I'm only in three Manhattan stores for now. But it's been a long time coming."

"Fantastic! With the prices at that place—you'll be rich!"

"Maybe some day," I said lightly. My mother wasn't the best audience for my host of financial concerns. I didn't tell her that our order from Kai had kicked off a massive cash outlay. First, we rushed a giant gift basket of muffets to Kai. The messenger alone cost forty dollars. *Ka-ching!* And that was just the beginning. Our website cost four thousand. An ad in the kids' edition of *Time Out New York* ("Now at Whole Foods!") cost three grand. We put in another freezer at Mr. Pastucci's club. So he raised our rent. *Ka-ching! Ka-ching!* My shoulders tensed with anxiety just thinking about it.

"So what are you doing to celebrate?"

I chuckled. "I'm going to the kitchen tonight to bake about three hundred more muffets. Right now I'm making a pizza for the kids."

"Pizza?"

"Well . . . sure. Whole wheat crust, veggies—"

"But *honey.* You live in New York City. Pizza gets delivered, you crazy girl. Who on God's green earth makes her own *pizza*?"

"Mother! What do you care? Mine is healthier!" Not to mention cheaper.

"I care because life is supposed to be fun. Take a shortcut every once in a while. God, girl. Live a little."

I gritted my teeth. Even if I'd felt like succumbing to another petty argument with my mother, there simply wasn't time. "I'll take it under advisement, Mother. I'd better get going."

"Julia—wait. The reason I called is that I'm just about to book those Thanksgiving tickets. Do you think Saks will be open on Thanksgiving?"

"No way." It was both an answer to her question and my own personal statement of disbelief. I guess that's what my mother meant by living a little.

"Okay. We'll probably come in Tuesday, then. My love to the boys!"

"Bye, Mom."

"Bye!"

I sighed. At least everyone else around me rose to the occasion of my now frequent absences. Luke made sure to come home every night in time for dinner. He put the kids to bed. And Bonnie put in extra hours. She didn't seem entirely thrilled with her new responsibilities, but the embarrassment of her recent run-in with the law seemed to quell complaints.

I tossed the phone back into my bag. Even my unreliable cell phone seemed to be holding up. For the most part it rang when it was supposed to, connecting me to the host of new vendors and distributors with whom I needed to negotiate. And I appreciated it, because money was tight.

The view from our tiny kitchen sink was a crumbling brick wall. Luke used to talk about selling our apartment and moving into something a little roomier. But lately he hadn't mentioned it. It was the only evidence I had of his growing unease about our financial situation. His only recent comment on the matter, as I filled him in on how much Julia's Child had "borrowed" from our savings, was that business capital was like love—you had to give some to get some back.

I wondered if this was exactly how intelligent married couples got into grave financial trouble. Maybe both of us were secretly terrified about the cash hemorrhage for Julia's Child, but each was too chicken to say it out loud.

I took a deep breath and went to find the children. When I stepped into our sunny living room, I understood why their laughter had sounded so far away. A couple of dining chairs had been pulled into the room, to an awkward spot in front of the sofa. The blanket from Bonnie's bed was stretched over the couch to the top of the dining chairs, where it had been secured with rubber bands. From underneath this makeshift tent came Wylie's giggles.

"Where fash-wite go?" I heard Wylie ask.

Bonnie murmured something in response.

"Want it. Peeeeease Bonnie."

A spot of light appeared on the inside of the blanket, moving back and forth across the tent's wall. Then it disappeared. "Night time now, Bonnie. You go seep."

From inside the tent I heard an exaggerated yawn and then the low rumble of a snore.

The boys had taken to Bonnie immediately. At first I'd thought it was because she was so young, and a little bit exotic with her Mary Poppins voice and her Briticisms. She said "shed-ule" and "trousers" and "telly." Lately it had sunk in, though, that they responded to something more fundamental about her personality. Bonnie lived in the moment. Just like children do.

She snored again—and not just any snore. A big, exaggerated chainsaw snore.

Wylie giggled.

I cleared my throat. "*Grrrr.* There's a bear in the woods!"

From inside the tent came happy shrieks. Wylie's head appeared at one end of the tent. His sandy hair was standing on end, the static from the blanket having electrified him. "Bear! Mama, come in!"

"I *am* the bear, Wylie. *Grrrr!*"

"You *not* a bear. Come." He beckoned forcefully.

There couldn't be much room under there, so I dropped to my knees and scooted just up to the opening of the tent. Maybe that would be close enough.

"*In*, Mama. Bear not eat you." Wylie backed farther into the tent to make room for me, ending up on top of Bonnie's legs, in the unconscious way that all toddlers treat people like furniture.

I obeyed, inching into the tight enclosure.

"Why 'ello Julia," Bonnie said politely. Like Wylie, she also had tent hair.

"Hi, Bonnie! Come here often?" I smiled as warmly as possible. These days we tiptoed around each other. "Say," I asked her, "did

Jasper ever find his missing sweatshirt?" I had ducked out in the middle of a drama this morning, hoping that it hadn't inadvertently been me who had stashed the thing where nobody could find it.

"Of course. He found it under his bed."

"Ah. So where is he, anyway?" I asked.

"Birthday party," Bonnie answered in the Queen's English. "He went directly from school."

"Oh! But I didn't buy a—"

"He and Luke were planning to choose a gift on the way to school. At the bookshop," she said. "The party is just a few blocks away, actually. On Ninetieth Street."

"Oh! The Hanson family." I vaguely remembered taking Jasper to that child's birthday last fall. In spite of my hectic new schedule, I thought I'd managed to keep all the balls in the air, but apparently some things were slipping by. "Thanks," I said uselessly. I tried to imagine Luke picking out a birthday present. I hoped they'd managed to wrap it somehow.

The tent was warm and airless. I wondered how long Wylie and Bonnie had been camping in there. Bonnie appeared completely unrushed, even serene. But after just a couple of minutes inside, I'd already had enough. I turned to peer out of the confined space, hoping to ease my growing claustrophobia. Lately, when the stress of my business got to me, I could swear I felt the rotation of the earth. I felt it right now, the living room rug shifting beneath me. Logically, I knew I was just overtired. But lately the clock in my head never shut up. Its constant ticking prevented me from enjoying myself, knowing I still needed to settle my obligations in the kitchen and then race back to work in order to save my company from certain ruin.

But Wylie had other ideas. "Bear out there?"

I inhaled slowly through my nose, hoping my discomfort would lift.

"*Mama*," he tried a stage whisper. "Make bear sound."

Wylie, being two, wanted the game to go on forever, but I was out of time. It was a routine state of affairs here in apartment 514.

Jasper had summed it up perfectly last weekend. He and Wylie had been playing house. As usual, he was bossing his little brother around, which Wylie accepted without complaint. Jasper gave himself the role of daddy, assigning the mommy role to Wylie. "You're getting the dinner," he'd instructed. "But do it fast. Because Mommy is always in a rush."

On hearing that, I'd felt as bad as if he had said, "Mommy beats me with a leather strap."

Because of course he was right. I *was* always in a rush. It had been true long before Julia's Child got off the ground and probably for years before Jasper was born. I was a high-energy girl, which was not always a bad thing for a woman with two rowdy boys.

Even so, the comment made me feel terrible. But the upshot was that it helped me appreciate Bonnie a little more, in spite of her penchant for leaving crumbs everywhere in the kitchen and the laundry loads that never quite got folded and her blossoming rap sheet. She led a more carefree existence than I did, and why shouldn't the children enjoy her?

I stuck my head outside the airless chamber and filled my lungs with fresh air. Then, ducking back in, I said, "Come to the kitchen with me, Wylie. I'll let you help me with the pizza dough."

He bounced off Bonnie and onto my knees. I wrapped my arms around him and maneuvered us into the daylight.

In the kitchen I felt a little better. I stood Wylie on a chair. I slipped an apron over my head, since kitchen work and Wylie were a volatile combination.

"Where *my* apron go?"

Wylie's apron had an inchworm appliquéd on the front. It was hard to believe that I'd done the needlework myself, before life had become so intolerably frantic. I plucked it off a hook and dropped it over his head. "Show me the back of Wylie, please."

"Here go." He turned around, and I tied the apron strings loosely around him, just above the diaper bulge.

"This is for our pizza." The ball of whole wheat dough had been defrosting on the countertop all day. Of course the moment I removed it from its plastic bag the phone rang. The outside of the dough ball was sticky with condensation, and so I stared at the phone, not sure what to do.

"Phone ringed," Wylie prompted. "I hold it." He reached for the dough.

"Don't drop it, okay?" I sighed, handing Wylie the sticky ball and scraping my hands on my apron. In an alternate universe, perhaps Bonnie would answer it. But in this one, it was clearly my job. "Hello?"

"Hi, Julia. It's Derrick. Do you have a minute? Can I run a couple of things by you?"

"Um . . ." I looked up at the clock. I didn't actually have a minute. I needed to make a pizza and then leave for Brooklyn within half an hour. On the other hand, my trusty Web developer had managed to make good on his promise to have my site up and running in record time. "Sure, Derrick. What's on your mind?"

"Mama, who talkin'?" Wylie asked.

"It's Mama's friend from work," I whispered.

"Hey! Is that your little man? How's he doing?" Derrick asked.

I squinted at Wylie as he manhandled the ball of dough. "He's thirty pounds of burning ambition. Now, what did you need to ask me about?"

"Tracking cookies, Julia. I need to know how deeply you want to embed them."

Wylie was happily poking his finger into the dough, over and over. I trapped the phone with my shoulder and began to slice an uncured nitrate-free pepperoni into discs. "Say it in English, Derrick. What are we deciding?"

"Do you remember what a tracking cookie is? We talked about it last week."

"Sure, tracking cookies," I said breezily. "They, um, track things."

Wylie put the ball of dough down on the counter. "Where tookie go?"

"Oh, Wylie," I sighed. "It's not a cookie you can *eat*."

"Want to eat it."

Derrick laughed in my ear. "At least you've got part of the idea. You can't eat a tracking cookie, but they're very useful. When customers visit your site, you can put a little bit of code onto their computer. Then, when they log back into your website, you'll be able to tell which other companies' sites they've visited. It's kind of like following them around the mall."

"That's what a cookie does? That's so rude! Who would do that?"

"Who wouldn't? If we look at your PC right now, I'll bet I can find fifty of them. It's business intelligence."

"Want tookie!" Convinced that I was holding out on him, Wylie began to cry.

So I set down my knife and began riffling through kitchen cabinets, looking for something to pacify him. "I don't know, Derrick. Let's not do that."

I found a box of wheat crackers in the back of the cupboard. They were probably horribly stale. I opened the box and handed it to Wylie. Sniffling a little, he plunged one of his hands into the box and then popped a cracker into his mouth.

"It's your show, Julia. You can always change your mind later. I'm almost finished with your webforms, and I'll show them to you tomorrow. Are you in the office in the morning?"

"Oh, I'll be there," I sighed.

"Great. See you then."

"Thanks, Derrick." We hung up.

"Okay, kid. Let's knock out this pizza crust." I dusted the countertop, and then my hands, with flour.

I began to press the dough into a disc.

"Mine!" Wylie shoved my hands out of the way, diving onto the dough with both hands. The disc began to resemble an undersize wheel of Swiss cheese. I was willing to share the work but poking holes in the dough was not getting us anywhere. I had twenty-four minutes to leave the house, and the kitchen was spiraling into a very messy circle of hell. I was a brittle twig, just about to snap.

The sound of my voice was shrill. "Rolling pin time!" When I handed Wylie the pin, he dropped the dough. I scooped it up at lightning speed, reformed it into a ball, and set it back on the counter. "Now, here we go!" I fitted our two sets of hands onto the rolling pin handles and guided the pin across the dough in smooth strokes.

But Wylie fought me off. "Do it b'elf," he kept repeating, and I thought I might cry. I'd always seen myself as someone who welcomed her children into the kitchen—someone whose career was supposed to bring her *closer* to family and hearth, not further away. And here we were wrestling for the rolling pin. I didn't let go, and Wylie began to scream.

Sweaty and desperate, I considered my options. I could break off a bit of dough for Wylie to handle on his own. But time and dough were short, in equal measure. I watched his little face redden from the effort and the insult of our struggle.

I closed my eyes and reached deep down, finding the last shred of calm in my soul, along with a tiny speck of remaining ingenuity. "Wylie," I whispered. "Would you like your *own* batch of dough? You could mix it up with a spoon."

He relaxed, nodding and sniffling. Not wasting a second, I grabbed a saucepan from the pot rack, scooped half a cup of wheat flour, and spilled it into the pan. When Jasper was a toddler, once or twice we'd made playdough together. I could almost remember how. I grabbed a carton of salt and poured some over the flour. Then I handed Wylie a spoon. He began to stir slowly, tracing salty circles into the brown flour.

You have to make hay when the sun shines. So I turned my back on him and rolled that pizza dough out in about thirty seconds flat. I flipped it onto the baking pan just as Wylie made a complaint. "Not gooey."

"Oh!" I said brightly. "You want *gooey* dough." I raced a can opener around a can of organic pizza sauce like an Indy 500 entrant. "Why didn't you *tell* me?"

"*Need* gooey dough."

I turned on the faucet with my elbow and poured a bit of water into Wylie's saucepan. He attacked it with his spoon. I began spreading tomato sauce over the pizza before he could notice or insist on helping. The work in front of me was finally beginning to resemble a pizza, and my blood pressure dropped accordingly. I had fifteen minutes left in the kitchen.

"Gooey!" he pronounced.

I took a package of shredded mozzarella from the refrigerator, tore it open with my teeth, and began to sprinkle it furiously over the sauce.

"Stuck!" Wylie gasped. The dough had begun to tighten up on him.

I scattered diced red pepper over the top of the pie, looking over his shoulder. Then I got out the olive oil, which I intended to sprinkle over the pie like a true Italian. "I'll bet your dough could use a drop of this, kiddo." I gave him a dollop.

He stirred but then turned to give me a funny look. "It smell funny now."

"Ah," I said, thinking that nothing smelled finer than olive oil. But it was his concoction. "What do you want it to smell like, then?"

Wylie's round cheeks were set in concentration. "Tookies."

I stuck my nose in his soft hair and kissed him. "You got it, buddy." I reached for the cinnamon. I eased his saucepan onto the stove and lit the flame. "Don't touch the pan now, okay? But here—add this to your dough." I handed him a teaspoon of cinnamon, and with a shaky hand he tipped it into the saucepan. Then we added some ginger, and I stirred like hell. By the grace of God, he didn't fight me for the spoon.

The heating dough began to hold together. And suddenly the kitchen smelled wonderful, like pumpkin pie or apple strudel. "Wylie, your dough is great." Seasoned playdough! It had never occurred to me. And not only was Wylie happy, but I felt the same tickle of delight that I always got from recipe development. It was a source of constant excitement for me—familiar ingredients recombined as a surprise. Discovery was my favorite drug. Perhaps Tookie Playdough would be a cheery addition to the Julia's Child website.

I moved the pizza out of the way and turned Wylie's steaming dough onto the countertop. "We'll just give it a minute to cool, okay? And then you can touch it all you want. This dough is *yours*."

"Mine!" His favorite word.

Together, we put slices of pepperoni on the pizza while we waited for Wylie's dough to cool.

## Wylie's Whole Wheat Gingerbread Playdough

*Ingredients*

**1 cup whole wheat (or any other kind of) flour**
**½ cup salt**
**2 teaspoons cream of tartar**
**1 teaspoon unsweetened cocoa powder (for color)**
**1 teaspoon cinnamon**
**½ teaspoon powdered ginger**
**½ teaspoon grated cloves**
**1 cup water**
**1 teaspoon vegetable oil**

*Instructions*

Have your child stir the dry ingredients together in a saucepan for as long as it interests him. (Tip: toddler + large spoon = flour flung about the kitchen. Give your child a chopstick or a fork to stir with. You can thank me later.)

Add the water and vegetable oil, and then stir.

On the stove, stir over medium heat for 3–5 minutes, until you see the playdough form a skin on the bottom when flipped. Turn it out of the pan and knead when cool enough to handle. Dough keeps well in an airtight container.

# Chapter 13

I grasped the handle of the freezer case and looked fondly through the glass. The Autumn Harvest Muffets looked back at me, at eye level, from their excellent position between the pizzas and the frozen organic vegetables.

Perhaps Marta suspected my ulterior motive when I'd volunteered to pick up lunch, but I didn't even care. It had taken long enough to finally get Julia's Child into the store of my dreams, and I would steal this moment to admire my muffets, shining under the expensive Whole Foods lighting.

It was impossible to see, from this side of the glass anyway, just how many costly rookie errors I'd made. But Kai and his team had been quick to point them out. Stacked cases of muffets didn't fit well on standard warehouse delivery pallets. Furthermore, we'd been told that the typeface we'd used to print the ingredients list on the side of our package wasn't kosher.

The only solution was a pricey redesign of our packaging. So I'd closed my eyes and agreed to spend the money. Last night I'd lain awake worrying that it wouldn't matter, that Kai would fit the glass slipper onto some other princess—one whose bar code was already perfectly aligned on her packaging for a good scan in the checkout aisle.

On the other hand, after a gut-wrenching two-week silence, the trade show had finally admitted us to its roster. So now Marta and I were hurriedly designing appropriate display materials. If Whole Foods dropped us after our probationary period, we'd need to snag another big order—Safeway, Price Chopper, or Piggly Wiggly—just to recoup all the cash we'd spent trying to impress them.

Unable to help myself, I opened the freezer door and squared the corners of the packages. There weren't very many muffets left. That might be good news. Or perhaps the store was just slow to replenish the shelves. I had no way to know.

"Just a few more minutes, sweetie! If you're a good girl, we'll head over to the playground."

The mom rolling toward me used the roof of her stroller in lieu of a shopping cart. Beneath the flap of fabric, which was sagging under the weight of organic yogurt and all-natural diapers, her infant daughter wore a look of squirmy protest.

Whirling around, I feigned interest in the items opposite the freezer case. There's always a chance . . .

The mother slowed in front of the freezer. As I pretended to scrutinize the jars of salsa, she opened the door and reached in.

I held my breath while she grasped a package of muffets, reading first the front and then the rear of the package.

"Eeeeekkkk!" her daughter shrieked.

The mom sighed. "Okay, pumpkin." She pushed the muffets back on the shelf, allowed the freezer door to snap shut, and moved quickly toward the checkout aisles.

I watched her walk away, feeling snubbed. She hadn't even bothered to set the rejected carton properly on the freezer shelf. It pitched pathetically toward the frozen flatbread pizzas, a situation I quickly remedied.

With one more proud glance at my babies, I headed for the deli counter.

"May I help you?" The team member behind the counter snapped a fresh pair of latex gloves onto his hands.

"Could I please have a half pound of . . ."

The organic roast beef that I often chose was $12.99 a pound.

"Yes?"

"Turkey, please."

"Organic honey roasted, organic smoked, all-natural roasted, pepper, or maple?"

I picked the cheapest price tag and pointed. If things didn't turn around soon, I'd be eating Spam out of a can in order to fund my investment in the world's most pristine organic toddler food.

My phone rang as soon as I left the store.

"*Hola, chica*. You answered your phone!"

"Of course. When my phone rings, I answer." The trouble wasn't my phone etiquette, rather my lazy phone. It habitually refused to ring. Hours later it would always confess its sins, guiltily blurting out its string of omissions: "Five missed calls." Marta had been leaning on me to buy a new one, but cell phones contain a mineral called coltan, and Congolese miners had lately been killing off gorillas right and left to get to the mineral deposits. Anyway, I didn't have two hundred bucks.

"Uh-huh. *Chica*, I'm picking up *un café*. You need one?" Marta sounded exhausted.

"No thank you, Marta. I'll be back with the lunch fixings in just a couple of minutes."

When I arrived, I found that my partner looked just as tired as she sounded on the phone.

"Morning," she grunted. I looked at the clock. It was twelve fifteen. Marta now spent nearly every night cooking at Zia's with her cousin Theresa. She got only a few hours of sleep before it was time to see her son off to school. Then, when Carlos had boarded the school bus, she caught a couple of more hours sleep before coming into the office for the afternoon.

"Greetings!" I put my shopping bag down on my desk as she put a giant cup of coffee down on hers. When I'd met Marta, she was caffeine free. "Is that really coffee in there?"

"Sí," she said tiredly. "I think they call this size the bladder buster"—she shook the computer mouse so that the system would come to life—"which is a problem for a lady who is too busy to go to the bathroom. So, any customer e-mails today?"

Now that our website was up and running, the first few consumer comments had begun to trickle in. We were riveted by the feedback. It didn't even matter to us that, by volume, most of it was negative. We'd learned that people usually kept their thanks brief. "The baby loves muffets! Keep up the good work!" Whereas people took their time with critiques. We'd received a couple of missives from people who felt that the packaging for the Apple and Cheddar Muffets was too similar to the Autumn Harvest flavor and who had bought the wrong one by mistake.

"Maybe they should swap," Marta cracked. "We'll tell the lady who accidentally bought apple about the one who bought the pumpkin." Instead, we'd added the problem to the list of packaging fixes.

I opened my e-mail now with the same hope as a child opening a birthday gift from a crazy elderly aunt. It would probably be another pair of socks, but there was always the chance of a shiny new toy.

The first letter was short and plaintive. "I really miss you" was all it said.

"Eh?" asked Marta.

"This one is from Luke. He promised this morning to look at our site and see if he could spot any bugs."

"Ay! The only bug he has is with you, *chica*. You should do something for that man."

I raised my eyebrows at her. "On one of my many days off?"

She shrugged wearily. "I'm just sayin'. Are there any more?"

There were two more messages. One was a brief "We love the new pumpkin flavor." The other one was short but nasty.

Dear Ms. Bailey,

I saw you on *The Scene*, and you seemed nice, but I couldn't find muffets at the Walmart where I shop. So I went to look at your website. It says that on your farm you fertilize with goat manure. I can't for the life of me figure out why you would spread GOAT POOP around vegetables that little children are going to eat. If that's what you mean by "all-natural," you can keep it.

Brenda Veertema
Kansas City, KS

"What the hell!" I yelled, leaping to my feet beside my desk. "What is wrong with people? Marta—please take this down."

Although her job did not usually involve taking dictation like a secretary from the 1960s, Marta walked slowly over to her own desk and took up a pen with an air of exaggerated cooperation.

"Dear Ms."—I checked the screen—"Veertema," I began. "For thousands of years, the only way to grow food was what we now call 'organic.' The human race steadily increased its agricultural output and also its lifespan. Then in just the last hundred . . . No, less than that. In the last sixty years, big agriculture money-grubbers decided that it's"—I made my fingers into quotation marks—"'conventional' to pour noxious chemicals all over crops. Suddenly our society is beset by higher rates of cancer, obesity, and type 2 diabetes."

I took a breath. "You have allowed yourself to be brainwashed, and therefore *you* are what's wrong with food in this country." I ran out of steam. "Did you get all that?" I asked Marta.

"Sí," she said. She held up a piece of paper with a lot of scribbling on it. Then she very deliberately tore the paper into four pieces.

"Marta!"

"*Chica*"—the exhaustion was evident in her voice—"you do not really want to send this message, even if it is all true." She held two of the torn pieces together. "I may not have a fancy MBA, but I'm pretty sure that '*you* are what's wrong with food in this country' is not going to sell any muffets. What happened to 'the customer is always right'?"

I put my forehead down on the desk. Some days the mountain seemed insurmountable.

"Why don't we have some lunch?" Marta changed the subject.

"Okay," I said weakly. "I'll do the honors." I peeled myself off the desktop. From our mini fridge I extracted a jar of mayo and a loaf of bread. On a couple of recycled paper plates, I began to assemble our sandwiches.

I was just adding my special touch—a razor-thin layer of sliced apple, for crunch—between the turkey and the bread, when the phone rang.

Marta answered. Whenever she was exhausted, she slipped deeper into her accent, so the name of our company took on a Latin pronunciation. "Hoolia's Child," she said into the receiver. "Marta speaking." She listened attentively. "Yes, sir," she said. More listening. Then she said, "That's fantastic," but the look on her face told a different story. She looked like she might cry. "You can have them tomorrow, in our existing packaging. *Or* you can have them next week with the new design." Her frown grew deeper. "Tomorrow, then. Excellent. Thanks so much."

Then she hung up the phone and leaned back in her chair like a stricken woman.

"What is it?" I asked.

Without opening her eyes, she said, "It's Kai. He needs more stock. You've nearly sold out at the Time Warner Center and in Chelsea. And you're sold out at Union Square."

I could hardly believe my ears, especially given Marta's lack of enthusiasm. "So it is true! What did he *say*? In spite of all the packaging snafus, people are actually buying them?"

She opened her eyes. "He was careful to say that it often goes like this with a new product. Lots of people try it. The second batch will be more telling. We'll either have repeat customers or we won't."

"But that's not why you're depressed?"

"I'm depressed because we're going to have to ship him all the muffets we just baked for the trade show. And I thought we were almost done."

I clapped my hands together joyfully. "Tell me what he said when you told him the muffets could be there tomorrow."

Marta stood up and maneuvered around the desk to reach for her sandwich plate, which I handed over. "He did seem a little surprised, now that you mention it."

"I just know he takes us for small-timers. I'll bet he thought we couldn't rise to the challenge."

Marta looked at me, blearily, over her plate. "This is the corporate titan taking a bite of her turkey sandwich."

"Marta, as soon as your coffee kicks in, you're going to agree with me that this is a good thing. We need the revenue from Kai to pay down our credit cards."

Marta nodded. "Are you cruising the suburbs today?" Marta asked.

"Tomorrow," I said, taking a bite. I'd been piloting my Subaru all over New Jersey, scoping out warehouses and food-production facilities—called copackers—searching for the right place to manufacture Julia's Child. This meant donning a hairnet to tour factory floors that seemed impossibly large and automated. And expensive. The search was not going well. As I watched cans or cartons twirl by on overhead conveyor belts, I had a hard time reconciling those impossibly industrial places with the company I wanted to run.

"It only takes one." But Marta's voice wasn't as optimistic as her words. I wasn't sure which of us she was trying to buoy up. But then she seemed to gather herself and sit up a little straighter in her chair. "Hey, the apple tastes good in here. Nice touch." Then the phone rang, and she set down her sandwich to answer. "Yes? Chris!" she said to her caller. "Of course I remember you."

I worried the rim of my paper plate. The trick was, as in all things, timing. I couldn't afford to change manufacturers until we got another big order, either from Whole Foods or another big buyer. Then I'd need to *instantly* switch, somehow, to a new facility, simultaneously increasing production, staff, and marketing. If I got the timing wrong, the business would lose cash flow and die. It seemed as impossible as a trapeze artist's fingertip catch of a swing in midair.

Marta hung up the phone with a joyful clap of her hands. "I met someone at my son's school!"

"A guy?" I asked through a bite of sandwich.

"No, *chica*. I met a journalist. From the *New York Post*. Her name is Christine. I chatted her up, you know, hoping for free publicity. And guess what? It paid off."

"Again, Marta! You have the touch. She wants to do a story? About Julia's Child?"

"Sort of," Marta said coyly. "It's a story about me."

"Oh!" I waited for her to explain.

"She wants to write about my life. Local girl goes from welfare mom to part owner of a fast-growing new children's company. Like that. Isn't it great?"

Her face was lit with excitement. But I didn't say anything right away. I hoped she'd think it over before she opened up to this journalist.

"What, Julia? You don't look happy for me."

"I'm just thinking about it, that's all. The angle . . ." I didn't know how to say it. I wasn't sure if it was me, that I'd be comfortable with it.

"The angle?" Marta put her hands on her hips.

I took a deep breath. "I just hope they focus on your smarts, Marta. On you, as a businesswoman, and not a caricature of a welfare mom. Do you know what I mean? I hope the journalist is smart enough to make it . . . human."

Marta's face creased in shock. Clearly, I had not made my point. She thought I was raining on her parade. "Never mind, Marta. You've met the journalist and I haven't. I'm sure she'll write really well about you. I shouldn't have worried."

"Well, I *never*," Marta spat, obviously upset. She stopped to swallow. "I never pegged you for the jealous sort."

"Jealous!" God, I dreaded media attention. And Marta knew that. "I am *not* jealous. I just want you to be portrayed as a whole person, you know? I . . ." I was at a loss. Somehow I had offended the only other person who cared as much about my dream as I did. At that moment I would have done anything to take it all back.

"Hoolia, tell me something. Will this interview, even if it's done by a baboon, have a chance at increasing the value of my ten percent and your ninety percent of the company?"

I blinked. "I, uh, suppose any mention of the company in the newspaper is a very good thing."

"Then what the hell are you worried about?"

I was speechless. The phone rang. Marta stared me down, making no move to answer it, so I grabbed it. "Julia's Child."

"Hi, this is Pam from Shonen Brothers Food Packing."

"Yes! Hi, Pam. This is Julia."

"Julia, I know we had you scheduled to visit us tomorrow, but it would really be so much better if you could tour today. We're getting a large shipment of organic kiwi tomorrow, and it's going to be really crazy here with all the peeling."

"No problem, Pam. I'd be happy to come today. It will take me about an hour and a half to get there, though."

"Terrific! We'll see you around two o'clock, then!" She hung up.

I put the phone down and met Marta's gaze once again. "I'm sorry, Marta. I don't have the best instincts about media. I don't trust it. But I'm sure you know what you're doing."

She crossed her arms. "We can't keep this up, you know."

"Which part," I whispered.

"This schedule. My nights away from my son. Neighbors watching him. His teacher calling me, telling me his homework isn't done. I haven't had more than one night's sleep in a row. And you—I'm worried you're going to crash that car in Jersey, you've got so much on your mind. We can't keep it up indefinitely."

"I know, Marta. Nobody expects you to keep it up forever. The trade show is next week. Then we regroup."

"We have to. Julia . . ." She hesitated. The look on her face was grim.

"Yes?" I was afraid of what she'd say next.

"Remember Lila? She makes the churros?"

"Of course I remember Lila."

"She got picked up by Starbucks. Fifty locations in Queens and Manhattan."

"Wow! Good for Lila." Starbucks—I'd never even considered it as an outlet. An awful lot of toddlers get dragged into coffee shops every day. Their mothers buy them bagels. There was really no reason at all why muffets wouldn't be a great product too, between the low-fat coffee cake and the madeleines. I was just about to make this suggestion to Marta, when I noticed that her face still wore an expression like death. "Marta, what's wrong?"

"She wants me to work for her. Nine to five."

"Oh." I swallowed hard. In my overtaxed and overextended recent history, I hadn't given enough thought to Marta's concerns. Too late. I now realized that the world must be full of people who would appreciate her superpowers. "Is it . . . a much better offer? Are there . . . benefits?" I meant things like dental insurance. But as I said it, it was clear to me that the real benefit of working elsewhere would be the security of having an employer who was not on the brink of failure.

"No," she sighed. "Lila isn't much further along than we are. I told her it wouldn't be right for me to leave Julia's Child in the lurch right now."

I felt a swell of relief and gratitude. I opened my mouth to speak.

"But I did say that if she hadn't found anybody in a month, to check in with me again."

I closed my mouth again and only nodded. "Marta, I . . . I know," I squeaked. "This is no way to live. And now I've got to go to freaking Jersey again. To try to get us off the night shift. This copacker could be the one."

She stared at me, unblinking. "We keep saying that, but then life gets harder instead of easier."

I picked up my handbag and dusted the crumbs off of my desk. I'd run out of words of encouragement. I should have realized before that Marta was near the breaking point. And now, with Julia's Child on her résumé, she could certainly get a nice nine-to-five job in any number of less-dysfunctional workplaces. And I couldn't even spit out the real reason that it made me so sad. But I'd miss you!

"*Chica*," she said in a low voice, "take the rest of that sandwich with you. And drive safe."

# Chapter 14

By 8:00 P.M. I had come to resemble the poem inscribed on the Statue of Liberty. I could have easily passed for one of the tired, poor, huddled masses. Though I'd been impressed by the small but tidy copacking plant I'd visited, the drive home from New Jersey was beset by horrible traffic. As I inched the car toward the George Washington Bridge, I tried to imagine making that commute several times a week. As I finally dragged myself toward my own golden door, I realized I had one more thing to do. I speed-dialed Marta.

"Hola, chica," she answered. I heard the din of Zia's kitchen behind her.

"Hi, Marta," I said gingerly, still wary from the fight we'd had. "I'm just calling to see if the pumpkins got to you on time. I was still begging the distributor at three thirty."

"Sí." Marta's answer was curt. "The first batch is out of the oven already. Theresa is pureeing it now for the Autumn Harvest.

"I'm so glad."

"But, Hoolia, today I did some checking. We can buy organic pumpkin in one-gallon cans for just about the same price as fresh pumpkins."

I bit my lip. It wasn't me who was about to stay up until two tonight steaming the flesh and scooping it from the shell. But I was not about to put canned *anything* in my muffets. "We'll take a look, Marta." I was too cowardly even to say no.

"Okay, *chica*. Ciao." Just before the call was disconnected, I heard her holler at her cousin. "Stop blending! You're stirring out the vitamins!"

Miserable, I exited the elevator and, while pocketing my phone, finally arrived at the door to my apartment. From behind the door, I could hear a strange sound. It was a soft keening, almost a whimper.

Concerned, I turned the knob and tiptoed into the darkened apartment. The shadowy living room was lit only by light reflected from the condo tower across the street. I searched for the sound. There in the darkness, I located two standing figures, their arms around one another.

I gasped, and they came apart. Bonnie and Luke, a nightmare unfolding before my eyes.

I held my breath, frozen like a scuba diver whose air hose had suddenly been cut. When I eventually remembered to inhale again, the rush of oxygen to my brain brought the picture into sharper focus. I began to notice details of the scene, and they altered my perception of what was going on. Luke wore his overcoat. His briefcase stood beside him on the rug, where he must have set it down only moments before.

Bonnie, on the other hand, was all dressed up. Instead of her usual skinny jeans, she wore a dress and heels. Tears were streaming down her face.

"Hi, sweetie." Luke's quiet voice was reassuring. "You're late."

I opened my mouth to answer, but no words came out. My brain was still busy catching up from its emotional roller-coaster ride. Eventually, his words penetrated, and I remembered that it was Thursday. I had been scheduled to make a rare dinnertime appearance, so that Luke could take a turn staying out later.

I put a hand over my mouth, still not trusting myself to speak.

Bonnie spoke instead, and the words were little chips of ice. "I had a *date.* At a nice restaurant. For my *birthday.* And you don't answer your *phone.*"

"Oh! Bonnie, I'm so sorry!" I took a couple of steps toward her, hoping to hug her too. But she brushed past me, swept her jacket off a chair where it lay, and strode out of the apartment in her heels.

The door closed with a thud.

I raised my eyes slowly to meet Luke's, feeling for all the world like a teenager who has just been busted for breaking curfew.

He said, "I was out with—"

"Ricky," I said miserably. "I remember now. You were taking him out for dinner, to thank him for the legal help."

"Yes, and you were supposed to be here."

"I . . ." My reason sounded so lame now. "I was touring a copacking plant in New Jersey. It was supposed to be tomorrow, but they called to reschedule. I just wasn't thinking . . ."

I couldn't finish the sentence. I wasn't thinking *about my family.* About Luke or Bonnie or the children. My crusade to succeed had finally reached a point of total self-involvement. And now I would pay for the oversight.

Luke took off his overcoat without looking at me. He draped it over the chair where Bonnie's had just sat. Then he disappeared into the kitchen.

Still not sure if I would be grounded for the crime of raising the family stress level to a record high, I held my position on the rug. From my pocket, the phone bleated with some sort of notification. With dread, I drew it out.

The screen read "Eight missed calls." Each of them, I noted, was from Bonnie. And all I could do about it now was feel guilty.

Luke appeared a minute later, with a bottle of wine in one hand and two glasses in the other. The corkscrew he carried in his teeth.

He set everything down on the coffee table. Then he went over to the mantelpiece, where the remote control sat. Aiming it at the fireplace, he pressed a button. The flames lit with a *whump*. The previous owners had done the gas conversion, to our amusement. It seemed so phony.

But now it filled the room with instant warmth, the orange flames licking the air.

Luke replaced the remote and sat down on the couch. He busied himself with opening the wine. "Come on, then," he said. "Sit."

I obeyed, taking the glass of wine he offered. Then Luke looked me in the eyes, for a long moment. His face was still. I had no idea what he was thinking. Eventually, I saw a familiar crinkle at the edge of his lips and then all at once he laughed. "Oh, Julia." He grinned. "The look on your face when you walked in here."

I reddened. "I thought . . . I thought she . . ." I couldn't even finish the sentence.

"I know what you thought. But *come on*, don't you think it's even a little bit funny? Like a bad movie? Man embraces sobbing nanny just as wife returns?" He laughed so hard that he couldn't take another sip of wine. Then he made a visible effort toward assuming a serious expression. "I'm so *offended* that you'd think that." But his lip quivered in a way that hinted he might begin laughing again at any moment.

The shame that had gripped me only moments before began to ease up. I smacked him playfully on the knee. "You're so offended? Because I thought a nubile young woman wanted you?"

Luke took a thoughtful sip of wine. Then he smiled again. "I see your point, but I could never stoop to such a cliché. If I'm ever to let you down, I promise to do it much more unconventionally. Say, with a troupe of circus contortionists or—"

I put up a hand to stop him. "Really, Luke, I know lately I've cramped your style, and you have a right to be mad about it. You're on duty at home every night. You've missed every card game with your college buddies."

Luke shook his head. "Julia, come on. Do you seriously think there's this much tension here tonight because I've missed a few poker games?"

I took a gulp of my wine. Somehow we were back to having a serious conversation.

"No," I said quietly. "And I know it's all my fault."

Luke put his glass down on the coffee table. He stared at me for a minute. "I love you so much, Julia. And you're a good person—you started your business for all the right reasons. But I don't think you see how dangerous this has become."

So now, finally, we were going to have a conversation about the money. It was overdue. Even so, the blood rushed to my face. "You don't think I know it? Of course I know it's dangerous. Every morning when my alarm goes off, the first thought in my head is always 'Dear God! I may be flushing'"—the number was so large that saying it out loud brought the taste of bile into my throat—"'forty thousand of our dollars down the toilet.' That's why I've been killing myself every day and night at work. Our savings are on the line, and I feel terrible about it."

Luke stared into our faux fire for a minute. He swirled the wine around in his glass. Then he brought his gaze almost back to mine but didn't look me quite in the eye. "No, Julia. That's not the problem. It isn't the money."

"What, then? Because I think the money is a pretty big goddamned problem!"

"I think you're stuck, Julia, between a rock and a hard place. On the one hand, you're terrified to fail. I understand that, because you've never failed at anything before. Everything you've ever done has been a raging success. Summa cum laude in college, good job on Wall Street, two healthy kids. So I'm sure you're filled with horror at the idea that Julia's Child could fail, and I'm sympathetic about that."

He looked me in the eye then, and I managed to keep my mouth shut, to let him finish.

"On the other hand, I don't think you *will* fail. In spite of the recession, Julia's Child, like all your other ventures, will probably succeed. But the problem is that you've got no endgame. Each new level of success will demand even more of your time and energy. It will take years until you achieve world domination and muffets are available even on NASA missions to Mars. In the meantime you're exhausted, and you don't spend enough time with the rest of us. We miss you, Julia. And I just can't figure out how that's going to change."

"But . . ." It was finally my turn to speak. "But it will! As soon as I get a decent order from a major . . ." I stopped. Because Luke was right. I had to admit that a successful launch at the trade show was no guarantee of familial bliss. Even if my money woes eased, I would still need to triple my production, potentially the most time-consuming project so far.

I gulped air. "Okay, I see your point. But once the business is solvent, I can really take a breath. I promise. I'm just so worried about losing our savings. It's all I think about."

But Luke had planted a tiny seed in the back of my mind, about my own experience with failure. Even as I spoke the words, I realized it wasn't really the money I craved.

"If that's the case," Luke mused, "then you need real funding. You need investors. It's the only way not to be a one-man band anymore."

"If I have investors, I can worry about losing someone else's savings too," I said darkly.

Luke threw his hands up in the air. "Goddamn it, Julia! That's just what I mean! The risk will always be there. You can *never* eliminate it. That's called running a business. And, at the end of the day, it's only money. The fact that you can't say that anymore—"

"The only people who say that are people who have plenty."

"Look around you! Even if your business falls flat on its butt, and even if I lose my job in the merger, nobody who lives here will starve."

I looked up at him with alarm. "Are you going to lose your job?"

He shrugged. "I don't have a crystal ball. But I'm trying to tell you something important. I care more about our family than I do about our jobs. Maybe . . . maybe the right thing to do is to quit my job."

"What?" It was just about the scariest idea I'd ever heard from Luke.

"Just hear me out for a minute. When Wylie was born, you quit because the boys were only little once, you know? I still think that's important. But I don't want you to feel like you have to be the little wife and give up your dream. So maybe it's my turn. Bonnie has been very helpful, but I think we have too much babysitting and too little time together."

"Luke!" I couldn't stand to hear it for even one more second. "It just defies logic to talk like that. Because this is the worst possible timing! You're the only one who's keeping us afloat right now. And I've got to dig our finances out of this hole."

Luke just shook his head. "But there's no end, Julia. If you open a factory, even if you get ten orders from the trade show, where does it stop? Then you'll just have to work seven days a week. How does this end? That's what I need to know. I can put up with almost anything if you figure that out for me."

It was the longest speech Luke had ever given on the topic of Julia's Child. I hated the way it sounded. As if I was a prima donna who lived for each mounting crisis. But his words had a ring of truth to them, and I had trouble answering. I had been counting on a big order to make my life easier, and I found I could not say how it would.

"Luke, if I don't get a big order at this show, I'm going to pack it in."

He nodded, without surprise. "Okay. And if you do get one, then what?"

I shook my head. I hated being on the defensive. I'd always imagined Luke and I were on the same page—worried about my failure. I never dreamed he was more afraid of my success. "I don't know!" I said, losing my battle with tears. "But don't make it sound like I don't care, okay? I lie awake every night worrying about every member of this family—if everybody is getting what they need."

Luke studied me. There was a peace in his expression that I'd always loved. I saw it now, as he moved closer to me on the sofa. "We'll figure it out." He sighed, pulling me to his chest. His shirt smelled of laundry starch and also of him. "Just get through the trade show, I guess. When is it?"

"Ten days."

"We can all manage another ten days without you. But then you'll have a better idea of your chances, right?"

"Probably."

"Fine. I guess there's no use making tough decisions beforehand. We'll talk about it again then. Just get to that point, do your best, and the result will announce itself. The family will wait a little longer."

I leaned on him, not answering. He seemed to feel better about everything, but I only felt worse. Until tonight I'd thought that failure was my biggest enemy. But now I had to add success to my list of worries. How could I possibly go on like this?

# Chapter 15

"Twickatweet!" Wylie pounded on the door of apartment 515.

Standing nearby, Batman giggled. "Mama, he caught on quick."

"He's a prodigy," I agreed. It was only the second conquest of our Halloween, but Wylie was already exhibiting a lot of enthusiasm for the project.

Marta and I had taken a rare evening off from muffet production and trade-show prep. I'd walked in the door at five o'clock—my earliest arrival in weeks. While the boys mugged in their costumes for Luke's camera, I'd performed a secret ritual.

In a shoebox on a high shelf, I placed a small quantity of individually wrapped dried fruit and yogurt-covered pretzels. Wylie was still young enough that I could swap out some of the scarier contributions to his treat bag with my less-toxic offerings. With my surreptitious healthy treats waiting in the wings, we'd set off down the hall of our apartment building.

Wylie banged again on the door to apartment 515.

Then, it swung slowly open to reveal a dimly lit interior. Mrs. Weinstein shuffled into view, sporting a startlingly effective witch costume, complete with tall pointy hat, shapeless black dress, and greenish face powder.

Jasper took a big step backward, bumping into me. He drew his Batman cape around himself, as if for protection.

I reached for Wylie, readying myself for his shriek. But none was forthcoming.

"Twickatweet!" he said again.

"Hello, my pretty," our neighbor cackled. "Would you like a piece of candy? Or an eye of newt, perhaps?"

Wylie squinted up at her. "Candy?"

"Good choice," Luke called from our own apartment doorway across the hall.

She dropped a lollipop into Wylie's plastic pumpkin.

"You too, dearie?" She reached slowly toward Jasper with another lollipop. The witchy hat tilted creepily. Mrs. Weinstein was really laying it on thick.

Jasper swallowed hard and then extended his pumpkin as far as his short arm would go without stepping closer to her.

"Boys, can I get a thank-you?" I prompted.

"Tank you!" Wylie yelled, and then he headed down the hallway without giving another thought to Mrs. Weinstein or her getup.

Luckily, ours was not a very big apartment building. That meant my children would not have more than two dozen doors to knock on—and fewer if I could somehow manage to skip a floor.

I blew a kiss at Luke as we paraded down the hall. He stayed behind to hand out treats.

"Have fun!" Luke called to the boys. But they didn't even respond, the quest for sugar burning too brightly inside them.

It goes without saying that Halloween is a fraught holiday for nutrition nazis like me. The deluge of high-fructose corn syrup and artificial colorings makes my skin crawl. The bitter truth is that I didn't want my boys to know how the other half lived.

But on the plus side, Halloween generated a rare moment of shared community in our creaky old building. I could hear children's voices echoing off the ancient plaster walls a floor below us. Even if it was for only one night, neighbors opened their doors—at least the ones who had signed up at the front desk. Participants found a pumpkin-shaped paper plate taped to their door by 5:30 on Halloween.

"Twickatweet!"

"Wylie, you're knocking on the elevator, sweetie. Look for the pumpkin plates, okay? Let's try downstairs."

But Wylie had spotted another of the sugar beacons—right on my dreadful neighbor Emily's apartment door. "Twickatweet!"

"Yeah! I wonder what Sadie and Bryan are giving out." My boys jostled each other to stand close to the door. Jasper had recovered from the shock of the witch in 515 and was ready to party.

The door swung open. "Oh!" Emily cooed. "What do we have here? It's Batman! And a—"

"Piwate," Wylie supplied. As if the meaning of the three-cornered hat and the eye patch might be missed.

"You are fierce!" Emily maneuvered a basket of candy toward the children, tilting it so they could help themselves.

Why do people do it that way? Doesn't it make more sense to simply hand an age-appropriate treat to my child? Preferably a small one?

Wylie readied his arm for a plunge deep into the loot. "Take only one," I said quickly.

"Go ahead and take two, sugar! This is the night to have fun."

I let a neighborly smile wax on my face, but inside I was boiling. "Go ahead and take two," she'd said. But if you eat them in public, I'll have the board write you another nasty letter.

"M&M's! And hey! I got a gummy *brain*." Jasper was gleeful. He dropped his two treats into his bag.

Then came the fateful moment when the thank-you was due.

I said a little prayer, right there on Emily's doormat, that one of them would remember.

Instead, Emily's older child appeared at her hip.

I had to admit that Bryan's costume was stylish. He had green fleece scales from the top of his head all the way down his back. "Nice dinosaur, buddy!"

Emily winced.

"Dragon! I'm supposed to be a dragon. Mom! You said it would work."

I tried backpedaling. "Oh! Of course you're a dragon. Silly me—only dragons have the . . ." I gestured wildly at my own head.

But the damage was done. "Everybody thinks I'm a dinosaur. Next year can we just *buy* a costume like other people?" He slunk off behind her.

"You made that costume?" I peered around Emily to see the dragon's retreat, down to the perfectly spiked tail.

She shrugged. "Fleece is easy. You don't have to finish the edges. The hard part is customer satisfaction." She tried flashing a grin, but it came off more like a baring of teeth.

Up until that moment I'd been pretty proud of myself just for making it home in time for Halloween. But I'd always admired anyone who could sew. It seemed to require a lot of personality traits that I lacked—artistic flair, a sense of design. The patience of a saint.

Wylie had lost interest in the proceedings and had begun wandering off down the hall, scanning the apartment doors for pumpkin plates, like a bloodhound on the scent. I would have to extricate myself from the little disaster I'd caused. It seemed there was no way to encounter my neighbor and come away unscathed.

I was just starting to apologize when Jasper brushed past Emily and took a few steps into the apartment. I was opening my mouth to call him back when I heard him say, "Bryan, can I look at your tail? It's really cool."

"Really?"

My heart swelled with gratitude for my sensitive son.

"Yeah. And maybe you should think about breathing some fire or something."

"Hey, Mom? Can I breathe fire?"

Emily perked up. "I've got an orange silk scarf you could borrow."

"Cool!"

That was our opening. "Jasper, we have to get moving if you want to do any more trick-or-treating."

Batman walked out of Emily's apartment, his cape following regally behind. "Thanks for the gummy brains!"

Emily beamed. "Come back anytime, Batman." At least she liked one of us.

I waved good-bye and then bolted down the hallway after Wylie. A few months ago he'd actually gotten into the elevator without me, and I'd had to run down flights of stairs, peeping into each hallway in turn, until I found him.

"Twickatweet!"

I laughed. He'd stopped to knock on an apartment only a few doors down. But it was our apartment door.

As I trotted toward him, Luke opened the door, treats under his arm.

"Daddy?"

Luke played along. "Oh!" he said with pronounced enthusiasm. "What have we here? What a cute little lion!"

Wylie giggled. "No! Piwate."

"That's what I said! What a cute little hippo."

Wylie had never heard a funnier joke. He giggled so hard he almost couldn't answer. "No, Daddy!" he gasped. "Pi-wate!"

"For the little . . . fireman, I have this lovely treat."

Wylie laughed on, but Jasper peered over the edge of the basket in Luke's hands. Then he straightened up in shock. "No!"

Uh-oh. The basket was full of individually wrapped muffets. I'd used packaging left over from our giveaway on *The Scene*. Personally, I thought they were adorable. And I also thought it was neighborly of me to give out something that kids could eat tomorrow for breakfast.

Jasper did not agree. He grabbed the basket out of Luke's hands and stomped into the apartment.

I followed in hot pursuit, having no earthly idea what Jasper planned to do with the muffets.

The bat cape flared as Jasper fled toward the kitchen. I would have gone pounding after him if Luke had not caught me by the hand.

"Tough night in Gotham?" A smile played around his eyes.

I loved that about Luke. He didn't always succumb to the children's drama. He was always ready to stop a moment and try to find the humor in the situation. "I'd better not find those muffets in the garbage," I complained.

But Luke simply kissed my hand. Then he released it, to step into the adjacent dining room and fill my glass with red wine.

I followed him to the table and sat down. "I don't know why he freaked out about the muffets. I know he doesn't like to eat them anymore, but I don't see why he should take it personally." The truth was that I'd assumed I had a couple years left before my boys became so easily embarrassed by their mother.

Luke opened his mouth to reply but then frowned. "Did you hear that?"

We were both silent for a moment. I heard it too—the sound of paper tearing, at very close range. My eyes met Luke's. At the same instant, we both ducked our heads under the dining room table.

Wylie was down there scarfing down M&M's straight from the "fun-size" bag.

"Wylie!" I gasped. "Daddy's making pasta for dinner."

But Luke just leaned back in his chair and took a sip of wine. "Melts in your mouth, and not on my rug."

I'm well aware that my nutritional neuroses are a bit over the top. But it made me feel slightly ill to watch a child eat candy before dinner.

The doorbell rang. "Trick or treat!"

Luke's eyes opened wide with alarm. And a second later, I realized why. Jasper had made off with all our Halloween offerings.

"We can offer them wine. Or maybe a couple of spitty M&M's!" Luke ducked his head under the table again. "No. Eighty-six the M&M's."

I stood up. My secret stash of healthy treats was about to come in handy. "Coming!" I called.

But Batman was faster. A little black streak flew past me and opened the door.

In the hallway stood a man I didn't recognize and a very young . . . girl? It was hard to tell because the child was disguised head to toe in a startlingly lifelike tree frog costume, complete with bulging red eyes and webbed feet.

"Wow" was all I could say.

"Lannie!" Wylie said. He'd emerged from under the table, with a lollipop in his mouth.

"Wywy!" croaked the tree frog.

The dad grinned. "I'm Thomas." He held out a hand. "We live on the second floor. Lannie just turned two."

"Julia." We shook hands. "I guess the children know each other from the playroom."

Thomas nodded. "Lannie is on the nanny circuit during the day."

The little tree frog was now holding a small package of M&M's. And it was then that I realized what Jasper had done. He'd given her one of his own candies from our brief stint of trick-or-treating.

"Lannie, say thank you."

"Tank you!"

"Nice meeting you, Julia." And then they were gone.

But two more forms filled our doorway. Under piles of pink princess garb, I could make out the twins from 404. "Trick or treat!"

As quick as you please, Jasper handed each of them a treat, one of which was the gummy brain he'd been so excited about only ten minutes earlier.

"Jasper! You don't have to . . ."

"Thank you!" The twins bounded off. And Batman shut the door. I was fairly certain that those were Jasper's blue eyes looking out from the slits in his mask. But otherwise, I couldn't be sure it was him. My five-year-old saw candy so rarely that he'd never give it away.

In one motion I swept the Batman mask off his face. "Jasper Daniel Bailey. What the heck is going on? Why are you giving away your candy? And where are my muffets?"

The fact that Jasper had mask head—his hair standing straight up like a hedgehog's—only magnified the intensity of his gaze. "We can't *give* the muffets away!"

"Why not?"

"You need to *sell* them. You and Marta."

"But . . ." So that was the problem? Really? If so, then I could find a way to make him understand that two dozen muffets were barely a drop in the muffet ocean. "Sweetie, these muffets are *extra*. It's really okay." I got down on my knees and hugged him, breathing him in. He smelled of tear-free shampoo, and also of stretchy nylon.

"Do you think you'll have enough muffets soon? And you won't have to work as much?"

God! Jasper was the sort of kid who could put a dagger straight through your heart. He was genuinely unselfish—not the sort of boy to keep tabs on whose pancake was the biggest or who got to choose the bedtime story. He was a super, easygoing kid, and I was so lucky to have him. "Yes, Jasper. There will be enough muffets soon. And less work. But there's only one Halloween night a year. Let's do some more trick-or-treating before it's too late. And then we're going to eat pasta with Daddy and go to bed."

"Okay." He was silent then, hugging me tightly. I wondered if he believed me. "Mama?"

"Yes, Jasper."

"Can I eat a piece of candy too? I still have one left."

I looked over my shoulder at Wylie, who had sticky lollipop goop all over his lips and candy wrappers strewn around him. Yet still Jasper asked permission.

"Go ahead, buddy. You enjoy it." Even if it turned out to be some really dreadful, neon-dyed dental nightmare, I promised myself I wouldn't say a word. "In fact, let's go and get you some more."

# Chapter 16

Standing in my office a week later, I sneezed for the five hundredth time.

Over the past few weeks, our tiny office space had come to resemble an overcrowded hay loft. I waited for Marta to heft one bale of hay out of our office door. I kicked another along behind her.

My allergies hadn't prevented me from choosing hay to be the cornerstone of our trade-show display. To make a table, we planned to stretch an old farmhouse door across the tops of the bales. It was pastoral and a little bit funky. Best of all, it was cheap.

After a week and a half of preparation, it was finally time to drag everything to the Javits Center for the show. With our signage under both of my arms, I followed Marta into the bull-pen area of the office suites.

"Have fun at the hoedown, ladies," Derrick winked at me from behind his desk.

"Aren't you a funny guy," Marta said over her shoulder, as she coaxed two hay bales toward the stairs.

"Keep those servers humming, Derrick," I called, maneuvering our signs among the cubicles. "If the trade show pans out, we should get a lot of Web hits."

He gave me a salute. Behind him, the room was packed with bodies. I had always imagined that the other denizens of Chelsea Sunshine Suites were slackers. I rarely saw them roll into the office before eleven in the morning. But now I knew the truth. They lived and worked in a different time zone than we did. Even though it was past nine in the evening, there were no empty chairs.

I sneezed again, fumbling for yet another tissue. "Hay is for horses."

"*Chica,* what horses?" Marta asked.

"It's just a saying. When I was growing up, if I said 'hey!' to my mother, she would respond that hay is for horses."

Marta chomped her gum. "I don't get it."

"I guess it isn't that funny."

"Where *is* your mother anyway?" Marta asked.

"What do you mean? She's driving a golf cart around South Carolina and playing bridge. Same as always." Gently, I set our pricey foam-backed posters against the stairwell wall.

"They don't visit so often, your parents. I'd think they'd want to be closer—pinch the boys' cheeks, see your business. Help out at your trade show."

That would be the day. "Well, my mother thinks I've got it made. She actually made a crack that my home is 'staffed.' "

"You mean, because of Bonnie?"

"Yes. They visit about once a year. It's tight in our apartment. We wedge them into the boys' room, on an inflatable bed. And then Wylie bunks with us. And my father snores. Or they can pay three hundred bucks a night for a hotel. New York is tough that way."

Marta was silent, maneuvering a hay bale down half a flight of stairs. Watching her, I remembered that Marta's own mother had left more comfortable quarters in Puerto Rico to share a tiny apartment with her daughter and little Carlos for a year—all so that Marta could start the classes at Zia Maria's and get off welfare. And then, right before I met her, Marta's mom had died.

Perhaps my own mother would make the same sacrifices for me, under those circumstances. But I never asked for her help because I didn't want to hear what she thought of my choices. I feared she'd view Julia's Child, not as a real job, to put food on the table, but as a kind of luxury to which I treated myself.

I didn't like to admit that her viewpoint had merit.

Either way, it was easier to go without help than to tease apart my own motivations, which tonight led me to sweat over bales of hay when I could have been enjoying a quiet night at home with my family.

It took us half an hour to manhandle our display materials into the entranceway of the office building. I was grateful to see Lugo's truck idling outside. When he spotted us, he came out of the cab to unlock the back, where a pallet of fresh muffets waited inside. Marta had slaved for the last two days, baking them on the eve of the show for maximum appeal.

We stacked our things carefully in the back of the truck. Then I opened the door to the cab and climbed in. "Evening, Lugo."

"Hi, missy."

There was only one passenger seat, but Lugo had placed an overturned milk crate on the floor behind the gearshift. So I maneuvered my way onto the crate and sat. I left the proper seat for Marta.

She climbed in and then did her best to align her bottom in a way that only part of the seat was used. "There's room," she said.

"I'm fine down here," I said brightly.

"Next stop, Atlantic City." Lugo rumbled with laughter at his own joke. The laugh turned into a coughing fit so violent that I feared for him. But the truck lurched forward anyway, forcing me to search for an object to steady myself should the truck stop fast. Marta gripped the back of her seat with the same idea.

Lugo's coughing died down. "You ladies gonna work all night?" he asked.

"God, I hope not," I told him. "Tomorrow will be another long day."

"So, Marta," Lugo asked. "You want a lift home?"

She frowned. "Lugo, I live way out in Queens. You live in Brooklyn. Why would you want to wait around to drive me an hour out of your way?" She gave him the fish eye.

He shrugged. "Can't blame an old man for trying."

I could feel Marta cringe in the darkness.

The Javits Center was less than a mile from our office, which was just about the only truly convenient thing about the trade show. The loading dock was three deep with trucks like ours, so we idled for twenty minutes, waiting to get near the door, or at least the sidewalk. Lugo lit up a cigar, causing Marta to hastily roll down the window. The smoke began to waft down toward me, and I pulled myself up to maximum height on my milk crate, hoping to catch a fresh breeze.

Outside, the commotion of the exhibitors on the darkened sidewalk reminded me of the leaf-cutter ants on exhibit at the Central Park Zoo. A swarm of busy bodies dragged enormous objects toward the gaping nest hole. "That can't all be . . . for the trade show," I wondered aloud. One group of movers carried an old-style diner counter into the building. Behind it followed a team of men with the cutest little retro stools I'd ever seen. The last person in the group staggered in with a sign reading "Leah's All-Natural Foods, Lennox, MA."

"Jesooz," Marta whispered. We watched as the next group of movers lugged a faux-brick hearth toward the door. A sofa and matching chairs followed it. "At least I haven't seen anyone else with hay bales," she said.

I moaned. "That's because they've all brought entire suites with them." I'd booked only the ten-by-ten-foot booth, the cheapest one. Surely there would be other modest displays? Or would Julia's Child, New York City, be the only country bumpkin?

Suddenly Marta leaped from the truck. By the time I extracted myself from behind the gearshift, she was walking back toward us, pushing an enormous mover's dolly along the sidewalk.

"Nice work, Marta. This will save our backs."

"Those other guys were done with it."

From the driver's seat came a loud creak—hopefully from the door and not Lugo's aging body. He got out, opened the back of the truck, and then retreated to the cab with his cigar. Marta and I hefted the hay bales onto the dolly, stacking our cases of muffets and then our meager-looking posters on top of our wooden door. Our only prize for being the least outfitted exhibitor in sight was that Marta and I could roll all our props and merchandise forward at once.

Through the driver's side window, I passed Lugo the fifty-dollar bill I'd been holding for him.

"Thank you, missy," he said, pocketing the money.

"Thank *you,* Lugo. See you tomorrow night."

We pushed our hay island slowly through the loading bay, into the cavernous expanse of the convention center. The ceiling was perhaps forty feet above our heads. I stopped to take in the hive of activity around us. The worker ants swarmed everywhere, building a temporary city. Walls were raised, furniture moved into place. Rugs were unrolled. If I hadn't been so appalled at the contrast to our own humble furnishings, I would have been impressed.

The most surprising thing was the bright sheen on every

exhibit. I'd been expecting something more in keeping with the all-natural theme—like booths in a giant and very upscale farmers' market. Instead, the displays were as flashy as Las Vegas. There were acres of slick surfaces, bright signage, and gleaming kiosks.

The exhibits made only the occasional nod to the all-natural theme. The sides of a booth for Nature's Toothpaste were embedded with smooth river stones, like you'd find in a Zen garden. And the wooden hangers for a perky children's clothing line hung from bamboo clothing racks.

"We're screwed," I said. "Look at all this."

Marta pressed on. "Let's just find booth number 307."

When we found it, booth 307 was nothing but a ten-by-ten section of concrete floor. I looked around. Things were only marginally more modest in our row. The neighboring booths, though smaller, continued to amaze. Most vendors had brought their own floor coverings, giving their areas a unified, streamlined look. Marta and I would be standing on the cement floor. And the lighting! Many of the custom-built displays incorporated their own little spotlights. I tilted my head toward the soaring ceiling and understood why. We would have to rely on the filtered ambient light from up high. It was fine for conversation, but it wouldn't add any dazzle to our product.

"If there's a prize for the most all-natural display, we'll take home the trophy," I grumbled.

"It will be fine, Julia. Don't worry." Marta had already begun hauling our stuff off the rolling platform, piling it in one corner of our vacant plot. Together we arranged our bales of hay just so, our rustic wooden door stretching between them to make a table.

I had to admit that it did look rather cute. Cute but small. "Okay, so tomorrow I'll bring the platters down in a taxi, and—"

"Evening, ladies." An older man with a clipboard had stopped in front of our booth. He peered through wire-rimmed glasses at the list in front of him. "Booth number 307. Julia's Child?" he asked.

"That's right," I told him. "I'm Julia."

"Great to have you here. You've found the correct spot. But I'm afraid we're going to have to change your setup."

"Why is that?"

"Hay is flammable," he said. "Have those bales been fire-proofed?"

"Yes," Marta said, at the exact moment that I answered no.

He squinted over his wire rims at us. "Carlos!" he called over his shoulder.

A sweaty young man, with a dark fringe of hair, bounded over. "Yeah?"

"Please help these ladies remove their hay bales. You will take them to the disposal room."

"Wait!" I gasped. I'd paid a hundred dollars for that hay. And after it was gone, my booth would consist of a wooden door, lying flat on the bare floor.

"The door too," the man said. "Unless the ladies would like to take it with them."

"Hey!" I put both hands defensively on my door.

"Hay is for horses," said Mr. Glasses. Then he burst out laughing at his own joke.

My blood pressure went up several points. My pulse rang loudly in my ears. I opened my mouth to argue.

But Marta stepped closer to Mr. Glasses, placing her hand sweetly on his wrist. "You know, my own mother used to say that joke?" She looked up at him. "Perhaps we could figure something out," she purred. "Tell me what we could do to make it okay. It's the only display we have."

He smiled down at her. "I'm sorry, dear, but the convention

packet states clearly that all structural items must be made of a nonflammable substance."

I pressed my fingertips into my temples. "We didn't receive the packet until two days ago, because the trade show rejected our application and then changed its mind and accepted it. I never got a chance to read—"

"Be that as it may," he sighed, "the hay has to go. I can't get a two-thousand-dollar citation from the fire marshal over this. Carlos!" He gestured toward our hapless bales.

A few minutes later, Marta and I were left with a nearly empty booth. We had muffets, and we had posters. And those were looking skimpier by the minute.

"Even if we had a way of getting it here, we couldn't use my dining table," I said. "It's wood."

"We're going to end up with a card table or something." Marta sighed. "If only I'd accepted that ride home from Lugo, at least we'd have him to help us."

"Ugh! A card table. Covered with a plastic birthday-party tablecloth. Shoot me. It's going to look awful."

Marta looked wistfully around at the shiny displays going up on either side of us. For once, even she was out of ideas.

Even cadging a card table at ten o'clock on a Thursday night was not going to be easy. I didn't own one. Maybe a neighbor had one, but knocking on doors an hour from now was out of the question.

"What about our metal office furniture?" Marta suggested. "It's kind of ugly. But what other choice do we have?"

I tried to picture the booth filled with our Chelsea Sunshine Suites desks, with their gray metal tops. But then I snapped my fingers. "Not *our* office furniture! But in the big room, that tall drawing table. In the corner? Whose is that?"

"Sí!" Marta said. "The girl with the blue hair—her name is Yona. And I think there are also stools."

"That's the one. Let's go!" I had no idea when the Chelsea Sunshine Suites emptied out for the night, but we needed to get there before it did.

Now, as we trotted past them on our way out, I understood why so few of the All-Natural Kid Stuff Tradeshow booths looked natural. All that gleaming plastic was nonflammable. Of course, in the event of an actual fire it would emit noxious gasses that might kill us anyway. But it was abundantly clear by now that nobody cared what I thought.

When we arrived back at our offices, the room was still packed with twenty-something-year-olds staring into screens. Yona stared into hers, twisting a lock of cobalt-colored hair. The blue light from her terminal compounded the effect, making her look for all the world like a manga character.

"Hi," I said, pulling up a chair. "Yona?" She looked up, surprised. I hoped she even knew my name.

"Julia, right?"

"Right," I said. "I apologize, but I have a favor to ask you. I'm doing a trade show at the Javits Center, and they just threw out my setup."

"Oh, no! That's so whack. The hay bales? I thought they were cute!"

"I thought so too, but the fire marshal did not. Is there any way I could borrow your drawing table for a day? And the stools? I could rent them from you."

Yona swiveled around in her seat and appraised the furniture behind her. Then she faced me. "Take it," she said. "No charge. Somebody might as well use them. These days, the only jobs I get are dopey logo designs. I should never have bought that furniture. I had such big plans."

The sound of her lament was familiar enough. "You know, if this trade show works out for me, I might need a dopey logo too."

Yona smiled. "Take the furniture. But how are you going to get it there?"

"It's, uh, only a dozen blocks away. Or so." I said. Marta and I would just have to carry the table there, and then come back and cram the stools into a taxi.

Yona's partner, Mack, spun around in his seat. "I'm just about ready to head out of here. I could give you a hand." He made a self-mocking display of his biceps for our inspection.

It was the second nice offer in as many minutes, and my eyes grew moist with gratitude. "Tell you what. I'll buy lunch tomorrow. From Pastis. For everyone who helped us tonight," I said.

"Yikes," Marta breathed behind me, probably thinking of the budget. Pastis was an expensive celebrity hangout ten blocks downtown. But I didn't care. We were down-and-out, and strangers were willing to help.

"I'm in too!" Derrick said, standing. "I'll carry something." He jabbed his sidekick, another aggressively pierced fellow. And suddenly there were six of us.

"You also had signs," Yona said. "They didn't throw those away too, did they?"

"We've still got them. They'll have to be propped up on the floor," I said.

Yona put her hands on her hips, scrutinizing me in the same way my mother used to when she appraised my outfit. "That will look terrible, and they'll fall down all day. How about taking the chalkboard?" She pointed to it.

The big green board had probably always been there, but I saw it for the first time. It had the same sort of retro, classroom styling as Yona's table. "Is it yours?" I asked her.

She shrugged. "No, but you'll bring it back. What's the harm?"

And so the chalkboard came along too. And by midnight, my hundred square feet looked much better than an empty concrete bin. Mack even made an extra trip back to the office for a couple of clip-on lamps, which now shone from the corners of the blackboard, like spotlights, onto our posters.

Yona's table also had a light inside. "Yeah, I sprang for the light-box top," she'd explained. "Stupid idea, it cost me a thousand dollars. But hey, your stuff will look great on it."

I gave Mack my credit card. "Have a lunch party, and cross your fingers for us."

"It will be killer," he said. I took that as a good sign.

# Chapter 17

It had been years since I was up until two in the morning for any reason other than puking children. But our booth looked so much better by the time I left the Javits Center that I didn't care how late it had gotten.

I happily woke at seven the next morning, because this was the day we would make it happen. My company would finally share airspace with some of the biggest buyers in the land.

I took a speedy shower and threw on pants and a sweater. Marta had ordered two matching Julia's Child aprons for us to wear at the trade show. They cost thirty-nine dollars, plus shipping. God bless Marta, I thought, as I blew my hair dry before dashing out the door.

The subway ride from my apartment to the convention center took only twenty minutes. The energy of New York City coursed through my veins. There were plenty of seats in the car, but I stood up, watching the stations come and go. Not only was my booth in decent shape, but I had a home-team advantage. The biggest organic trade show in the nation was in my own backyard. Getting off the train at Thirty-fourth Street, I rode the escalator back toward street level, an anthem playing in my head. Today would be my day.

I flashed my participant pass to the security guards at the door of Javits Center and trotted, through the glittering trade-show city, in the direction of our booth. It was a sleepy city, just waking up for the day. Plastic sheeting still covered the wares on many of the tables.

Turning into our aisle, I slowed down to take in the neighboring displays. They were just as beautiful and intimidating as they'd seemed the night before. But at least the shock had worn off. I passed an enormous display for Samba Smoothies, which appeared to be one of those whole-meal-blended-into-a-drink products. An enormous faux smoothie in an enormous faux glass towered overhead. The red-and-white striped straw, probably seven feet tall, was particularly cheerful. Jasper and Wylie would have loved it.

But the world was already full of smoothies, wasn't it? And that sort of product was often chock-full of sugar. I strode on. I passed Organic T, which proudly displayed a whole lot of shirts. I passed Herbal Cure, some kind of cold remedy. Its booth sported a giant-beanstalk-size box of tissues.

I had made it to the middle of the row without finding our booth. Could it have been on my left while I passed by, gazing at the products on my right? I spun around, scanning the other side of the aisle. And that's when I saw them.

It was the photograph that grabbed me. It must have been five square feet—a high-resolution shot of a baked good with a strong resemblance to a muffet. The photography was obviously professional: the crumb appearing moist and tender, bits of carrot emerging from the crust.

I tore my eyes from the image to read the gigantic gold lettering above: "Melissa's Munchers, Philadelphia, PA." On the left panel, clippings were stylishly arranged to highlight media attention the company had received. The right-hand panel showed, in giant type, the ingredients list and nutritional information for each muncher. It was a gorgeous booth, telling Melissa's whole story in a couple of easy-to-read images. And it seemed to be standing in the very spot where my own things had been the night before. I began to wonder if I was dreaming.

"Julia!"

I spun around. Marta was waving both arms at me from the next aisle. I could just barely see her behind part of a display. I ran toward her, ducking under a rack of hemp dresses to reach the next aisle.

"Julia, are you lost?" Marta grinned at me.

"I . . ." I gulped. "Did you see that booth over there? Melissa's Munchers?"

"No. Stupid name. What are they?"

"They're . . . They look a lot like muffets."

Marta stopped, her bloodred fingernails frozen in place on a carton of muffets. "Oh."

I took a deep breath. "It had to happen sooner or later, you know? Maybe ours taste better?"

Marta nodded. "Damn straight."

"Maybe ours are cheaper."

"Doubt it! Not with our expenses."

"Well, Melissa just blew several grand on a convention display booth. That's all I'm sayin'."

Marta laughed, shaking her head. "Where are the platters?"

"Oh! Here." I held up the shopping bag I'd been carrying. I put two platters onto Yona's table. I switched on the lights, and the surface was suffused with a white glow. "Where's the box of brochures?"

Marta pointed at a carton with her foot. I set about arranging our literature in piles. We would talk to as many people as we could; hand out samples, business cards, blessings. Whatever it took. We were there to network.

We tied on our new green aprons. It was time to set out the merchandise.

"Let me show you what I was thinking," Marta said. On the cake stand I'd brought, she arranged one muffet of each flavor. Into each she inserted a little toothpick flag, carefully printed with the flavor's name.

"Gorgeous! I'm going to start calling you Marta Stewart."

She grinned like a cat. "You go ahead, *chica*. Because that old blonde lady makes a lot of money. But wait until you see this."

We'd brought about five hundred muffets. Some were packaged as if for sale, but most sat in plastic bins, unwrapped, for tasting.

"See—I made loaves," Marta informed me. She took the plastic off, revealing giant, rectangular muffets.

"Wow. I guess if we're cutting them anyway, that makes sense. Do you think the centers are cooked?"

"I'm Marta Stewart, remember? I fiddled a bit with the moisture content and the baking temperature. Worked like a charm. Greasing every one of those muffin tins wasn't working for me."

We sliced the muffet loaves into one-inch cubes, each with a little toothpick for easy tasting. We arranged them as attractively as we could on the platters I'd brought.

At eight thirty, convention attendees arrived like a tidal wave, just as Marta and I were managing to eat a bite of bagel and sip coffee. It was showtime.

The first plates of muffets disappeared in a heartbeat. Marta cut up more while I attempted to greet each visitor. The tradeshow attendees drifting into our booth were men and women, young and old. Any adult who wanted to pony up thirty dollars for a badge was welcome to the show. Attendees all wore the same square plastic passes, usually hung around the neck. We looked like so many items at a tag sale.

I studied the faces in the crowd. Some would be food store buyers (yes!), writers for the trade press (okay!), and a few were probably competitors (boo!). I scrutinized everyone, wondering how I would identify the VIPs.

"I'm Elmer," an older man said, offering his hand. His long gray hair was pulled back into a ponytail, atop of which he wore a ten-gallon hat. "I run a health-food store in Dallas. And I *love* your product! Do you think you can ship these to me?" He munched an Autumn Harvest Muffet.

Flattered, I tried to imagine how that would work. Styrofoam coolers with dry ice inside? FedEx overnight? That would just about double my production cost. "I'd sure like to think about trying," I said. "Do you have a business card?"

"Sure, little lady." He tipped his hat to me. I put the card in my pocket, holding a hand over it protectively.

But then that conversation began to repeat itself. I met scads of buyers with tiny retail operations far from New York. Sure, a few of my admirers were more local. It was possible to imagine delivering to Jersey or Long Island. But for every friendly buyer from within a hundred miles there were three more from the ends of the earth. As much as I enjoyed chatting about muffets, in my gut I knew that these smaller orders would not save my company.

Still, I repeated my pitch dozens of times to these buyers who had traveled so far. I didn't mind. It was like attending an enormous party where every guest was just as excited as I was about natural kids' products. I recited ingredient lists. I extolled the virtues of flash-freezing. I waxed nostalgic about my organic farmland in Vermont. I tried to believe my own hype.

I grew sweaty in my efforts to greet everyone, all the while scanning the crowd for Mr. Big, whoever he might be. And sometimes I would actually sense the presence of heavier firepower. More than once I watched as a stealthy attendee sidled into our booth. I would invariably be trapped in conversation with one of the Elmers from Dallas. The stealthy ones held a folder in front of their ID tag. They would take a taste of the product, or inspect the brochure, and then disappear again into the crowd.

"Marta, did you see that?" I asked once. "Was that guy covering up an ID that said Costco? Or am I having paranoid fantasies?"

She stared after the man, probably in his forties, slipping away into the crowd. "I don't know," she said. "But if I were a buyer for a company that big, I'd keep it under wraps. A guy from Costco would practically need his own security detail in this place."

I nodded grimly as another clump of people arrived at our booth.

Then, after the initial rush, the pace of muffet consumption slowed. I began to realize that our earlier popularity had more to do with the hour—breakfast time—than buyer interest. Now people began to skip our booth. I had to hope that it was because they were, say, apparel buyers and not because we looked like shabby losers.

Sometime around noon I ducked behind our chalkboard and wolfed down the congealed cream-cheese bagel I'd brought that morning. I took gulps of bottled water, stretched my arms and legs. There was music pulsing from somewhere nearby. I realized that it had been on all morning, but I had internalized the driving tempo as the soundtrack to my ambitions. Things were happening, right here in this room. While some of the mom-and-pop exhibitors were bound to come away with nothing, others would be discovered, their dreams brought to fruition.

The products around us varied from inspired to downright stupid. On my only sprint to the ladies' room, I'd glimpsed heirloom-quality wooden toys and gorgeous children's clothing made domestically, not by child labor in China. But I'd also spied a group marketing the Sick Bunny Bowl, for kids to puke into in the car. That one left me scratching my head. "Two handles! Just the right size! Comforting for upset tummies!"

The product that tickled Marta's funny bone was the PeePee TeePee. "It's a paper cone that you're supposed to set over your baby boy's weewee while you're changing his diaper, so he doesn't pee on you."

"So he . . . pees on himself instead?"

"I guess. They got a twenty-foot booth, and five people working it, all dressed like Indians."

"Then at least we're not the craziest people in the room."

"Not even close."

I dove back into the fray. We had another wave of muffet consumption around lunch hour. I unwrapped more muffets while chatting about sodium levels with a health-food-store owner from Berkeley. I quartered them while discussing distribution with a store owner from Northampton, Massachusetts. Meanwhile, my pocket filled up with business cards for far-flung buyers, the likes of whom I could only support if I went truly national. They weighed me down, like another missed opportunity.

Then I watched a pair of people enter our booth, a man and a woman. He was tall, with a prominent mustache. She had rather heavy calves poking out from underneath her skirt. But the oddest thing about them was their empty hands. Unlike every other visitor to the trade show, they weren't laden with pamphlets or samples.

"Morning!" I greeted them cheerfully.

"Hiya," the man said. He went right over to the chalkboard and began to read our signage.

"Would you like to try a muffet?" I asked the woman.

"Sure." Her brown eyes darted between Marta and me. She took up a chunk of the Autumn Harvest flavor and nibbled daintily on the corner. "Delicious," she said.

Mr. Mustache came around to the front of our table. "You make these products yourself?" he asked.

"We sure do. Every one of them."

"And you do that where?"

"In sunny Brooklyn," I answered. His manner was abrupt, but I was all charm and salesmanship today.

"You store them where? Who do you use for distribution?"

So many questions. I looked for his convention tag. But he wasn't even wearing one, which was against regulations. I tried to keep the smile on my face. "We have freezer space in Brooklyn. Our truck driver does local deliveries, and we're just now working on our national, um, distribution. Would you like a sample?"

"Sure," he said. He reached for the nearest muffet—Focaccia Fiesta. He popped it in his mouth. "Nice to meet you," he said. He nodded at his partner, and they retreated quickly down the aisle.

"What was that all about?" I asked as they walked away.

"Spies!" Marta had a flair for drama.

I shook my head. "I doubt it. A spy would ask about the recipes."

"Not me," Marta argued. "I'd want to know about production. Let's send somebody over to grill Melissa's Munchers. Let's ask if they manage to make their product during daylight hours. We're like vampires, you and me."

It was a couple of hours later when Marta's voice sang out purposefully. "Oh, Julia!" I turned to her. "Meet Kai from Whole Foods!"

Aha! Hours ago, I had thought to wonder whether he'd turn up. I looked him up and down. Kai was tall, dark, and handsome, perhaps half Asian, half skater dude. He had coffee-colored skin, straight brown hair, and big brown eyes. "Ladies, it's a pleasure," he said warmly. "I thought you weren't going to make the trade show."

"I decided that wasn't wise," I said evenly.

"So how's it going?"

"Good! It's good," I insisted. "I can't believe how much product we've moved today. And I'm going hoarse, and it's only . . ." I looked at my watch. Oh. It was five thirty already. I had an hour left to meet the buyer of my dreams.

"Hang in there," he said kindly. "These things can kill a person. Look at me! I'll need a chiropractor if I don't get out of here soon."

In each hand he had a heavy shopping bag full of product samples—every one of them, I was sure, made by one of my competitors.

I stared at those bags with the feeling of doom, wondering if Melissa's Munchers had made it inside. I tried for a joke. "Well, Kai, you don't really need all that stuff. With muffets selling out at three of your stores already . . ."

He laughed. "I hear you, Julia. We'll talk soon. When all this madness is over." As he walked away, I said a silent prayer that those bags were full of twenty-five brands of yogurt smoothies.

Marta read my thoughts. "You know, Julia, possession is nine tenths of the law. You're already on his shelves. Why would he take the trouble to replace our product with another one just like it?"

"From your lips to God's ears, Marta." I could only pray that she was right.

"Anyway, it looks like we brought enough." Marta showed me what was left—a few cartons of muffets. "With only an hour to go."

One more hour. I spun around to squint at the stream of people trickling past our booth. Maybe this would be the moment when one of them would appear. Yes! That must be how it would happen. Someone who tasted muffets earlier in the day would come back now to talk to us about a deal. There was no reason it shouldn't play out that way. A serious buyer would sample everything before circling back to make up his mind.

Wouldn't he?

I was like the survivor of a shipwreck, treading water in the ocean: I knew I couldn't go on like this forever, but I wasn't quite ready to slip beneath the waves yet.

I brushed a few crumbs off Yona's table and then stepped over to the chalkboard to smooth down the flapping corner of a poster. It was a blow-up of Wylie, his arms stretched wide, looking upwards. We'd superimposed the various flavors of muffets in an arc above him, creating the illusion that Wylie was juggling them like a circus performer. The flavors were labeled over each picture: "Apple and Cheddar!" "Focaccia Fiesta!" They sailed above his rounded toddler head like a rainbow.

I'd studied my dog-eared entrepreneur magazines while designing those signs. They'd cautioned me that it usually took a few rounds on the trade-show circuit to find your audience. But I'd really believed that this one day would do it for me. I *needed* ANKST to work for me, and so I'd believed that it would.

Wallowing in my disappointment, I almost didn't notice the suits stroll into our booth. The two unfamiliar men wore pinstripes. I glanced over at Marta to see if she'd noticed them. But she was busy with a gray-haired lady, probably a health-food-store owner.

"Hello there," I greeted our visitors.

One of them held a map of the trade-show booth assignments, marked up in ink pen. The other one checked his ANKST catalog and addressed me. "Are you Julia Bailey? I'm J. P. Smith."

"Yes, sir." I shook his hand. "How can I help you, Mr. Smith?"

He definitely wasn't a health-food-store owner. He looked more like a corporate lawyer. His starched white shirt collar stood up just so. "I'm from GPG. We were wondering if you'd take a meeting. Say, next week? You're based in New York, correct? Our offices are just in midtown."

I blinked at him for a minute, trying to decide whether or not to admit that the name GPG didn't ring any bells. Some of the big grocery chains were part of large corporations.

"A meeting?"

The two men nodded in unison.

I'd prefer an order, but sure I'll take a meeting. The subway fare would be the cheapest business expense in Julia's Child's history. "Certainly," I said. "Next week in midtown."

"Super. My team and I look forward to hearing more about Julia's Child." He handed me his business card.

I promised to phone his assistant on Monday. Then they were gone.

I turned to Marta. "GPG?"

She shook her head. "*Chica,* I never heard of it. But that don't matter, as long as their checks don't bounce."

# Chapter 18

"GPG? I think it stands for Gulf Pacific Group," Luke said. "It's a big conglomerate. Why?"

I'd arrived home from the trade show in the midst of bath-time and bedtime madness, so I'd been waiting an hour to talk to Luke about my whirlwind day. "Well, I hope it's a conglomerate that owns a chain of grocery stores. They turned up at the end of the day. They want to meet with me, but I don't know why."

I handed the business card to Luke. He looked at it, shrugged, and handed it back. It was only marginally more forthcoming than what you'd expect to receive from a CIA operative. It contained just a name and phone number under the gray letters *GPG*.

"Interesting," Luke said. "So let's Google."

"Oh, baby!" I teased. But I trotted after him toward his computer. He sat down in the desk chair and I sat down on his lap, and together we stared at GPG's corporate Web facade. There was a long list of food brands, brands they owned. We recognized a Napa winery and a luxury ice cream.

There weren't any grocers on the list.

"What do you suppose these guys are after?"

"I don't know, honey." Luke scratched his chin. "Maybe they want to buy your business, not your products."

I sat up straighter on Luke's lap. It was an idea I'd never considered.

Luke skimmed the list. "You'd be in good company with these brands." We clicked through the meager information on their site. After reading every word, I still wasn't even sure what gulf the first *G* in GPG referred to. The corporation had offices on every continent except Antarctica. I chewed on my lip. "They didn't tell me a thing, Luke. But it says here that they acquire a brand every two weeks."

"This is really wild, Julia. I'd better get some champagne out of the fridge."

I shook my head. "Don't pop the cork yet. Why on earth would they want my unprofitable company? These other brands are all big-time. Maybe they've mistaken me for someone else."

Luke laughed. "Don't you think *they* started small? Whatever they're after, you'll have an interesting meeting. Shall we have a cocktail now?"

I followed him into the kitchen.

Luke sliced a lime, while I stared out the window, lost in thought.

"Did any of the chain grocery stores you were looking for turn up?"

I shook my head miserably. "Not unless they were incognito. There were dozens of independent stores that showed interest. But without a big distributor behind me, that will never work."

"It's not nothing. Maybe health-food stores are your brand's niche?"

"If I could sell to every single one in the country, then maybe it would work. Otherwise . . ." I didn't finish the sentence. Unless GPG had big ideas for my company, it might be curtains for Julia's Child.

From: marta@juliaschild.com
To: julia@juliaschild.com

If we ever have to do another trade show, I'm going to quit my job. So here's my version of our Squash-Carrot-Raisin Muffet Bread!

Best,
Marta

P.S. Joking!

*Ingredients*

**⅞ cup white flour**
**¾ cup whole wheat flour**
**1 teaspoon cinnamon**
**¼ teaspoon nutmeg**
**Pinch ground ginger**
**½ teaspoon salt**
**1 teaspoon baking soda**
**¾ stick butter, softened**
**½ cup honey**
**⅓ cup vegetable oil**
**½ cup golden (or regular) raisins**
**2 eggs**
**1 teaspoon vanilla**
**½ cup finely grated yellow summer squash or zucchini**
**¼ cup finely grated carrot**
**⅓ cup sunflower seeds**

*Instructions*

Grease and flour a 9 × 9 square baking pan. Preheat oven to 325°F. Grate the vegetables if you haven't already.

In a bowl combine the flours, cinnamon, nutmeg, ginger, salt, and baking soda.

In a food processor fitted with a blade, cream the butter and honey together until well combined. Add the oil and raisins, and process until the raisins are well distributed. Add the eggs and vanilla, and process again until combined. (Alternatively, use a mixer, in which case you should chop the raisins first.)

Stir the wet ingredients into the dry and then stir in the squash, carrots, and sunflower seeds.

Bake for 35–40 minutes, until a toothpick inserted in the center comes out clean. Muffet bread will be a beautiful golden color on top.

Cool for ten minutes in the pan, and then turn out the loaf onto a rack and cool completely, or cut squares from the pan.

# Chapter 19

Clutching a visitor's pass, I walked through the crowded lobby of an enormous office tower on Sixth Avenue. The place gave off a familiar smell: corporate culture. It buzzed with the self-important energy of a big-city firm. It was early afternoon, and many of the corporate drones were returning to the building with their lunches in tidy white bags. They moved in twos and threes toward the elevators, their ID tags hanging around their necks or clipped to their belts.

I watched two women ahead of me march toward adjacent automated turnstiles. Without breaking stride, they swiped their IDs in front of the machines' laser readers. The Plexiglas gates parted neatly, allowing them to pass. Once upon a time, I was one of them. I too wielded that bit of laminated power—a card marking me as a member of the inner circle.

Now, as I stepped toward the monolithic granite security desk separating the insiders from the outsiders, I had never felt more like a frumpy mom. Sure, I was wearing the right clothes. My nicest suit still fit me, and my blouse was fresh from the dry cleaner's plastic. But the clothes felt stiff and unfamiliar, and I was certain that anyone who bothered to glance at me would peg me as an imposter.

Corporate land was like a foreign country that I had once inhabited comfortably, but which had turned on me and become unfamiliar.

"Photo ID, please!" barked a voice from the other side of the marble desk. I slipped my ID and a visitor's pass through the slot. "Nineteenth floor, thank you!" My papers were returned to me, and the door swung open.

The guard, in his blue uniform, pointed toward one of the elevators. I pressed the "up" button and a set of doors parted instantly. I stepped in alone.

The GPG building had the sort of polished brass elevator doors that were reflective enough for finger-combing one's hair. I used the last few moments before my mystery meeting to neaten up.

"Welcome to GPG," chirped a receptionist as the elevator doors parted. She wore a gray GPG blazer, the exact shade of the granite wall behind her. The granite, I noticed, had an enormous "GPG" carved into its face.

"Hi. I'm Julia Bailey," I told her. "I'm here for a meeting with J. P. Smith."

"One moment, Miss Bailey. I'll let him know you're here. May I take your coat?"

She rose from behind the desk and opened a closet, which was perfectly camouflaged by the maple paneling on one wall of the reception area. I handed over my coat and tried to look around. But the place was built to conceal. The granite and maple swooped around me, offering only an oblique glimpse of the passageways that led to where the real work was done.

"Ms. Bailey," said a voice. "Thanks for coming by."

I spun around to find the speaker. At the trade show I'd been too overwhelmed to get a good look at J. P. Smith. Now I saw a thin, bookish face and a very expensive suit. His dark hair was perfect and neat. He might have been sent by central casting to play the role of corporate titan.

"It's my pleasure." I offered my hand.

He had a titan's handshake. "Would you step this way?" He slid open another neatly camouflaged door, revealing a tiny, windowless conference room. Apparently, I wouldn't be getting the nickel tour. This must be the room where they held meetings of little consequence. The visitor could be coughed back off the premises in mere seconds if the fit wasn't just right.

"One moment while I grab my colleague," Smith said, disappearing.

I chose one of the matching gray mesh chairs. There were only four of them, pulled close to the slab of maple that served as a table. The room was lit by large translucent panels on the wall, providing the illusion of windows. GPG, whatever it was, did not give up its secrets easily.

Smith reentered the room, followed by his tidy sidekick.

He too offered his hand. "I'm Paul Smythe," he said. "It is a pleasure to see you again, Ms. Bailey."

Smythe looked a lot like Smith—the slightly younger model. As we shook hands, I smiled. "Ah, the team of Smith and Smythe! But you must get that all the time."

They both stared back uncomprehendingly.

"So, Ms. Bailey . . ."

"Julia," I prompted.

Smith made a pup tent out of his hands and leaned back in his mesh chair. "Julia, let me tell you what it is we do here at GPG."

I nodded, waiting. I'd been eager for an explanation ever since his mysterious business card crossed my palm.

In spite of my eagerness, J. P. Smith spoke slowly and deliberately, as if doubtful that English was my first language. "At

GPG . . . we look for companies that are well loved . . . and well positioned . . . but struggling."

The pauses in his delivery gave me ample time to feel self-conscious. I wondered what it was about my company that tipped him off that we were struggling.

"We use our resources and our experience to make those companies profitable. You see, manufacturing is our expertise, although we're also pretty good at marketing. But when we take on a brand . . . we try not to tamper with its quality or integrity—we simply take control of the input chain, the supply lines."

Each word was spoken so carefully and so correctly that I began to wonder if there was something about me that conveyed a deficient IQ. Still, I sat as straight and still as possible, doing my best to wear an expression of attentiveness.

"We harness our experience to slim down the cost side of the equation, thereby turning the company profitable. We asked you to meet us here today because we're always on the lookout for companies that could benefit from this kind of intervention. Companies that have developed a loyal following but are not as profitable as they could be, usually because their unit costs are too high."

In spite of his irritating delivery, J. P. Smith's words were starting to sink in. My unit costs are too high?

Yes. Yes, they were.

The men in front of me had a simple name for my troubles: "unit cost." Sitting in this spotless corporate setting, with its commercially beige carpeting and ergonomic furnishings, the problem sounded so benign. My mountains of steaming hot anxiety, when analyzed by a conglomerate, could be reduced to a crumb of accounting jargon.

At that moment I felt a surge of appreciation for J. P. Smith and his sidekick. Maybe we were meant to be playing on the same team after all. There must be something they saw in Julia's Child, some diamond-in-the-rough quality that brought them to my booth at the trade show. I leaned forward more earnestly. "I think I understand. But tell me—do you have children? Have you tried the muffets?" I studied their faces expectantly, but my newly found admiration for them wasn't reflected back at me. Instead, they both looked mildly uncomfortable.

Smythe spoke up. "No, can't say that I have. Not yet."

I assumed that went for both the children and the muffets. "Well, then how did you come to be interested in Julia's Child?" With a twinge of discomfort, I began to fear that they'd requested a meeting with every vendor at the trade show.

"Well, actually it was our proprietary model who chose you," Smythe admitted.

It was my turn to show no glimmer of recognition. "Model?"

Smith took over again, going back to his dumb-kid speak. "We've built a robust computer model. We enter into it all the data that describe the current marketing environment. Then we use predictive technology to calculate which products can thrive . . . and which are doomed to fail."

"So . . . you have a computer that likes muffets?" I'd meant it sarcastically. But as the words came out of my mouth, I realized that they made me sound like a dumb blonde. And I'm not even blonde.

Luckily, Smith laughed, proving that he had not had his sense of humor surgically removed. "My computer model likes profits, Ms. Bailey. The downturn in the economy hurts our brands' prospects. But lately our model has identified three important trends." He ticked the points off on his fingers. "First, people are eating at home. Second, sales are up for the toddler age group, while expenditures on babies and older children are flat, and third, organic products continue to gain market share. Do you see? At the intersection of all of those trends is you."

I stared at him, unmoved. I'd assumed that he'd found my company innovative, or at least charming. But I was just a math problem to him.

"But even so, it's not a slam dunk," Smythe broke in.

"Why not?" I asked. Because according to their model, I'd won some kind of statistical lottery.

"Several reasons. First, there's the problem that your customer outgrows your brand in a heartbeat. And also, we're not sure about your price point. When we invest in a brand, it can't just work on the coasts, it has to play in the flyover states too. We're not sure soccer moms in the Midwest will pony up for your product."

I took a deep breath. "Sir, I think you have *no idea* how much money people are willing to spend on their children." It came out a little more forcefully than I'd meant it.

He stopped smiling. "Really? Tell me."

"First of all, the growth in big families is most pronounced for people earning the most money. Haven't you heard? Four is the new three."

There were no grins at my little joke.

"I'm not kidding. It's the wealthier families that are having more children, even in urban areas. And my brand stays with a family for longer than the toddlerhood of one child. I don't make pureed food for infants. Children eat muffets from nine months to nine years. Mothers tell me they're eating them too."

Somehow I'd hit on a point that awakened Smith and Smythe. They sat up straighter, nodding to each other. "Crossover!" Smythe said to Smith.

"Right!" exclaimed Smith to Smythe. "It probably accounts for some of the diagrammatic shift we're seeing into the category."

I plunged ahead. "It doesn't even matter that the economy sucks, and I'll tell you why—because spending money on one's children is the only status symbol that some mothers have left.

They wouldn't dare buy themselves another designer bag, but spending on the children is not a personal indulgence—do you understand? For proof, I give you the Froggaroo stroller. Five years ago, two hundred bucks was a fortune to spend on a stroller. But the stylish Froggaroo costs eight hundred dollars. It's imported from the Netherlands. And you can't swing a diaper bag without hitting one. Even in the suburbs."

"Go on," Smith said. Smythe scribbled notes onto a yellow legal pad.

"But getting back to food—thirty blocks from here there's a chain baby store, called buybuy Baby. It's aptly named, because when you have a baby there are suddenly five hundred new things you have to buy for it. The biggest section in the store is the feeding section. It's the size of a terminal at JFK. They sell *dozens* of different sippy cups, with every combination of spouts, straws, and no-spill valves. Then there are the bowls: Bowls that stick to the table with a suction cup. Divided bowls for picky eaters. Bowls with a reservoir for warm water, to keep the baby's food warm. Then there are the spoons: Ergonomic spoons. Spoons shaped like a bulldozer, an airplane. Spoons with rubber tips, to protect baby's teeth. Spoons that—"

"I think we get the picture, Ms. Bailey. Parents spend a lot of money feeding the baby. But then the baby grows up."

"No, you *don't* get the picture, gentlemen, unless you understand why parents spend so much. It isn't just a fad. It's because of anxiety. Parents harbor a lot of anxiety about feeding their children. And that trend, sadly, is only getting bigger."

Smith and Smythe had begun nodding at each other like a couple of bobble-head dolls. So I kept going. "That's where organic comes in, and the customer becomes truly blind to the price tag. A mother will pinch pennies for some things. But 62 percent of mothers report that an 'all-natural' designation is either 'important' or 'very important' to their purchasing decisions."

I watched Smythe scribble down "62%" on his legal pad and then circle it. And I took a deep breath, ready to deliver what I considered to be the most important reason to love Julia's Child.

"The last few years have proven—even to the doubters—that these things matter. We can thank those recalls—I'm sure you've heard of them—of toys with lead paint. The troubles with 'Totally Toxic' Thomas and 'Poison-Me' Elmo have helped to swing the pendulum pretty far into my court."

I was mixing metaphors like crazy, but the GPG guys were still with me. Behind their spectacles their eyes flashed. "Yeah! And melamine in baby formula!" Smythe nodded. "The organic sector probably has a sales bump, maybe *three points*, every time they mention a sick baby on television."

It was right then that my speech lost steam. The mention of those poor Chinese babies with kidney failure drained me of excitement—and quick. As much as I wanted the world to believe in Julia's Child, I stopped short of celebrating sick infants as a sector booster. I sat back in my chair, trying to breathe normally. That tragedy was not my fault, nor was it Smith's or Smythe's. But in the crisp offices of the Gulf Pacific Group, I suddenly felt far removed from the toddlers I wanted to feed.

"Would you like to take the nickel tour, Ms. Bailey?"

I snapped to attention. "Sorry?"

"Perhaps you would like to see where some of the work gets done on our food brands? It's right here on the nineteenth floor. If you have time, that is."

# Chapter 20

I probably hesitated a beat too long, wrestling with the idea of placing my little gem of a company onto the GPG conveyor belt. But I *was* a businesswoman. A tour might be my only chance to peer over the fence at the inner workings of a successful food business.

So I followed Smith and Smythe past the reception desk, around a corner, and into a bull-pen area. A row of offices lined the exterior walls. Daylight filtered coolly through the frosted glass on the office doors. "We house our smaller food brands here," Smith said. "The brand managers have their offices close together, for cross-pollination of ideas. And, of course, support resources are pooled *here*." He indicated the dense forest of cubicles crowding the center of the room.

The cubicle farm looked nothing like the Chelsea Sunshine Suites. It was cleaner, for one thing, and oddly quiet. Behind upscale tweed-upholstered walls, the workers were completely concealed. There were no neighborly voices in cheerful conversation. Instead, I could hear the sound of keyboard strokes from all around, even if I couldn't see their makers. It was the corporate equivalent of standing in a country field, listening to the chirps of crickets hidden in the tall grass. You know they're in there, but you can't see them.

Smith and Smythe moved on, down another corridor, and I hurried to keep up. "There's someone I want you to meet," Smith said. "But first let's run you past our marketing team, so you can get a feel for the breadth of resources bestowed upon every brand at GPG."

The beige corridor opened out into another cluster of offices, this one with a dramatically different feel. Instead of cloistered tweed walls, there were glass rooms, sprinkled with furniture in playful colors and shapes. In one of them, a group of youngish people convened. Instead of the suits that Smith and Smythe sported, these employees wore faded jeans. Their blazers were natty and their self-conscious eyewear was too cool for school.

"I'm sure you can tell, but we've reached the *idea people,*" Smythe chuckled.

It was true that the furnishings functioned like a billboard announcing: "You Have Reached a Creative Space."

"What are they doing?" I asked. Several pictures were pinned up on the conference room wall, with the participants clustered around them.

"Brainstorming. Ideas for a new product or maybe a new direction for one of our labels. That's one of the big advantages here—so many heads to put together. An entire team to think about the public face of each brand."

They must have been discussing a dairy product. Two of the pictures were of cows—Holsteins. It was always Holsteins, with their cheery black-and-white splotches, that got the starring roles on the dairy cartons of the world. The equally hard-working but less photogenic Jerseys and Guernseys were doomed to chew their cud in obscurity.

I stood rooted to the rug, trying to imagine how any of this related to Julia's Child. Did I have a future in this building? Could it be me in there, whiling away the day with a team of young faces staring earnestly at the image of a muffet? I would park myself like a queen bee on one of those expensive-looking beanbag chairs. I would exhort a posse of twentysomethings to wax poetic about bucolic, nutritious vegetables.

On the one hand, how could any product fail with so much energy and attention? But on the other hand, these expensive ideas would be conceived by urban youths in a hermetically sealed think tank nineteen floors above street level, while taxis honked outside. We were far, far from the pumpkin patches we'd be imploring our clients to picture.

Before I had a chance to digest this conundrum, my tour guides raced onward at warp speed. Perhaps the GPG secret to profitability was doing everything at a breakneck pace. "Our marketing department is formidable," Smith chatted as I labored to match his strides. "But I also want to show you something else. Usually, there's at least one session going on." He waved me into a darkened room.

Smythe brought up the rear, tiptoeing in and closing the door behind us. "This is where we hold focus groups," he whispered.

One wall of the glorified closet we'd entered was entirely taken over by an oversize window made of one-way glass. In the adjacent room, a group of casually dressed women about my age sat around a conference table, sipping coffee. At the head of the table, a woman in a lime green suit held up an unfamiliar cereal box.

Smythe pressed a button on the wall, and the conversation from next door was piped through to our side of the magic mirror.

"Now," said the lime-jacketed leader, "I'd like to hear your thoughts, comparing the last package to this one. Would you be inclined to assume—given the picture—that this product was *more* or *less* wholesome than the previous one?"

The women tilted their heads to one side, scrutinizing the photograph of cereal flakes in a bowl, with milk. I realized there was no text at all on the box the woman held—just graphics.

Smythe whispered an explanation. "Consumers, we have found, form very substantive opinions about a product just from the colors used on the packaging."

My eyes went wide with fascination. The box and the cereal pictured were both reddish brown, the bowl and the berries were blue, the milk was white as the driven snow.

Could it be that most shoppers made a hasty, subconscious decision about whether or not to buy my product simply based on the color of the package? Could it be that Julia's Child was sending the wrong signals straight into harried mothers' brains from the freezer shelf? Or the right ones?

"Ms. Bailey?" Smith whispered to me, his hand on the doorknob.

But I didn't budge. I was desperate for the women to hurry up and tell me how they felt about the reddish brown box.

"It reminds me . . . ," began one of the participants.

"Julia?" Smythe prompted. "We'd like you to meet the CECO now."

"Of chocolate milk," the woman said. "And I don't serve chocolate milk, at least not at breakfast."

Reluctantly, I followed Smythe and Smith into the corridor. I was suffering from sensory overload thanks to the whirlwind meeting and cyclone tour. I wished Smith and Smythe would forget me for a half hour in another one of their numerous conference rooms, so I could remember my own name and figure out what I was doing here.

But they had other plans. Smith was actually rubbing his hands together in anticipation. "And here we are, Ms. Bailey, at the office of the special executive in charge of eco-issues. It is very fortunate that he's not traveling today, since I can't imagine anyone at GPG with whom you'd be more eager to talk." Smith knocked on an office door. Through the glass I could see a man on the phone.

He was dressed with neither the formality of my deal-making tour guides nor the casual garb of the marketing people. He was in the middle—khaki gabardine trousers and a crisply ironed shirt of green and white checks. He wore fashionably retro horn-rimmed glasses. He waved at us, motioning that we should enter.

Smith opened the door and gestured for me to take a seat. I slid quietly into a chair.

"Yes, we want to get as much mileage out of it as we can," the man said into his telephone. "But it doesn't make sense to label a product both as 'locally sourced' and 'fair trade.' The brand manager is going to have to choose which virtue best serves the brand's narrative."

I glanced around the office. Instead of the standard-issue corporate furnishings, everything in this office was aggressively eco-friendly. The desk was bamboo butcher block. On its surface sat one of those trendy Swiss aluminum water bottles. A sign posted over the laser printer in the corner commanded, "Think Before You Print." And the wall decor included a "Go Green" page-a-day calendar.

Next to my chair sat a familiar end table. I'd seen it in the Pottery Shed catalog. It consisted of a solid stump from a tree, perhaps sixteen inches across. The bark had been sanded off, revealing luscious wood grain. The varnish was supposedly an ecologically friendly mix of beeswax and linseed oil.

I'd coveted that table myself, before I'd checked the price. It was $249 dollars. "Crafted from *fallen* wood. No two alike!" bragged the catalog copy. But in Vermont, we paid about half that much for a cord of seasoned firewood standing eight feet long, four feet wide, and four feet high. The Pottery Shed must make a pretty penny selling stumps.

His conversation over, the stump's owner hung up his phone and flashed us a winning smile. "J. P.! Who have you brought me today?"

"Ralph," Smith began. "I'd like you to meet Ms. Julia Bailey. Her company makes organic food for the preschool demographic. I think you'll find that her interests and yours are very much aligned. And Ms. Bailey—"

"Please, call me Julia."

"Julia, Ralph DaSilva is our new CECO."

I held out my hand to shake. "Um, *seeko*?" I asked. My growing exhaustion was evident in my less-than-brilliant greeting.

Ralph DaSilva stood up to shake my hand and let out a braying laugh. "I'm the CEO of all things 'eco' here at GPG. So that makes me the CECO, get it?"

"Ah." I gave him a stiff smile. "So it's your job to monitor the ecological impact of the food brands?"

"Of *all* the brands at GPG, actually," he corrected. "But I'd say I'm really the earth's advocate. That's my role."

"Ralph," Smith broke in, "can you spare twenty minutes? I'll leave you two to chat." Smith looked at his watch.

"Certainly!" The CECO beamed, waving off my host. "Julia," he said graciously, turning back to me, "with a business focused on organic products, I'm sure you have a lot of questions for me. You must be wondering how you can entrust your organic business to a massive conglomerate like GPG. Right?"

The bluntness of this observation caught me off guard. "Well . . ." I was tentative. "The thought had crossed my mind. Surely not every brand at GPG has a history of . . . ecological compassion and sensitivity?"

"And it's my job to fix that!" DaSilva boomed. "I want GPG to be known as the most environmentally friendly organization on earth."

His enthusiasm was encouraging. But I wondered how he could really expect to give Greenpeace a run for its money. It totally made sense from a PR perspective to have a "CECO." But it also made sense for a corporation with thousands of shareholders to try to appear eco-friendly rather than to actually be eco-friendly.

"So . . ." I decided to test him. "That means you'll be switching every single food brand over to organic practices?"

He laughed, and I narrowed my eyes. Because I hadn't been joking. I'm on to you, buddy, I thought.

He stopped smiling. "I hope so, Julia," was his answer. "But a complete conversion will take years. Imagine what would happen if we did that next week. I'm sure you realize that the unintended result would be GPG pricing its brands right out of the grocery store. That would, in turn, bankrupt the company, helping nobody. But I'm preaching to the choir here, right? You surely feel those same market forces pressing upon you every day."

I swallowed hard. "True enough," I conceded. My opinion of GPG and DaSilva was whipping back and forth like a tennis ball at Wimbledon. After all, my failure to properly consider the bottom line was what brought me into the jaws of a conglomerate in the first place.

"But let's take a look at your product." DaSilva flipped open a file that Smythe had handed him. It contained pictures of my product labels. "Let's see . . . Cute titles. And organic, of course," he said. "Recycled packaging. Excellent, Julia! Do you also use soy-based inks?"

I shook my head. It was too expensive.

"Hybrid delivery trucks?" he asked.

Picturing Lugo's ancient truck nearly caused me to snort with laughter. "Uh, no. But since I use locally sourced ingredients, our carbon footprint shrinks by an even wider margin."

"Touché, Julia!" Ralph DaSilva seemed delighted by our round of eco-jujitsu. "But there's always something more we could do, isn't there? No grocery store product on earth can claim to be a hundred percent green. It's our job—yours and mine—to burnish the ship as well as we can without sinking it. Right?"

Across his bamboo desk, I stared hard at Ralph DaSilva. It was going to be trickier than I imagined, figuring out if his real role at the company was to be its conscience or its greenwasher in chief.

"Now, Julia, what's your line?"

"My what?"

DaSilva frowned. "Here at GPG we're very focused on each brand. Every single one of them can be summed up in a single sentence. One line. Inside these walls we believe that if a brand cannot be summed up well in one line it's likely unmarketable. Fair enough?"

I gaped at him, wishing for the first time in my life that I'd gone to business school. This must be the sort of thing a person learned in business school. How to sum up the enormity of one's ambitions in a single phrase.

"So dazzle me, Julia. What's your line?"

My mouth was dry. The only word that flashed through my feeble brain at the point was "organic." I was just about to utter some drivel about how good organic food was for kids when I had a flash of recollection. My "line" had been handed to me on a platter a few months ago. In an elevator no less.

I cleared my throat. "Julia's Child"—I made my fingers into quotation marks—" 'Saving the world one little bite at a time.' "

"Wow!" DaSilva leapt out of his chair and reached for my hand. He pumped it up and down. "Terrific! Just wonderful. I can tell you've really done your homework on GPG." He paced excitedly back and forth in front of his desk. "So tell me about your audience, Ms. Bailey. Exactly who *is* she?"

"She's . . ." I hesitated. I was beginning to understand that big companies like GPG played the game on another level, with sophisticated market research at their fingertips. I had none, except what I'd gleaned chatting up mothers in Brooklyn. So I decided just to describe myself. "She's a mother," I told him. "A mother who wants to do the right thing—for her children and also for the environment. But she doesn't always have enough time to make everything from scratch, so she's hoping to find a shortcut here and there."

"Continue." DaSilva leaned back in his desk chair. It was a colorful modern design, one of those new ones fabricated from recycled water bottles.

"She's . . . got sufficient discretionary income, at least for food. And food and health issues are important to her. She's heard about the Prius, of course—"

"She drives a Prius?"

"No, because you can't drive carpool in a Prius."

He nodded thoughtfully. "I see your point. Julia, that's absolutely a customer that we'd like to add to the GPG family. I can see why J. P. likes your product so much."

"I can deliver her," I said solemnly. "I understand her needs. And her fears."

"I'll bet you do, Julia. I bet you do. So let's *really* think outside the box for a moment, okay? Let's go off the reservation. What is the single most ecologically friendly thing you can think of that Americans could do with regard to babies and children?"

It was an easy question. "Diapers." I smiled. "They could use cloth diapers, at least in the major metropolitan areas where diaper delivery services are available. The landfill reduction would be staggering."

DaSilva put his feet up on his bamboo desk. "Diapers are a big one," he said. "I'm happy that here at GPG we don't make them. Because, of course, there is so little I could do to improve them."

I knew what he meant. Consumers were not about to switch back en masse to cloth. They just weren't going back to the era of scraping stinky poop into the toilet and then either washing or balling up the offending cloth diaper and dropping it into a smelly plastic can to await its pickup.

"That's not it, though, you know."

"It's not?" I asked.

"Nope. That's not the most ecologically effective thing American families could do."

"Well, are you going to tell me what is?"

"The most ecologically significant change Americans could make would be to stop having children at all." He winked at me. "Don't look at me like that. It's true. The world is flooded with children, many of them hungry. If we care so much about the environment, it would be the most effective stance."

"But that violates the life force!" I couldn't tell whether he was kidding.

"Of course it does," he said quietly. "And that's our challenge, isn't it? Those of us who care about the environment. I care very much about the environment, whether or not you believe me. But I work at a company that exists to sell products. And the best way to be green with regard to products is to simply buy fewer of them. But I can't possibly advocate that, right?"

I began to feel dizzy. "Of course."

"Instead, I put concentrated laundry detergent into smaller bottles, and I make sure that our yogurt is packaged in BPA-free vessels, you got me?"

I nodded.

"The shareholders essentially sign my check every month, and that's not going to change. If they don't make a return on their investment, I'll eventually be fired. So my best course of action, then, is to convince the firm that we can do well by doing good—that consumers will favor us with their dollars because they approve of our actions."

"But does that mean if the green frenzy dies down GPG will change your title and cease to care about the environment?"

"What a cynical girl you are!" He laughed. "I like you, Julia.

Because you're an idealist, but you also have your eyes open. So I'm sure you realize that your choice is to either bring your brand to the big corporation, where you will lose some amount of control over it, or to go it alone and never make a dime of profit."

I gulped. Were those really the only two choices?

"If you join us here, I *promise* you'll have the opportunity to set the new standard for consciousness! You could help me, Julia. You could be a force for good at GPG."

There was a tap on the door. Smythe stuck his head in. "How are we doing?"

Ralph swung his feet off the desk and rose. "Where did you find this feisty entrepreneur, Smythe? She's a firecracker."

Smythe grinned. "So you found something to talk about?"

"Plenty. Didn't we, Julia?"

I was just about to answer when Smythe said, "Hey! Is that the new xPhone?" He pointed at a sleek titanium device on the CECO's desk.

"Yeah! It's pretty great. I thought the G5 was awesome, but this one is even cooler." He picked it up, touched something on the screen, and handed it to Smythe, whose face lit up.

I watched the two of them fondle the phone. Surely the CECO would have heard about unconscionable coltan mining? Wouldn't he?

Smythe set the phone longingly down on the desk. "I'm supposed to walk Ms. Bailey back to Smith's office now."

"Later, man. And, Julia—it was truly a pleasure to talk policy with you. I do hope we can do it again in the very near future." He shook my hand graciously.

I followed Smythe back through yet another corridor.

"There she is!" Smith said, appearing from inside an office. "Ms. Bailey, thank you so much for meeting with us today. If it's okay with you, we'd like to learn even more about Julia's Child.

Can you have your lawyer draw up a nondisclosure agreement you can live with?"

Just as I began to process his request, my attention was drawn away by a series of posters on the wall beside us. Each was a framed advertisement for food, obviously GPG brands. I recognized the California vintner Luke and I had spied on the GPG website and the premium ice cream. But one of the posters really caught my eye, because the picture was already so familiar to me.

It was an advertisement for the Zamwich.

I felt dizzy then, as if the merry-go-round had just sped up to twice the speed.

"Julia? Ms. Bailey? After we sign the nondisclosure agreement, we'll be able to look at your books, orders, facility, products in development. That sort of stuff. Okay?"

Woozily, I forced myself to respond to Smith's request for a second date. "My lawyer. Yes," I stammered. "I'll call you."

"Excellent! Excellent. We like how you're thinking, Julia. Good stuff."

Still feeling light-headed, I allowed myself to be steered toward the elevators. My coat was produced and my hand was shaken a couple of more times, and then I was on my way back into the real world.

I rode the escalator toward street level. The corporate bees still buzzed around me, but the lunch bags had been replaced by afternoon coffee cups. Nobody wore a coat, in spite of the fact that autumn was firmly advancing toward winter. In corporate land, any human need could be met without leaving the building.

I pulled my coat tightly around me and headed for the revolving doors. I didn't know if I could do it. Could I really sell out? *Sell out*. I tried out the words my head: I'm a sell out.

I sighed, stepping into the wind. First I had to get them to make me an offer. Then I would worry about the moral implications.

# Chapter 21

On any other day, I might have rushed back to the office for two more hours of work. But with the business teetering between bankruptcy and corporate domination, I had reached a point where I could safely say that the additional effort wouldn't make or break Julia's Child.

So I went home, where, when I walked into the living room, I was treated to a look of joyful surprise from both Jasper and Wylie. And they were all too happy to ditch Bonnie for an unexpected excursion with me.

The taxi ride to Sixty-third and Fifth Avenue was short. I even let the boys take turns jabbing at the touch screen controls of the TV that some nitwit decided should sit in the back of every yellow cab. These days, instead of looking out the window at some of the finest prewar architecture in America, my children watched restaurant reviews on Taxi TV.

I was just about to give a ten-dollar bill to the driver when Wylie snatched it out of my hand. "I do it *b'elf*!" he cried, thrusting the bill through the Plexiglas window.

"He always gets to pay the man," Jasper grumbled.

I opened the door. "Let's not fight," I said with forced cheerfulness. "I can't take grumpy boys to the petting zoo!"

I waved our membership card for the lonely soul in the ticket booth, and the boys sprinted up the ramp ahead of me. I watched them disappear through the concrete entrance gate, which had been molded to spectacular effect into the shape of a hollow tree. I parted the plastic strips that hung down like a curtain, meant to deter the escape of any of the animals, and entered Central Park's children's zoo.

Jasper and Wylie were already climbing on the cement bunny sculptures. We'd been coming here since Jasper was a baby. While the animals weren't exotic—overweight rabbits, waterfowl, and farm animals—the exhibit itself was inspired. It had been whimsically designed by some genius clearly still in touch with his or her inner child. Every sculpture was climbable. There were three-foot turtle eggs from which to hatch and rubberized giant lily pads to leap upon.

The children found their way over to a cave containing a generous tank in which enormous catfish circled. Jamming my hands into my pockets, I found my phone.

Luke answered on the first ring. "What did they say? How did it go?"

"It went well, I think," I told him, "with Mr. Smith and his sidekick, Mr. Smythe. And now they want to know more. So they told me to ask my lawyer for a nondisclosure agreement, and then they'll look at the guts of the company."

Luke whistled. "That sounds serious. So then what would happen? If they like what they see, would they buy the brand? Would you work for them? In their office?"

"I . . . I'm not sure," I admitted.

"Well, would they just buy a stake in it? Or do they buy the whole company and then hire you back to run it?"

"We didn't, um, cover those details yet," I stammered. In retrospect, I realized how little information I'd gotten from the meeting—and how much I'd given. Though I'd done a poor job of explaining it to Luke, the experience had been less a meeting of the minds than a ride on the Tilt-A-Whirl at the state fair, leaving me breathless and sweaty.

"Okay," Luke said gently. "You can tell me all about it tonight."

"Perfect," I said, "because right now I'm at the zoo with your sons."

"Sounds like fun. Love you," Luke said before the click.

"Want it goats." Wylie tugged on my coat. His cheeks appeared even rounder underneath his fleece hat.

"Okay, honey," I said. I took his mittened hand, and we sidled up next to Jasper, who had pressed his forehead against the aquarium wall. I took Jasper's hand, too, which he allowed. Together we navigated the rubber lily pads and made our way to the petting area.

Jasper went straight for his favorite feature of the children's zoo—a giant spiderweb made of fisherman's rope, where he could climb away and play out his Spider-Man fantasies. I dug in my purse for change to buy some feed pellets for Farmer Wylie. I let him put the quarters into the machine, but then I quickly turned the crank myself, because he didn't have enough torque to manage it, which usually made him scream.

"Why we not have dis in Vermont?" he asked, patting the shiny red dispenser.

"Well . . ." *Because, Wylie, this is an urban construct that only pretends to show you life on a farm.* "Because in Vermont we just keep our feed in a bin."

"Dis one better," he proclaimed, before marching toward the goats. I sat down on a concrete bench, one that pretended to be a fallen tree.

Predictably, Wylie managed to drop his handful of pellets on the ground in front of the goat enclosure. But that was okay with him. He got down on his knees, pulled off his mittens, and commenced picking up the pellets one by one and passing them through the metal bars to a couple of eager goats on the other side.

This was where the rich Upper East Siders brought their children to experience nature. And it was arguably as tidy and inspired as a children's zoo could be. But it was also utterly artificial. There was none of the authenticity that stepping over cow pies in a real meadow delivered. That sweet mixture of sunshine and the air tinged with gently composting manure—it was missing from this urban oasis.

Instead, we had a rubberized mat on the ground, so nobody got hurt if they fell down. And there were Purell dispensers on the wall, so we wouldn't encounter—dear God!—any country germs.

It was November, a gray month when New Yorkers forget about the zoo. There were only a couple of other families around us. One mother encouraged her one-year-old to "Look at the cow! Look at the cow!" I guess she hadn't looked under the hood. I checked my urge to correct her. That's actually an arthritic bull, dear.

The only other family was also feeding the goats. I studied them. They were dressed awfully nicely for a petting zoo. The father stood a little apart from the animals, perhaps so his cashmere coat wouldn't get soiled. I smiled to myself. Cashmere comes from goats, of course, but Cashmere Dad would want to keep their saliva off of the wool. They, too, had purchased some feed pellets from the machine. The well-coiffed mother held them in her cupped, leather-sheathed hands so her own toddler didn't have to pick them off the ground like Wylie.

My children were happy. So I pulled out my phone again to make the necessary call to my lawyer. The faster she drew up my nondisclosure document, whatever that was, the faster I could unravel the mystery of whether or not GPG could help me.

"Hello, Julia!" Nina Schwartz, Esq., was at my service. And that meant that her meter was running—at two hundred and fifty bucks an hour.

So I gave her a speedy description of my meeting with GPG and the document they'd requested. "So what is it really for, anyway?" I asked her, when I'd finished my download.

"The document I'll draft, and that they'll sign," she said, "will forbid their company from using your proprietary market information to compete against you. It binds them to secrecy about all aspects of Julia's Child's business and any future plans and products you disclose to them."

"Great." There went another five hundred dollars down the drain. It was a nice idea, this document. But my secrets probably had a wholesale value of approximately zero. Last week I'd stood on the floor at ANKST, blabbing to anyone who would listen about every aspect of Julia's Child. I was an open book.

The true purpose of the nondisclosure agreement, then, would be to maintain the illusion that I knew what I was doing. I'd show up with my slick little document, play the role of the hard-hitting, successful businesswoman. If that didn't work, I could always resort to throwing myself prostrate across the GPG corporate logo, begging for salvation.

"All right, Nina. Draw it up," I said. All the past year's optimism had been replaced by resignation.

"Are you sure you want to do this, Julia?"

"Yes, but why are you asking?"

"Well, nondisclosure agreements are a good idea. But if this group really wants to rip off your ideas, this won't stop them. And you won't find out for months, until you see the competing product on the store shelves. Of course, you'd have grounds to sue them, but that would be expensive and slow. Do you trust these guys?"

I considered the question and its relevance. If I sat down to rank my anxieties about Julia's Child, the idea that they'd poach my business model wouldn't even make the top ten. Whether or not they were trustworthy, I would be forced to walk my poor old mare of a business into the glue factory. "I don't know if I have a choice," I told her truthfully.

"Hey!" someone shouted. "Who's watching that baby?"

I looked up fast. A zookeeper, in his tall rubber boots and uniform jacket, pointed at Wylie. My enterprising toddler had climbed the goat enclosure, thrown a leg over the top rail of the fence, and was trying to figure out how to drop down onto the other side.

"Uh, can't wait to read it! Gotta go," I managed to say to Nina. I snapped my phone shut, stuffed it into my pocket, and trotted toward Wylie.

The well-coiffed mother reached him first, throwing her arms around his back, as if rescuing him from the lion's den. "No, honey!" she said to a startled Wylie. "Dangerous!"

I arrived in time to pluck him off the rail myself. "Sorry, Wylie," I said quietly. "At the zoo, we're not allowed in there."

"You should be more careful," the cashmere father said.

My neck got hot. I was partly embarrassed but also indignant. After all, Wylie was used to climbing in with the goats in Vermont, thank you. And goats don't *eat* toddlers, although sometimes they nibble on them a little bit.

But I held my tongue.

"Me a goat farmer," Wylie whined when I set him on the ground.

"You'll have to do your farming from this side of the fence," I told him. "That's the rule here."

My face continued to burn. The other family probably expected me to thank them for "saving" Wylie, but I let the moment pass. They moved off toward the alpacas.

Jasper wandered over. "Whatsa matter, Mama?"

My eyes fluttered. *Everything.* "Nothing. Now, who wants to go find a hot pretzel with me?"

# Chapter 22

If you can't stand the heat, you're supposed to get out of the kitchen. I was already sweating through my carefully chosen shirt, and Smith and Smythe hadn't even arrived yet. "Okay, girls!" My loud voice betrayed my nerves. "Do you suppose we should prop the recipe on the countertop, which will make us appear organized? Or should we make it from memory, like we always do, and appear experienced?"

I fanned myself with a spatula and looked for the five hundredth time toward the double metal doors.

Marta's cousin Theresa was a young woman of few words. She shrugged. Theresa had expressive brown eyes, but she rarely spoke up.

"*Chica*, calm down," Marta ordered. "Stop staring at the door and help me unpack these ingredients."

I attempted to comply. Marta looked piqued. She was sweating too. And we hadn't even turned on the oven yet.

"Damn," she said.

"What's the matter?"

In answer, she held up an industrial-size bottle of organic vanilla extract. It was nearly empty.

"Oh, shit!" I stared at the empty bottle. "I forgot to order more." Organic vanilla wasn't easy to find. And we were supposed to bake pumpkin muffets, which were flavored with a fair dose of vanilla. "I guess we'll just . . . leave it out? We have to make *something* when Smith and Smythe are here." The only other choice was to switch recipes, which would leave us short of some other ingredient.

"But the muffets will taste bland," Marta objected. "And they *are* going to taste them, right?"

I sighed. "What are our options? We can make just a small amount, with the last bit of vanilla, or make some more without and then throw them away."

Theresa looked stricken. "We can't throw them away! We need eight cases. *Mañana*."

"I'm goin' in." Marta inhaled. She reached up to the hairnet she wore, removing a bobby pin from over her ear. Then she squared her shoulders and marched toward the back of the building, which contained Zia's office and the closely guarded storeroom. Marta had told me the lock on Zia's pantry was pickable, but I'd never seen her do it.

I took a deep, cleansing breath and tried to tell myself that this wasn't a disaster. A disaster was the Ebola virus. Or a tsunami. A lack of vanilla was an inconvenience—but of the sort with which my life was increasingly peppered.

We'd never managed to screw up in precisely this way before. Cooking—unlike business savvy—was our core competency. Obviously, the stress was getting to us. Inviting the suits from GPG to scrutinize our production facility had made me feel incredibly self-conscious. Allowing them to paw through my underwear drawer might have felt less invasive.

If we had a sufficient amount, I might have helped myself to a swig of organic vanilla extract.

As I stood there, attempting to think Zen thoughts about

vanilla theft and my visiting corporate judging committee, Marta trotted quickly back out of the hallway, followed by Zia Maria herself.

"And a-where were you headed, Marta dear?" Zia sang out. Zia stood about four feet eight, the gray bun on top of her head adding a couple of additional inches. In her arms she carried a broad tray, piled high with colorful gift boxes. She swept past us, hoisting her tray onto the workstation in the middle of the room.

"Hello, Zia," Marta said weakly. "I thought I heard . . . something rustling around back there, and so I went to check. But it was *you*."

"Of course it's me," Zia snapped, as if we always saw her at that hour. We hadn't spied her on a night shift in weeks. Now she stacked the shiny gift boxes on the stainless steel worktable. She opened a tin of Christmas cookies and a pastry bag for icing, and then set about arranging all the ingredients on the table.

The unusual incidence of Zia decorating cookies in the Cucina on a weeknight necessitated a whispered conference between the employee-owners of Julia's Child. "What the hell is this all about?" I hissed. I had never seen Zia making cookies. And the thought of her making gifts—to be given away *for free*—was almost incomprehensible.

"Hmm," Marta whispered. "The holidays are coming. I'll bet she's greasing the wheels of bureaucracy. Maybe for the borough officials who certify the Cucina?"

I felt my blood pressure soar. "We're toast! What's she going to say when Smith and Smythe show up to look around? This is terrible."

Marta chewed on her lip. "We'll have to tell her they're coming. Zia doesn't like surprises. You want me to do it? She likes me more than you."

That certainly was true, but I didn't wish to hide behind

Marta. I scrutinized the back of our cheerless leader. Zia's apron strings were cinched so tightly around her rail-thin body that the two sides of the apron fabric overlapped at the knot in back. Underneath, I noted her typical black stockings, black skirt, and black turtleneck.

I took a deep breath and strode toward her. "Good evening, Ms. Maria. Those are beautiful boxes."

She didn't look up at me but rather knitted her dark eyebrows tightly into a knot. She squeezed the pastry bag in her hands, and a bead of perfectly round white icing curled from the metal tip. Even frosting was afraid to cross Zia. "Yes, my dear, presentation is everything, isn't it?"

"Absolutely," I agreed as cheerfully as possible, reminded of the attractive way in which my sweaty shirt was sticking to me. "In fact, tonight I'll be presenting my little business to a couple of men from a food conglomerate. They want to see the spotless kitchen I've been telling them about."

At that, Zia put the pastry bag down, the metal tip clanking onto the stainless steel table. She whirled to face me, and reflexively I flinched. "People coming, tonight? Here?" Her mustache twitched.

"Just two. They won't stay long."

"*Cara mia!* Are you saying that if all goes well, I will have a graduate?"

"A graduate?"

"Your business hits the big time, with my Cucina responsible. This could be big. *Mamma mia!* This is news!"

"Oh!" It took a minute to adjust my psyche. I had expected to get a lashing. "Well, then, I'll let you know how it goes."

Relieved, I turned back to our corner of the room to tell Marta everything was okay. But she had vanished. Instead, her cousin

Theresa stood worriedly in her place, glancing toward the back of the building, her doe eyes heavy with remorse.

"Where's Marta?" I asked.

In answer, my partner appeared at the end of the short hallway that ran back toward the storeroom and Zia's office. She peered around the doorjamb, toward Zia's back, and then scurried over to our table. "Got it," she hissed at Theresa. "Cover me."

Theresa positioned herself between Zia and her cousin, and made herself busy with the ingredients on the stainless countertop. Marta slipped a very large bottle of vanilla from under her apron, holding it just beneath the edge of the table, and decanted some of Zia's extract into our empty bottle.

"What are you doing?" I whispered. "That's not organic!"

"Julia!" a voice rang out from the middle of the room.

"Shit!" Marta said, diving into a crouch near the floor.

I whirled around to find Zia advancing toward me. "Yes?" I chirped self-consciously, meeting her halfway between our stations.

"When those men come to see your production, I will help-a you. Over here. Help you with the muffins. They'll see you have a big staff, yes?"

"Muff*ets*," I corrected. "And that's a kind offer but . . ." I sensed trouble. Zia meant well, but she was prone to making scenes. I was anxious enough about the encounter without adding some forced role-playing to the mix. "There's probably not enough work to go around," I said lamely.

"Nonsense! I do your work on the muffins while you talk to the nice men. Where is your purse? We need some more lipstick on you." Zia gave me a gentle shove toward our workstation.

There was a scramble and a bump. "Ow!" Marta said. She emerged from under our steel table, rubbing her forehead. I was afraid to look, but her hands held only my purse and our own bottle of vanilla. "Here it is," she said, thrusting the bag at me.

"You!" Zia pointed at me. "Put on some makeup. And you"—she pointed at Marta—"need some ice for that bump. You're a-going to have a goose egg." She turned on her heel toward the ice machine in the corner.

"What are you doing?" I whispered again to Marta. "If we use that stuff, the muffets won't be one hundred percent organic."

"*Dios mío!* It's just vanilla. A tiny drop."

"But the organic regulations require that every *ingredient*—"

"Hoolia!" Marta shrieked. "God will forgive this one transgression. Stop playing saint for a minute and—"

"*Playing?*" I sputtered. "This is not a *game* for me. It's serious."

"Serious? Let me tell you what's serious. If tonight goes down the drain, you'll spend your days strolling around your fancy neighborhood, drinking five-dollar lattes. But me, I might be back on welfare." She brandished the bottle of vanilla. "I'm just asking you to remove that stick from your ass if we're going to make it through tonight."

Blood rushed to my face, and I had the sudden urge to belt Marta on the uninjured side of her face, but Zia pushed me aside and pressed a bag of ice with a great thunk onto Marta's forehead.

"Ow!" Marta yelped.

And that's when Smith and Smythe arrived.

# Chapter 23

I will never forget the look on Smith's face as he took in the kitchen. I'd already worried that he'd find our operation to be laughably small. But as I saw his eyes sweep the space and so quickly return to me, I knew it was even worse than I thought.

The others did an amazing transition, lunging into a pantomime performance that could be entitled *Kitchen Hard at Work*. Theresa, eyes down, began breaking eggs into the enormous bowl of the commercial mixer. Marta flicked the ice pack into a trash can and began sifting whole wheat flour. Zia Maria, stealing looks at my corporate raiders and clicking her tongue at Theresa's handling of the eggs, took up a giant carrot and began to peel it.

"So this is where it all happens," Smith said coolly.

"Yes, for now." I was defensive. "But we're bursting at the seams here. We need an automated facility to keep up with demand. I've toured six or seven copackers in New Jersey already, to get a feel for the market."

"I'm glad to hear it," Smith chuckled. "I don't think I can even calculate a labor coefficient on an operation this small."

*Whack!* Zia Maria's knife hit the chopping board with surprising force for a lady who must weigh eighty pounds dripping wet. A carrot top rolled off the table, like the head of a guillotined French rebel.

"We're . . . uh . . . off to a good start here, though," I said, trying to find something conciliatory to say.

Smythe peered over his clipboard, his eyeglasses glinting in the bright kitchen lighting. "And who handles your health department certificates?"

"That's the good thing about this space—"

"One of *many*," Zia grunted.

"I don't have to maintain them myself," I explained, ignoring her. "This is an incubator kitchen, designed to help small businesses get off the ground. The owner maintains the certifications and documentation. I rent space by the hour. This has allowed me to avoid the overhead of running my own certified commercial kitchen."

"At the expense of scale," Smith noted.

"Exactly," I said. Scale was a well-placed euphemism for "small."

"Ahem," said Marta, putting down her sifter on the table in such a way that she managed to jab me in the ribcage with her elbow.

"Oh! I'd like you to meet Marta Rodríguez," I said then. "My partner, friend, and general manager."

Marta removed her latex kitchen gloves to shake hands. "It is a pleasure to meet you, sirs."

"So what are you manufacturing tonight?"

"Muffets, of course," Marta answered. "We've had to drop our other product lines because of Whole Foods' insatiable appetite for this particular product."

"I see," Smith said politely. "And where do the ingredients come from? Julia's farm?"

"Some of them do, of course," Marta replied. "But most arrive from the distributor each night just before production."

"So, you don't need to store them," Smythe noted.

"Right," I volunteered. "We have very limited storage space for raw ingredients. We spend our storage dollars to warehouse the finished product." I'd said it hoping to make the point that we took good care of our product, but then I cringed. It would be impossible to show Smith and Smythe my freezer space. If I walked two men in dark suits up to the door of the Sons of Sicily Social Club, Pastucci might take one look at them and bolt, imagining they were cops coming to inspect his liquor license.

"If you had adequate storage, you'd save money in the long run," Smythe said. He scribbled again on the clipboard.

"Of course," I said. "I could save money on everything if I bought in greater bulk, especially packaging materials and nonperishables like flour."

"Yeah," Smith sighed. He stared toward the door. I seemed to be losing him.

"What else can I show you?" I asked, desperation creeping into my voice.

He leaned against a stainless steel countertop, and I worried that there'd be a line of flour chalked across the back of his navy suit. "I guess we'll take a look at the books," he said noncommittally.

Marta and Theresa were flash-freezing muffets when I emerged, alone, from Zia's office.

"How's it going in there?" Marta asked, over the clanking of the machine.

"I really don't know," I said truthfully. "I don't have a good feeling about it. I left them alone, because I couldn't stop hovering."

Marta shook her head. "*Qué será, será*. We did our best."

"I can't believe Zia volunteered her office," I whispered, to lighten the mood. "I don't know anyone who's ever been allowed into her inner sanctum."

"Listen," Marta stole a glance toward Zia, who was bent in concentration over her cookies. "Do this right now!" she hissed. "Take the vanilla back into the storeroom. The door is open. Put it on the left-hand shelf, next to the almond extract. Once the Smiths leave, we don't have any more excuse to go back there. Go!"

I found Zia's vanilla under Marta's coat and quickly headed for the storeroom. Marta was right—the door stood ajar. It was a big walk-in closet, lit by a single overhead bulb. On the shelves, cartons of baking powder and bottles of spices stretched from the floor to the ceiling.

Just as I placed the vanilla on the shelf near the other extracts, I heard laughter. And it was loud.

I glanced around, forgetting to breathe. The wall between the storeroom where I stood and Zia's adjacent office did not meet the ceiling. So I was effectively standing next to Smith and Smythe—invisibly—as they discussed Julia's Child.

The laughter alarmed me.

"I said this would happen, didn't I? If we went slumming at the trade show." The voice was Smythe's. It had a more nasal quality than his boss's. "I told you it would."

"The way I remember it, this was your idea. But look, I *know*. This brand is small. Laughably small. It's a problem."

"Small? Small? We're talking . . . lemonade stand. No—even smaller than a lemonade stand. This brand is like a contact lens. Let's not drop it on the rug, we might never find it again."

Smith snorted with laughter, while my face burned.

"Look, dude," he addressed his younger colleague. "Don't forget why we're here. We'd tour a larger competitor, if only there was one. But this market sector—it's just emerging. There are other companies, but they're all this size."

"But we're wasting our time. How could we possibly make a meaningful profit this year?"

"It's not what we're used to. I'll give you that. But the economy is in the dumpster, and we're trying to think outside the box here, okay? This lady, she walks the walk and talks the talk. Her business is actually growing, and every one of our lines is just treading water."

The blood rushing to my head might have impeded my hearing, but I thought Smith had just defended me. A little bit.

"But—c'mon, Smith. We're not venture capitalists. This isn't Silicon Valley. In New York, we don't start up companies in the garage. This place isn't even as *big* as your garage in the Hamptons. The executive committee is gonna laugh us out of the room."

"Then riddle me this, whiz kid—what are you and I going to do next quarter? We could sit around and wait for one of these organic brands to get bigger. But while we're sitting on our thumbs for a year, the executive committee is going to wonder why they're still paying for your Beemer. Not to mention that this company will just cost more after it grows."

"That's the silver lining, right? I guess we can buy it cheap."

"Real cheap. I just might have enough change in my wallet." Smith snorted at his own joke.

Someone laid a hand on my shoulder, and I nearly jumped to the ceiling. Whirling around, I was horrified to find Zia Maria.

But she didn't yell at me. She didn't ask what it was I was doing in her private storage room. She didn't say a word. Instead, she put a finger to her lips and winked. Then she brushed past me and pulled the bottle of vanilla from the shelf—the same one I'd replaced less than five minutes before—and turned around and left the room.

It was well known that theft of baking extracts was a capital offence in Zia's kitchen. But somehow eavesdropping was totally fine.

# Chapter 24

Smith and Smythe's parting directive had been, "Don't call us. We'll call you." And with their laughter still ringing in my ears, I was happy to forget I'd ever met them.

But my cash-flow problems had not magically dissipated. And as often as I replayed the supply closet encounter in my mind, I had to admit that the worst thing they'd said about my company was that it was small. Even as I bristled, I knew that I needed their help. Unless GPG became my fairy godmother, by the next American Express billing cycle the whole enterprise would be as valuable as a few mice and a pumpkin.

I began to wonder if they'd ever call.

As a cure for waiting by the phone, I stayed busy. I noodled around with the website design, and I reorganized our files. I caught up on all the e-mail that had trickled into our website. There was a new variety of complaint that we'd begun to receive from a few of our loyal Brooklyn customers.

Dear Julia's Child,

My daughter really liked your Cheese and Thank You pasta. And Give Peas a Chance was her only green vegetable. Where did they go? The health-food store in Cobble Hill now only carries your muffets. Please tell me where I can find those other foods.

Sincerely,
Shalom

I had no reply. It was hard to explain that the company's entire direction had been altered by one ninety-pound daytime television star.

One afternoon, in a burst of optimism, I finally called the bigger organic outfit, in Massachusetts, and inquired about its certification process. More attempts to reach Kevin Dunham, my mysteriously disappearing organic inspector, had failed. I faxed the application I'd originally prepared for him to Massachusetts. Then I spoke to someone named Mary, and the new outfit, Organiquest, agreed to visit the site within three days.

If GPG thought my company was too puny, I would try one more time to impress them. I called Kai Travers at Whole Foods, to try to persuade him to expand Julia's Child to the rest of the Northeast region.

It only took me three telephone calls to get through to him. "Hi, Julia!" Kai's voice was cheerful enough.

"Hi, Kai. It was great to meet you at ANKST," I began.

"The pleasure was all mine. But listen, I haven't made any decisions yet about my lines for children. The market is changing so fast, and I'm learning a lot from the products I'm testing—yours included. It makes sense for me to give it another month or so before I firm things up. Besides, it gives you some time to figure out how you'd deal with a much bigger order, right?"

As if I could think about anything else.

"Actually, Mr. Travers, that's why I'm calling. A sizeable food company is interested in backing Julia's Child. And it would really help with my ramp-up, if only I could show them . . ."

"Great news, Julia! That's terrific. You let me know how that turns out, okay? I'm late for a meeting, but we'll speak soon."

It was the unmistakable sound of the brush-off. So I let him go to his meeting, real or imaginary. I couldn't meet Marta's eyes after that call. Things in our little office weren't as harried as before the trade show. But our formerly easy rapport was strained by a new, unspoken reality.

The Thanksgiving holiday rolled around then, which meant I would shortly be cooking a feast as well as hosting my parents. Eager for the distraction, I ordered a turkey at the farmers' market and planned my menu. But Thanksgiving dawned rainy and cold, foiling Luke's plan to take the kids out to watch the Macy's parade from Columbus Circle. The confining weather, the change in routine, and attempts to compete for, as Wylie called them, "Bama and Bampa's" attention made the boys rowdier by the hour.

Mostly, I hid in the kitchen. Cooking a big meal is 40 percent competence and 60 percent confidence. It had been months since I had attempted to prepare anything resembling a traditional feast, and frankly I was off my game.

The turkey was coming along nicely, but the side dishes were giving me trouble. I'd forgotten to put the corn pudding into the oven early enough, and now it looked soupy even as the turkey began to brown.

"What's the matter, honey? You look stressed." Luke was pulling citrus fruits out of the refrigerator.

"Nothing, it's . . ." I grabbed the lid off the pot of potatoes just a second before it would have begun to boil over.

"You need some help in here? I was just about to make my famous sangria." He pushed my bag of cranberries aside and began to slice a lemon on my cutting board.

I tried not to be annoyed that Luke would commandeer the only two feet of prep space our cozy kitchen offered.

I watched my husband confidently juice an orange. "Are you sure that's a good idea? My mother doesn't hold her sangria very well," I whispered.

"It's not nearly as strong as martinis," Luke said. "And I think Bonnie's head will blow off if your mother gives her one more piece of child-rearing advice."

"Yikes," I said, adding a bit of milk to the mixer bowl in which I planned to mash the potatoes. "Maybe you should send my mother in here to 'help' me."

"Okay," he said, chuckling. "But it's not bad theater. And your dad likes Bonnie. Scotland is apparently the golf capital of the universe."

"Does Bonnie play golf?" I asked, trying to picture it.

"Who knows?" Luke poured wine and then orange liqueur into his concoction. "I don't think it matters to your father." Before he left the kitchen, Luke poured me a glass of sangria and left it on the counter. It was a nice gesture, but I was busier than a one-armed mom in a diaper-changing contest, and it would probably just sit there on the counter with the ice melting.

A few minutes later my mother swept in, her sangria glass already half-empty. For her sake, I hoped Luke hadn't added too much Cointreau. She clutched her glass and grinned at me. "So tell me, dear," her voice boomed off our ancient tile backsplash. "How's business?" Her fingernails were painted flawlessly in a coral color, the nails of a retiree.

Leave it to my mother to select the one topic capable of stressing me out more than an undercooked corn pudding.

"It's fine, Mom. There's not much to tell."

"Julia, how could that be? You say you're too busy to call me, and it's because of business. So when I ask you about business, your answer is that there's not much to say? I haven't heard a word about it since your big TV interview. It was a big hit on Kiawah, by the way. Everybody loved it."

Jasper popped into the room. "Um, we're playing that I'm the daddy and Wylie is the mommy and I'm a pirate and do you want some cheese?"

I squinted at him. "Real cheese or pretend cheese?"

"Real cheese. Daddy told me to ask you. He's going to put out some snacks for us and Bonnie and Grandpa."

"No thank you, honey." I sighed. Luke meant well. But only a daddy would make the mistake of putting crackers in front of the children right before I served a five-course feast.

"Jasper!" my mother bellowed. "Do you think your mother works too hard?"

The question was so obviously a loaded one that Jasper stared wide-eyed at his grandma. Then, having no easy answer, he bolted.

"It's not going well," I said in a low voice. I noticed the cranberries, still on the countertop. "Shit." I cranked up the heat under a saucepan on the stove, and then dumped the berries, a bit of water, and a quarter cup of sugar into it, stirring furiously.

"Good God, dear. You won't even use canned cranberry sauce? No wonder it's not going well."

"*I don't mean the berries!*" I yelled. "I mean my business! It isn't going well."

My mother blinked at me.

"There, are you happy now? Now you know." I hated the adolescent sound of that statement. I was devolving.

But she just shrugged and finished her drink. She set the empty glass down on the countertop. "Well, honey, what difference could that possibly make? I mean, really. You have these two gorgeous, healthy children, so how could you possibly care that much if it isn't going well?"

I wrenched open the oven door. That was the question now, wasn't it? The almost fifty-thousand-dollar question. I'd been trying not to think about it while I labored over the turkey. But my mother's words restarted the mill of tortuous logic in my mind. And why would she put it that way? If my two children were ugly and obnoxious, would it be okay if I cared a little too much about my business?

I stabbed the bird with my instant-read thermometer. Cooking is a simple technology. Apply heat to the food and then wait until the appropriate physics and chemistry rendered it done. But the higher you set the bar for success—perfectly crispy skin, perfectly juicy breast meat—the easier it is to fail.

The idea for Julia's Child had started simply. My idea was pure and true—to make a great product and do things my way. But the process had become overwhelmingly complex and perverse along the way. The very idea that I'd end up waiting for a multinational conglomerate to bail me out would have been unthinkable only a few months ago.

The turkey was done—and the side dishes weren't. I turned the oven temperature way down and tried to think of a plan.

I turned my attention to the undercooked corn pudding on the rack below the bird. The center wasn't set—it jiggled when I tapped the dish.

My thirty-year-old range had two ovens side by side. So I turned on the other one, the littler oven that I never used because the dial wobbled. I set it to what I hoped was four hundred degrees, hoping to preheat it fast enough to finish the corn pudding in time.

Still lingering in the kitchen, watching me work, my mother said, "You should have sprung for a Butterball. With that pop-out thing that tells you when it's done."

I could barely unclench my teeth to answer her. "Mother, this is a locally raised, organic bird from heirloom breeding stock. They don't come with a pop-up."

"That's my Julia, always doing things the hard way." My mother sighed.

I bristled, throwing down my oven mitt. "I know you don't care, but I do. Conventional turkey farming is disgusting."

She laughed. "Turkeys aren't pretty birds. Your great grandfather used to keep a couple. And they always tried to peck at us."

"Well, industrially raised turkeys wouldn't have bothered. They're too docile to notice you. They're bred for one trait alone—to get so fat that their legs break and they end up dragging themselves through their own poop by the wings."

"Gross, Julia. Why are you telling me this?"

"Because it's true, Mother. And it gets worse. Inbreeding has completely erased the turkey's sex drive. They don't even remember how to reproduce."

My mother rolled her eyes. "Then how do the evil farmers get more of them?"

"The female turkeys have to be artificially inseminated, which is weird enough—"

"People do that too. So what?"

I turned to her. "Yes, but for them it's voluntary. And they don't have to hire a professional turkey wanker to extract the semen. By hand."

"Eew! Julia. Talk about doing things the hard way."

I turned my back on her and stirred the cranberries violently. But she addressed me anyhow.

"Something's got to give, Julia. You can't possibly take perfect care of the turkey *and* the people who are going to eat it *and* the strangers who buy your muffets. No wonder you're stressed out. Here—have some sangria."

Stirring my cranberries, I ignored her. But she didn't take the hint.

"The thing I'd really like to know is—why," she said. "*Why* do you care so much about the turkeys? It isn't even like Save the Whales. You're going to eat them, anyway!"

She laughed at her own joke, and I finally turned around, my face reddening with fury. There were only about ten things wrong with her logic. "That's the point!" I sputtered. "You're going to *eat* this, right? You put food in your body. How can you not care what it is? How can you not understand that I don't want to feed just anything to my"—I paused to remember how she'd put it—"two beautiful, healthy children?"

She leaned against the wall, sipping her sangria. She didn't seem bothered that she'd upset me. "But what are you afraid will happen? So what if we eat something we can't even pronounce."

I just shook my head. There was apparently no way to make her understand. "It's . . . the journey," I mumbled, poking at one of my boiling potatoes with a fork. If we handed over the business of our food to the factories, my children would never grow up knowing the taste of a ripe summer peach just off the tree. They'd never know the smell of yeasty dough as it rose on their own kitchen counter.

"Ah, the *journey*," my mother scoffed. "Julia, we all die someday. Even if we follow your regimen. Meanwhile, you're trapped in the kitchen, or your office God knows where. Your journey doesn't look so great. I might die from too much . . . maltodextrin or whatever. But I'm going to try to have a little fun first."

I finally thought of a plan to shut her up. And not a moment too soon. I dumped the pot of boiling potatoes into the colander, filling the kitchen with starchy steam. My mother, with her heavily applied makeup, was forced to run for cover.

Luke stuck his head in the door. "Julia? I smell smoke."

"It's probably coming out of my ears." I'd smelled something burning too. But it couldn't be coming from the turkey, because I'd just checked it. And it couldn't be the underdone corn pudding or the cranberry sauce. "It's just the left-hand oven, honey, it's preheating. Some old crumbs must be burning up in there."

Luke sniffed the air. He crossed the little room and forced open the old double-hung window over the sink. The rain was still pouring down outside, but the air smelled wonderful—freshly scrubbed. "I don't know," he said. "That's a lot of smoke for a few crumbs." He opened the left-hand oven, and black smoke billowed out. But otherwise, the oven was empty.

Then we noticed that the smoke seemed to be leaking out from *underneath* the oven. Luke jerked open the old broiler drawer. "Aha!" The handle of a wooden rolling pin peeked out. It had been so long since I'd used that oven, I'd forgotten things were stored under there.

Luke grabbed the handle of the rolling pin and yanked it out. "Ow!" The other end was completely aflame. I backed away from the sink to give him clearance, and Luke lunged. But instead of dropping the pin into the sink, as I expected him to do, he hurled it completely out the window.

"Honey!" I shouted. "We live on the sixth floor! Why didn't you throw it into the sink?"

"It was on *fire*," he said. "Would you rather have a fire in our kitchen?"

Both children came running into the tiny room, drawn by the sound of our raised voices.

"But you could *kill a person* with that," I gasped. "What if you hit someone down below?"

"Is somebody killed?" Jasper asked, all concern.

"No!" Luke said quickly. "Julia, there's that . . . garden down below," he said. "The one that nobody sits in. Especially in November. In the *pouring rain*."

I looked out the window. From our height, the little seating area wasn't visible. The space between buildings was so tight; we could only see the neighboring wall. Though he was right about the garden. It was a forlorn little alcove.

Still, a hurtling rolling pin would make a fiery missile for any unfortunate souls below. I pictured a little old lady, flattened as she bent down to feed the pigeons. "Just go and retrieve it, okay? So I can know for sure."

Luke rolled his eyes and left the room. Just one more person who thought I was crazy. "Boys!" he called. "Who wants to run an errand downstairs?"

There was a chorus of "Meeeeee!" and the apartment door clicked shut on them.

I turned the cranberries down to a simmer, stirring them. I moved the corn pudding into the preheated left-hand oven. I scurried into the dining room to see if Jasper had complied with my request to set the table.

He had. Mostly. As I straightened out the forks where they'd been flung on the napkins, my mother addressed me from the sofa. "I thought you told me that the fireplace was gas. It smells so," she sniffed the air, which was still permeated by a faint aura of wood smoke, "genuine."

Wordlessly, Bonnie gulped her sangria and then poured herself a refill from Luke's pitcher. The doorbell rang as I folded the napkins. It rang again, and then it rang three more times. Wylie adored the doorbell.

Luke entered, holding the unburnt end of a blackened rolling pin. "I hit a Japanese maple." He started to laugh.

The phone rang, but I was distracted by the boys, still lingering in the hallway.

"My turn!" Jasper said.

"*Mine!*"

"Boys, come inside, please." The phone rang again, and I grabbed it off the hallway table. The caller ID read "GPG."

I bolted for the kitchen, pressing "talk" only when I was almost there. "Hello?"

"Hello, Julia. This is J. P. Smith."

"Mr. Smith, how can I help you?" The doorbell rang loudly again, accompanied by a wail from Wylie, who must have been shoved aside. I pressed my finger into my free ear, but even so it was easy to hear the ding-dong, ding-dong—like the soundtrack to an insane asylum.

"Do you need to get that?" he asked.

"Uh, no." I closed the kitchen door with a snap. It dampened the family mayhem behind me. "J. P." I took a deep breath. "What's on your mind?"

"I have a document I'd like to messenger up to you," he said, as if it were the most normal thing in the world to be swapping documents on Thanksgiving. "I need Marta's full name, though," he said. "Since she is part owner of your company, there's a set of papers for her too."

"Oh," I said. "The papers . . . they are . . ."

"An offer for Julia's Child," Smith said cheerfully. "You can think it over for the weekend. Actually, take until Tuesday, because you'll want your lawyer to review the language."

"Um, great! Thanks! Wow . . ."

"Her name, though?"

"Oh! Right. Marta Florinda Rodríguez."

"Thanks, Julia! We look forward to working with you." He hung up.

I set down the phone, my hand shaking, just as Luke carefully pushed the door open and entered the kitchen. He took one look at my startled expression and closed it behind him. "Who called?" he asked.

Instead of answering, I picked up my neglected glass of sangria.

The ice had melted and it was a little sad looking, so I dumped it down the drain.

Luke clutched his chest in mock horror. "What'd you do that for?"

"Honey, open up a bottle of champagne."

# Chapter 25

By Monday morning, the flush of victory still hadn't worn off. And it wasn't just me. Opposite me, in our small office, Marta was all aglow. I could tell she'd treated herself to a few hours in the salon over the weekend. Her curly hair had been cut into an attractive frame around her face. It also had taken on a suspiciously lighter tone, with caramel highlights that I'd never seen before.

"That's $285,000 in stock," our attorney's voice rang out, on speakerphone, "which breaks down to $28,500 for Marta and $256,500 for Julia." It gave me pleasure to hear the sound of my quarter million dollars bounce off the walls of our office. While Nina read aloud the terms of GPG's offer, we listened happily, like two junior high school girls at an awards ceremony.

"Well done, ladies," she paused. "But of course you won't be getting the money in cash. You'll be getting shares of GPG's publicly traded stock." She paused to read ahead. "And you won't be able to sell the last of them until three years from now."

"Gotcha," I said, so she would know that we were sort of listening.

"That's risky because GPG's share price might decline before you can sell."

"Okay, Nina." I thought she was belaboring the point. But I suppose that was what I paid her to do.

"The good news," our lawyer continued, "is that the additional fifty thousand dollars of debt extinguishment is in cash. All the money that Julia has lent the Julia's Child *Corporation* will be repaid in December, by check."

This was indeed good news. So good, in fact, that I could weep with joy. I would no longer be a fool who bet the ranch on her business the very minute a major recession blew into town. Our original egg would be returned to its nest, safe and unbroken.

"You are each offered a three-year employment contract as part of the deal. Julia will receive a salary of one hundred thousand dollars per year plus a performance-based bonus, Marta will receive a salary of forty-two thousand plus bonus. Payment is biweekly, in cash. Health benefits equivalent to other GPG employees . . ." The lawyer droned on. The two of us swiveled happily to and fro in our chairs and smiled at the ceiling.

"Julia's title will be CEO and brand manager of Julia's Child. Marta's proposed title is vice president for the brand." She stopped reading. "Ladies, titles are often more negotiable than the financial terms of the deal. Are there any changes you'd like to stipulate?"

Marta opened her mouth to say something but then hesitated. She hit the "mute" button on the phone, preventing Nina from hearing her question. "Do you think I'll get business cards that say 'vice president' on them?"

"I'm almost positive it won't be a problem," I said. When I'd worked at the bank, just about everybody with a pulse had eventually become a VP. With business cards.

Marta unmuted the phone. "That's fine," she said breezily.

"Moving on." Nina cleared her throat into the phone. "I'd advise you to take a hard look at the 'brand control' language."

"Why?" I asked. It would be hard for Nina to ruin my mood with something as trivial as contract language.

"It's a potential source of difficulty whenever an entrepreneur is subsumed into a big organization. You might have unanticipated differences of opinion. You might have different standards."

"But if I'm CEO of the brand, then I'll be able to determine—"

She cut me off. "That's just a title, Julia. The contract states that you'll report to the head of Food Brands. It's pretty clear that you won't have de facto control over everything. So you need to give this some thought. At the very least, we should try to specify veto power over the things you feel most strongly about. Say, changes to the package design or advertising copy."

"Okay," I said, feeling the day's first wave of uncertainty. Obviously, I cared very much about the product. But GPG had just thrown me one hell of a lifeline, and I very much intended to take it.

I checked the clock. It was nearly eleven. Usually, the waves of uncertainty hit me well before breakfast, so I figured I was already ahead. And it was all thanks to GPG. "Nina, I hear you. But part of selling the brand to GPG is trusting that they're ready to do the right thing. The only change that might give me a serious case of heartburn would be inferior ingredients. Why don't we ask them to give me power over that?"

"Okay," our lawyer said. "I'll add veto power . . . changing ingredients." I could hear her scribbling. "Do you ladies have any questions so far?"

"I have one," Marta said. "Do the benefits kick in right away?"

"You're pari passu with the other employees of GPG as soon as you sign. That usually means health and dental immediately. The 401(k) plan might start after a few months, though. Any more questions?"

Marta shook her head.

"I think that's all," I told Nina.

"Okay! So let's review the contingencies now, and then we'll be just about done."

"Contingencies?" Marta asked. She had received her own set of documents over the weekend, but I imagined she'd gone starry-eyed from the numbers on page one. It was doubtful that Marta had read all the way to the end.

"The group has given itself a couple of loopholes that would allow it to cancel the contract. The first contingency refers to product-packaging claims. GPG reserves the right to declare the contract null and void if any of Julia's Child product packages contain information that is untrue or misleading."

Marta harrumphed. "We are as pure as the driven snow."

I laughed. "You are not."

"But the product is," she argued.

Then I felt a pain in my chest, like indigestion. I stopped laughing as I remembered the great vanilla caper. That made for at least one batch of organic muffets that wasn't strictly by the book.

There was also the farm.

I halted my swivel chair to think it over. Luckily, I'd already asked the new organic inspectors to step in. Because if the farm certification wasn't complete, I could not legally claim that the muffets were organic. And a stickler might find the word "organic" on every package of muffets to be . . . How had they put it? "Untrue or misleading."

I would call the organic inspectors immediately. "Is that all, Nina?"

"There's one more thing here. The terms of this contract will prohibit Julia from using her name again on a food or children's product."

That was easier. "So if it doesn't work out with GPG, I can't quit and start a company called Julia's Other Child?"

"That's what they're driving at," Nina cautioned. "But this clause is far too broad," she scoffed. "I'm going to change the language to refer only to your first name."

It was hard for me to imagine a world in which it could possibly matter. As if I'd have the energy to ever try to start another company from scratch. "Thank you, Nina. What do we do next?"

"Sit tight while I talk to their lawyers about some of this language. Are you going to make a counteroffer on the price?"

I chewed on my lip. "I really don't know."

"Think it over, and I'll be back in touch at the end of the day."

I hung up, pondering the question. "Luke thought it wouldn't hurt to try to get them to raise their offer a little."

"Really?"

"He said that 285 sounded like it was just begging to be rounded up to 300."

"So are you going to ask them for 300?" Marta admired her manicure.

"I really can't decide. Does only a sucker say yes to the first number? But of course I have no leverage. I can't really pretend I'd walk away at 285."

"You're the one who used to work on Wall Street."

I shook my head. "In the accounting office."

"Hey, Julia!" Marta beamed at me from across the room. "You used to be a bean counter. Now you're a bean *cooker*!" She doubled over with laughter at her own joke.

But I really wasn't listening. I still had a bean counter's attention to detail. And the missing organic certification had begun to nag me. It was the one point on which we were vulnerable.

I dialed the Massachusetts number for Organiquest and asked for Mary. I needed to make sure that they'd inspected my farmland and could turn around my certification right away.

"I was just going to call you," Mary said.

"You were?" I asked, happy to hear that my new organic inspector might know how to pick up a phone.

"Yes. We inspected last Wednesday, and your application is good and complete. But we've found something awfully peculiar in your soil test results."

"Really? What do you mean, 'peculiar'?"

"It's the nitrogen level. It would be difficult to imagine," she spoke carefully, "how you could test at that level using the fertilization described in your application."

I was silent for a moment, trying to figure out what Mary was saying. "We used only goat manure this year. Before that, the land was used for organic dairy farming. My nitrogen is too low?"

She cleared her throat. "No, it's sky-high. That's what's so weird. As if you dumped a truckload of commercial fertilizer on it."

"But . . . that's impossible!" Kate would never put anything unholy on her precious soil. She was a born-again, proselytizing organic zealot. It just didn't make sense. Maybe they'd tested someone else's field? "Mary, we can figure this out. Tell me exactly where you tested."

But after I listened to Mary, I had to admit that the folks at Organiquest were organized to a fault. She described my property in exacting detail. She'd carefully parked her car in our driveway and crossed the road for the inspection—all to avoid compacting the soil with her tires. She'd inspected the goat pen, the marked plots, and the compost pile. "But not the barn," she'd said. "Only the outdoor hayloft. Listen, I'm just going to set your application aside for now."

"Set it aside?" That's just what Kevin Dunham had done.

"Just until you can take a look around, figure out what's going on with the nitrogen," she reasoned. "Something doesn't add up. Why don't you buy a kit from a garden center and do some tests yourself? With that nitrogen level, you should be able to duplicate my results. If you can't, then maybe it would be worth meeting us up there to test it again. But I can't really go further with this certification until we explain these numbers."

"But . . ." Panic rose up in my throat. "It was my understanding," I tried, "that the soil tests weren't really necessary for the certification. They're extra, right? To help me learn about—"

"That's true, but now that we have these numbers in hand, something doesn't make sense. So I think you need to take a moment and figure out why."

Mary was polite about it, but she was not about to solve my problem. Surely, she had no idea that my entire life hung in the balance.

Ten seconds later, I was dialing Kate, and mercifully she answered. "Hello?" That dreamy voice was unmistakable.

"Kate, it's Julia Bailey," I said breathlessly.

"Happy harvest festival, Julia!" I supposed she was referring to Thanksgiving.

"Um, thank you. I hope you had a nice holiday. Listen, Kate, I've got a little bit of a problem. The new organic inspector just told me that our soil tests came out a little funny. I was hoping you could tell me . . . if you put anything on the soil besides the manure?" I tried to make the question come out as innocently as possible.

But Kate didn't hear it that way. "Put anything on it? Are you serious? I don't even like to walk on it, which is more than I can say for your team of inspectors. There were four of them tromping around out there last week!"

"I'm sorry about that, Kate. But Kevin Dunham never gave me the paperwork I needed. I'm not sure if he's up to the task of certifying a farm."

She sighed. "Poor Kevin. Such a talented boy. So sad."

"Talented?"

"He's actually an exceptionally knowledgeable organic farmer. He really is. But he smokes all the produce. If he'd only switch crops, then everything would come out all right. I just don't know what to do for him."

I gripped the phone, wondering how to steer the conversation back toward my needs. "Well, the folks from Organiquest would be happy to certify us. But there's a problem with our soil test numbers."

"Seriously, Julia!" she erupted. "You've got this all backwards. Why do you care what they think? Why do you want to let other people tell you how to farm?"

The conversation was not going where I'd hoped to take it. "Kate, I'm sorry that you feel that way," I tried. "The thing is—some people are very interested in helping me expand the business. Some investors. And they need a way to know—"

"Investors? You mean . . . you're going to *sell out*?"

The words hung there in the air while I tried to think of what to say. "Kate, it's not like that. I'm not selling the land, just the—"

"Like *hell* you're not selling it. You said you were different, Julia. But I should have known better. People with money are all the same. One year in, and you're going to sell out to a big corporation for a quick profit. That's disgusting!"

Then she hung up on me.

I closed my eyes, the phone still clamped to my head. I could picture my farmland, quietly sitting next to the big red barn, the wind playing gently over the yellowed grasses, waiting for snow. What the hell had happened there? And how could I figure it out by tomorrow?

It was eleven in the morning. Luke was at work. Jasper was in school. And I needed to be in Vermont, right away. I stood up from behind the desk. Marta grinned into her own phone. "I'm going to transfer my shares of stock into a college fund for Carlos."

I put on my coat, picked up my purse, and left without saying good-bye. I didn't want to scare her.

As I trotted toward the subway, I reached Bonnie on my cell phone. "I'm sorry," I told her. "But can you come up with something for dinner? I'm not going to be around tonight or tomorrow morning."

"Sure. Is anything the matter?"

"I have to drive to Vermont for business. I'll call the boys later and explain it to them myself."

# Chapter 26

There were 245 miles between New York and Gannett, Vermont. That was almost one mile for every thousand dollars I might earn on my sale of Julia's Child to GPG. As I pressed my foot down on the accelerator on Interstate 91, I tried to imagine that the coincidence was significant.

The drive had never seemed so quiet or so long. Without Luke, the kids, the complaints, and the Elmo, I felt lost.

I tried the radio, but it was too chirpy for my mood. Instead, I tuned myself to an inner channel, one featuring several uninterrupted hours of self-recrimination. I measured myself against the hum of the motor and found that I came up lacking. I knew there'd been plenty of mistakes on the business end of things. That much was obvious. But I'd always been sure I had this one part right. My products' purity had never been in question. It was brutally obvious, however, that now things were completely out of control.

It was just as Luke, Marta, and my mother had been trying to tell me, or maybe worse.

If I couldn't find the answers fast, then the messy side of the business, my debts and obligations, would claim Julia's Child for good.

With each passing highway stripe, I said a silent prayer. Please, God. Let there be some explanation. Otherwise I'd brought everything to the brink, only to disappoint my family and Marta at the last minute.

I needed to get to Vermont before dark, but I couldn't do it without gas and at least a short break. I pulled off the highway in northern Massachusetts.

As part of my self-punishment plan, I visited the drive-through window of a fast-food restaurant. Then I pulled into a parking spot to make the necessary phone calls home. On Luke's voice mail, I left a meandering message on the topics of my love for him, a problem with the farm, and hitting the road to inspect it.

Then I dialed our apartment.

"Heddo!"

"Wylie?" I didn't know he could reach the phone.

"Mama! I having a treat. Wook!"

Wylie had not mastered the idea that although I could hear him on the phone I couldn't see him. "What are you eating, honey?"

"Apple pie. I buy it with Bonnie."

"Apple pie? Where did you find that?"

"At Old McDonald's. I already eat the chicken and fench fies."

I cringed. I'd been out of town for just a few hours, and Bonnie had run for the nearest fast-food restaurant, completely against the family rules. It was bad enough that I had to poison myself on the road with partially hydrogenated oils. But there was no reason the kids should suffer.

"Let me talk to . . ." I bit my tongue before I could ask for Bonnie. None of this was really her fault. There'd be no point fighting with her now. "Your brother," I finished. "Let me talk to Jasper."

"Hi, Mom." My big boy sounded so grown up on the phone. He had just started calling me Mom instead of Mommy. Coming from two hundred miles away, it broke my heart.

"Hi, sweetie. I'm sorry I won't be able to tuck you in tonight. But I'll see you tomorrow, okay?"

"Okay. Hey—Mom. Do you know what a Happy Meal is? There's a *toy* in it."

"Wow. Did it . . . make you happy?" I asked lamely.

"Yeah," he said.

"Love you, honey." I hung up, sad and confused.

Having dined that afternoon only on a diet of reproach, I was starved. Sitting behind the wheel in the lonely parking lot, I unwrapped my cheeseburger and took a bite. It had been years since I'd had fast food. It was saltier than I remembered. But the burger had a pleasingly soft texture. Fillers, of course, gave it that texture. But it slid down easily. I tried the fries. They were tasty. So this was how the other half lived. I munched in silence, watching the sun sink lower in the New England sky and trying not to think.

When my lips became salt puckered, I gave up on my McMeal. A tank of gas and several gulps of iced coffee later, I was back on the highway, speeding for the Vermont border.

It was a lucky break that I didn't get pulled over. Vermont isn't heavily patrolled, but I'd never driven faster. I was racing the daylight, the GPG deadline, and my own sanity. At least I had the good sense to slow down when I left 91 for the curvy road to Gannett. I wasn't too far gone to realize that a number of people required me to avoid wrapping the Subaru around one of the northern white pines along the route.

The sun had already set, but the sky was still light when I finally gunned the motor up our dirt road. I pulled up hastily on the barn side of the road and hopped out of the car. I didn't have a soil test kit, just a burning desire to see the dirt and touch it and try to understand.

After two minutes of squatting over the clods of soil, the cold brown dirt still hadn't spoken to me. Why had I thought it would?

I didn't know farming, yet I'd bought a farm. I didn't know

the food business either, yet that hadn't stopped me from plowing straight in. At that moment it was painfully obvious that I should have remained a corporate accountant, employed and flush with cash. If I had, I might be standing in my kitchen at home right this minute, cooking the most glorious organic meal for my family. My kitchen countertops would be covered with the purest ingredients—purchased at the farmers' market, of course, from somebody who knew what they were doing.

Instead, I hunched alone in the darkness over dirt that was afflicted with some mysterious chemistry that I had no idea how to cure.

My back was killing me. I rose to look around. The tall grasses of summer had fallen, brown and dried. But the earth was still soft underfoot. Several sets of footprints circled me. Kate must have seethed as the Organiquest folks tromped here, compacting the soil with their shoes.

I followed the tracks to our second plot, marked off with stakes and string. The footsteps became muddled here, as if people had stopped to chat or perhaps to take a sample. Then they went on back toward the final planting area, mingling again near the goat enclosure.

The light was nearly gone. I gathered my jacket more tightly around me, feeling the day's urgency slip away. There was nothing to be learned from staring at some footsteps in the lonely dirt. Even the goats were missing. Kate housed them for the winter in a shed adjacent to the Barker farmhouse.

A single set of heavy footprints diverged from the others and headed toward the barn. In the dim light, I followed it. We went around the corner, the footsteps and I, until we came to face the great sliding doors. That was a little odd, because Mary from Organiquest had mentioned skipping the barn. It was hardly a big deal, but I slid open the great red door anyway, wondering if the footsteps' owner had done the same.

Messy. It was my first thought when I saw all the little empty cartons thrown just inside the door. Who would leave such clutter? But as I stepped over them, I saw that they weren't just any boxes. The package design was familiar from my childhood—its green and yellow colors, with the prominent juicy tomato on the front—my father had used this product every summer. He'd carefully mix the right amount of bright blue powder with water from the hose. He had drizzled it lovingly onto the roots of his beefsteaks and Early Girls. They were his only contribution to the family cuisine.

Miracle-Gro.

There must have been fifty empty packages. This simple commercial product—the blue stuff, of a peculiar color not found in nature—was the very last thing I expected to see in my own barn. But it certainly would make a soil test sky-high for nitrogen.

But who would do this? And then leave the boxes here? Surely not Kate. And not the folks from Organiquest. This product, carefully applied by home gardeners all over America, might as well be arsenic. Once doused with an industrial fertilizer, three years would need to pass before the farm could be considered organic again.

The only person who would want to pour Miracle-Gro here would be someone who did not wish to see an organic farm succeed on the hilltop.

With that thought, my stomach clenched. I knew only one person who was against our farming here. One guy who would rather see condos than veggies. It was, I understood as tears pricked my eyes, a genius plot. To "poison" my land in a way that most of the world would consider harmless, except for me and a few other uppity organic purists.

I'd been defeated, and by a guy who had simply to make one trip to the local nursery in his pickup truck. I put my head down on my knees and cried.

# Chapter 27

I woke up to the taste of fire.

The salsa. It had been too spicy. A few stale chips had been all I could find in the house to eat. That and plenty of beer.

Bracing myself, I sat up and opened my eyes. Our Vermont bedroom swam before me. I sank back down onto the pillow and closed my lids again. Thank God I'd stopped short of Luke's single malt scotch.

The house was quiet—too quiet. I'd never slept there alone before. In spite of the familiar surroundings, I could have been on the moon. The silence was that deep.

This is what my life will sound like if I totally fuck everything up. I turned the idea over in my mind. It was a sobering thought. So I sat up again, more slowly this time, and came face-to-face with a Playmobil figure on the bedside table. He stood there, all three inches of him, staring at me.

He was a cop, I could tell by the uniform. But not an American cop. Playmobil was made in Europe, so he looked like the Eurotrash equivalent of a police officer. His tight plastic pants were tucked into his plastic boots. He wore an empty holster on his hip, because—pacifist that I am—I threw away the tiny plastic gun during assembly, before it was spotted.

Eurocop reminded me of something Luke had done a while back: a couple of times I'd found abandoned figurines like these lying in compromising positions on the bathroom sink top.

I blinked back tears. The deep quiet and my sour stomach made even the stupid memory of Playmobil hanky-panky tear at me. I missed my husband terribly.

Eurocop just stared.

"We should hang out," I whispered to him. "Neither of us was meant to be left here alone."

I heaved myself out of bed and into our tiny bathroom. It took a long time for the creaky plumbing to agree to pour hot water all over me. But when it finally did, I stood for a long time under the spray, piecing together the previous night's disasters.

It had not been my finest hour. I had called Luke in tears, blubbering with suspicions and defeat. But he'd been irritated with me for flying off to Vermont.

"What now?" he'd asked, exasperated. "I thought you were supposed to meet with GPG tomorrow—and *accept their offer*."

His anger had startled me, although it was hard to blame him. I'd been out on the ledge over Julia's Child for too long now. He wanted the drama to end.

I pled my case as well as I could to Luke. Eventually, he calmed down and tried to help me sort it all out.

Then I'd started drinking. I now felt the weight of the caloric imbalance. Through it all, I could not stop thinking about revenge.

Calling the police had been my first inclination.

"But, honey," Luke had pointed out, "I doubt the penal code carries a statute against rogue fertilization."

That had sent my mind spinning through all the cop dramas I'd ever seen on TV. What could I peg him with? Trespassing? Vandalism? Those charges sounded more fitting for preteens with peashooters than for a builder with a vengeance. Conspiracy! That was more like it. But how? I wondered if fingerprints could be retrieved from moldering fertilizer boxes.

I toweled off, letting loose another groan of misery. Pulling on the spare pair of jeans that I kept in Vermont, my mind was swamped with "if only's." If only I hadn't gotten myself in debt. If only Kevin Dunham had just signed off on my farm in July. But then what? Then I wouldn't *know* that the farmland was spoiled. Would that have been better?

Yes. Yes, it would be better. Because then GPG would have already cut me a check.

My hangover clouded my ability to reason. So it took longer than it should have for the time line of the alleged farming fiasco to really sink in. I was brushing my hair when it hit me. The greedy developer could not have dumped Miracle-Gro on my land until *after* harvest time. The boxes were a recent appearance. In fact, Kate and I had been standing on the very spot where they now lay scattered when she'd admired the hummingbird in September.

That meant that I hadn't polluted any muffets with industrial fertilizer. It was only *next* year's crop that could not be organic.

As I hastily pulled on my socks, I also realized that there was somebody who could help me prove the purity of last year's veggies.

This hopeful notion propelled me down the narrow stairway into my kitchen. I paused only long enough to grab a half-eaten box of stale whole wheat crackers. I was out in the car a few minutes later, wet hair and all, heading for South Hill, where I rarely ventured. But I remembered Kate telling me once where Kevin Dunham lived.

The place was easy enough to find. The rusty VW van was parked outside a double-wide trailer. The van and the trailer looked like hell, but the farm plot next to it was as tidy as can be, especially for November, when many farming tracts sported the

Vermont version of a bad hair day. Kevin Dunham's plots were mounded into neatly mulched rows, awaiting spring. I remembered that Kate said he was one heck of a farmer.

I got out of the car and banged on the trailer's metal door. There was no answer. For a stoop, the trailer had an inverted extra-large plastic milk carton. I checked my watch, discovering that it was only eight in the morning. I banged again. "Open up, Kevin. You have something I need!"

"Lady, come back at noon," a voice finally whimpered. "I don't have anything bagged."

"Kevin Dunham, open up. It's Julia Bailey. You took my FDA application and my soil samples, and I need them back!"

A minute later, the door opened a crack. A sliver of face, pale as moonlight, peered out at me. Dunham had several days' growth of beard. "I remember you," he said. "The place on North Hill. With the goats."

It wasn't poetry, but it was progress. "Of course you do," I said. "Because I paid you six hundred dollars."

The bloodshot eyes opened a little wider. "I don't have that money right now."

"I'm sure you don't. But I just need my soil samples back. Even if you didn't test them. *Especially* if you didn't test them. I need them back."

He frowned. "Just a minute." He disappeared into the dim recesses of the trailer. I waited, tapping my finger on the flimsy doorjamb. Just when I imagined he'd done a face plant onto the bed and was sleeping again, he reappeared, with papers and test tubes. "I don't know if all the pages are here," he hedged. "But the soil—I didn't test it."

"Fine," I said stiffly, my eyes locking onto the precious test tubes. He pushed open his screen door, and I grabbed for them. "But we're not quite done here," I said, holding his door open. "I need you to write something for me. Something like: 'To who it may concern, I certify that these samples were taken at the farm on North Hill in July, and since I was stoned out of my mind I didn't test them.' " I stared him down. "And sign it."

He winced, either because of my demand or because the daylight pained his bloodshot eyes.

I held out the back page of my organic-certification application and a pen. After a beat, he took them. "Look, I'm sorry," he said. He pressed the page against his flimsy door and scribbled for a minute. Then he handed it over to me.

Grasping the page, I considered him for a minute. On top of every other way of being disheveled, he needed a haircut. He peered at me from behind a shaggy curtain of bangs.

On the one hand, it would be easy for me to add him to the arrest list that I dreamed of handing over to the police. He took six hundred of my dollars, for nothing. Forget about the drugs.

On the other hand, that wouldn't solve any of my problems.

"Take care of yourself," I said instead.

"Yeah," he said noncommittally.

"No, I mean it. Because you don't look like you're having so much fun here. Kate Barker says you're talented." I didn't know where all this empathy was coming from. I really needed to get off the sagging plastic stoop and back on the road.

"Thanks," he said. "I'll think about it."

I backed myself down onto terra firma. But just before his door closed, I had one more thought. "Hey—do you know Randy Biden at all? The developer?"

The door opened again. "Sure," Dunham said gruffly. "He plays cards with us sometimes. Usually wins all my money. Why?"

I felt another flash of anger. Of course he won at cards. That cheater. He won at everything. I brought my rage under control for long enough to ask one more question. "I just wondered if Randy Biden ever mentioned my land."

Dunham shrugged. "One time he asked me whether you're going organic. That's all. Probably because he knows I . . ." He came to a halt, embarrassed.

"Deal with that?" I volunteered.

"Yeah."

I sighed. That rat. "Thanks, Kevin." Thanks for nothing. I stumbled into my car and pointed it toward Massachusetts. With any luck, I could get to Organiquest in the next hour and a half. If I could prove, at the bare minimum, that last year's crop had been pure, then maybe—just maybe—I could put the whole sorry twenty-four hours behind me.

# Chapter 28

"What did they *say*?" Marta shrieked, when I finally walked through the office door. The poor woman must have been pacing our ten-by-ten office since I'd called her, three hours ago, from the car.

"I think it's going to be okay," I said, to her visible relief. "Organiquest is going to test the old samples, in order to certify the farm as organic—but only for last year's harvest. I had to tell them the whole tale I told you over the phone—the boxes of Miracle-Gro, the builder, the pothead. I must have sounded like a raving lunatic, but I think they believed me." I tossed my purse down on the desk and flopped into my chair.

"When will we know? We were supposed to call GPG this morning, with our answer."

I nodded slowly. My eyes felt sanded from lack of sleep and from driving for nine out of the last twenty-four hours. But at least I'd had sufficient time during the drive home to consider the situation. "I think we can call GPG anyway and proceed. The old samples will show that our soil was fine last year. I know they will."

Marta's round face broke into a broad grin. "So let's call them! I want to order my business cards."

I hesitated. "Marta?"

"What?"

"Does it bother you at all? The idea of selling out?"

Marta whirled herself all the way around in her swivel chair—the way Jasper might if he visited our office. "No," she said firmly. She stopped her pirouette with one hand on the desktop. "And I'll tell you why. I know that corporation won't want to do everything the same. But that's half the point, isn't it? Just think—you get to give up all the parts of the business you hate, like worrying about the money, and get back all those hours to focus on the things you really love. Like inventing new recipes. What's so bad about that?"

As always, Marta had a perfectly sane outlook. But all the same, I stared at the phone on my desk, feeling grim. It was hard to put my finger on it, but I didn't have any of the exuberance I'd expected to feel at the moment when Julia's Child finally made the big time. I told myself it was just fear. Or exhaustion.

Marta looked at me expectantly. I dug Smith's business card out of my purse and slapped it onto the desk. I jammed the phone between my ear and my shoulder and began to dial.

The call was answered by a perky receptionist. "GPG!"

"This is Julia Bailey for J. P. Smith." There was a quaver in my voice, but, across the small room, Marta grinned from ear to ear. Hopefully she had enough excitement for the two of us.

"There she is!" Smith said heartily. "The queen of muffets."

"Indeed," I answered. "And Marta is also on the line. We are calling to let you know that we look forward to working with you."

"Terrific!" he said. "Your lawyer and ours have already hammered out new language for several clauses, so we're sending over a fresh set of papers. You can sign them and messenger them back over later this afternoon."

"Great," I said, swallowing hard.

"Listen—our timing couldn't be better. I need you to call our corporate travel department right away, because on Monday all the food brands for the Americas are having an offsite in Monterey. And I very much want to have you there, Julia."

"Monday, in Monterey," I repeated.

"Right!" Smith continued. "And while you've got travel on the line, I think you should also accompany Ralph DaSilva to D.C. on Friday to meet our lobbyist. He's doing a lot of work down there to try to hammer out the next version of the FDA's organic standards."

"Your lobbyist? To the FDA?" I hesitated. "That could be an interesting meeting, depending on whether he's trying to strengthen the organic rules or weaken them."

"Exactly," Smith said. "Good stuff."

I felt a ringing in my ears. What was I doing? The corporate wonks were closing in on me, and there was nowhere to hide. And Friday night was supposed to be Jasper's seasonal concert at school. The kindergartners were preparing to sing about Frosty the Nondenominational Snow Man. My son had been thumpety-thumping all around our apartment for weeks.

I looked over at Marta. She was scribbling down my travel plans, as if there was going to be a test later. She took no notice of me or of the panic attack I was starting to have.

"Look, uh, Mr. Smith," I said, overwhelmed. "There's just one more thing I wanted to talk over with you before we sign."

I was still watching Marta, and now she stopped writing and met my gaze, her eyebrows arching questioningly.

"And what is that?" Smith asked, unworried.

"The price," I said as casually as possible. "Your offer was $285,000. I ran some numbers, and I figured out that it would cost you closer to $400,000 to start up a company like mine from scratch."

I didn't have the slightest idea whether this was true or not.

And I hadn't planned on saying it. Asking for a higher price might be savvy. Or it might be suicidal. I wasn't sure which. But my mouth had brought it up all the same.

All the levity was gone from Smith's voice when he answered. "First of all, the cost to us at these figures *is* four hundred thousand. Don't forget—we're taking on your salary, benefits, and retirement. Plus, we're extinguishing your debts. So congratulations on a math problem well done, because we're already paying the higher figure."

I gulped for air. I hadn't expected to outmaneuver the corporate raiders at GPG, but it would have been nice if it took him longer than ten seconds to mow down my argument.

"Last but not least," Smith went on, his voice cold, "the two hundred eighty-five is more than a hundred percent of your annual sales revenue, *including* the regional order from Whole Foods, which you don't even have yet. In comparison, last month we bought a fair-trade coffee company for barely half its annual sales."

Across from me, Marta's mouth was dangling open. I had managed to turn a celebratory conversation into an awkward one, and now I didn't even know how to get off the line.

"I'll . . ." I hesitated. "I just need to think about it for a couple of hours," I said quietly.

"You do that," Smith said, his tone backing off just a little bit. "We want to make Julia's Child part of the GPG family. But there are other fish in the sea. Every company we look at takes up our valuable time. So I want to hear from you this afternoon."

"Fine," I said. "I'm going to make some deliveries to our retailers in Brooklyn, and afterward I'll give you a call."

"Okay," Smith said. "But you should know that at three o'clock I'm meeting with another company that we met at the trade show. It might be wise to call me before then."

As I tried to process this threat, he hung up.

The second our telephone receivers were back in their cradles, Marta began hollering at me. "Hoolia! Have you lost your mind?"

I put my head in my hands. "I don't know. Maybe."

"How can you do that? That man just told us he's taking a meeting today with our competition. We've gotta call him back and tell him we're on board!

My heart thudded in my chest. When I'd given Marta 10 percent of the company, I'd never guessed that it might pit us against each other. I wanted Marta to get her $28,000 for Carlos' college fund. I really did. But GPG scared me, and I wasn't sure I'd given enough thought to what we were getting into. Their jet-setting travel schedule and their lobbyist were terrifying.

"Marta, I know you deserve to get the money, but . . ."

"But what? It's a perfectly good company, with really good health care. Why on earth wouldn't you say yes?"

There was no easy answer. I was scared, and I needed some air. So I jammed Smith's business card into my purse and pulled on my coat. "I'm going to Brooklyn," I managed to choke out.

"*No.*" It was surprisingly forceful. "*I'll* do it." Marta stood up.

"No, really," I said, practically running for the door.

"Julia! Come back here a minute."

"Marta, I just need some time."

# Chapter 29

Mr. Pastucci's sunken eyes watched my progress as I filled my little rolling cooler with muffets. "How is Brooklyn treating you?"

He had asked me that question many times, but today it brought tears to my eyes. Mr. Pastucci didn't know it yet, but I might not be back. At GPG, my product would be manufactured in New Jersey or Pennsylvania. I wouldn't be there to taste each batch as it came out of the oven. It wouldn't be me who tucked each package into a cooler for delivery.

I forced myself to remember that Julia's Child's Brooklyn roots were *supposed* to be temporary. I'd never meant to store the product in the rear of the Sons of Sicily Social Club forever. I'd meant it as a way station before moving on to bigger and brighter things. But now I found myself terrified to cut loose from it. And I had only a couple hours to figure out why.

"Yes, Mr. Pastucci. Brooklyn always treats me very well." I put four ice packs on top of the muffet packages and zipped up my rolling cooler. "Did Lugo tell you? He's coming by later with the truck. Whole Foods needs another shipment."

"That's my girl," Mr. Pastucci rasped. "She's making the big time."

The lump in my throat expanded.

Mr. Pastucci limped over to the back door and opened it a crack. He peered around the edge of the door in both directions, in his characteristic way. Then he opened the door wide.

I rolled the muffets out the door, then turned around to give him a wave.

He returned it arthritically and then shut the door.

Cold breezes buffeted me as I bumped along the alley toward the sidewalk. Winter would soon be here. My first stop was just a block down Court Street, at Luigi's Convenience Store. My little cooler just barely fit through the door of the place.

"*Bella!*" Luigi called out from behind the counter. "How are you today?"

"Excellent, Luigi. How's business?"

"Pretty good, *bella*. See for yourself."

I parked my wares in front of the tiny freezer case and peered inside. There wasn't a single muffet to be found in there, and the ice creams were encroaching on the shelf where they usually stood. "Can I do the honors?" I asked Luigi, my hand on the freezer-case handle.

"Be my guest," the old man said, patting the belly that protruded beneath his old white apron.

I restacked the ice creams, on their own turf. I didn't mind doing the stock boy's job. It only took a second, and it guaranteed that the muffets would be visible.

The set of bells dangling from the doorknob jingled as a young mother pushed her Froggaroo stroller into the tiny shop.

"*Bella!*" Luigi called out again. "How are you today?"

I'll bet he says that to all the girls.

"Terrific, Luigi," the mother said. She had a super-cheery tone that made me wonder what she poured on her breakfast cereal. "And you?"

"*Perfecto!*" He kissed his fingertips and threw his blessings into the air overhead.

There was really no place like Brooklyn.

Between me and my cooler, and the mother and her stroller, nearly the entire square footage of the shop was now occupied. The newcomer shimmied past the enormous wheels of her stroller to reach the frozen foods. But I was standing in her way.

"Hang on," I said. I put twenty boxes of muffets into the freezer and then wriggled out of the way. I could tidy up my display after she had finished.

"Muffets!" the mother said. "We love those. Don't we, Liza!"

My heart soared, though the toddler said nothing because she had fallen asleep, the pacifier dangling precariously from the corner of her mouth, like one of Lugo's cigars.

"That's so nice of you to say!" I told her, slimming myself down to an impossible width, like a city rat, to pass by. "I'm Julia of Julia's Child."

"No *way*," she shrieked cheerily. "I'm Pam!" We shook hands. "Did you happen to bring Apple and Cheddar today?"

"I sure did. They're right on top." We executed a cooler-stroller tango worthy of *Dancing with the Stars*, and I pulled a packing slip out of my pocket for Luigi.

"Say." I turned to the mother. "I'm thinking about a new flavor for springtime. What would you think of sweet peas, corn, and mozzarella as a combination?"

"Yum!" she enthused. "Our housekeeper is from Ecuador. She told me her grandmother cooked corn together with white cheese. I think she said it was made like a pancake."

"Interesting . . . Thank you!" I made a mental note to look up Ecuadoran corn recipes. I'd already wondered if ethnic combinations would be the next toddler-food trend. I'd been brainstorming about Indian flavors. What, with yoga being such a rage. But Ecuador . . .

Cheery Pam chose three boxes of muffets, after which we tangoed again so that she could get to the cash register and I could get back to the freezer case. I gave each flavor its own stack and was just squaring their corners when I heard the bell jingle at Pam's departure.

"Ciao, bella," Luigi called after her.

I rolled my cooler toward the door.

"You see that, *bella*? People like your stuff just fine. You don't need a heavy like Pastucci fronting for you."

I stopped. "Luigi, what do you mean?"

"*Bella*, I understand why you get protection from Pastucci, I really do. You pay him a little on the side to look out for you—"

"Luigi! I just rent freezer space."

He held up a hand as if to silence me. "I know. I know. He's a very convincing guy. But Brooklyn's changing, *bella*. The streets are safe. I don't stand behind bulletproof glass anymore. And I got nice people like"—he waved his hand out the door, in the direction where Pam had just gone—"*bella* buying baby food at my store."

"That's . . . great, Luigi. But what does that have to do with Mr. Pastucci?"

He shook his head. "Guys like Pastucci—they think it's still okay to push guys like me around. They think if I'm not with him, then I must be against him."

My mouth must have been hanging open. I'd always assumed it was just luck that had brought me a flood of Brooklyn orders right after I'd begun renting from Mr. Pastucci.

"I tell you, *bella*. He's not a nice man. I do what he says. I sell him beer at the prices he sets. I look the other way when his guy is running numbers out of my store. But when he finally kicks the bucket, there's gonna be a thousand people at his funeral, all happy he's pushing up daisies. You don't need him. You'd be successful anyway. I can see that about you."

"Luigi, are you saying that Mr. Pastucci pressured you to carry my product?"

"*Bella,* I love your product. I'd carry it anyway. That's all I'm saying."

"God . . ." I didn't know what to say. "I'm sorry, Luigi, for any trouble I may have caused. I didn't know."

He waved a beefy hand dismissively. "If I was you, I'd probably listen to him too. You take care of yourself, *bella.* I see you next week."

Stunned by this new complication, I opened the door and pushed my cooler out ahead of me. "I'll . . . see you around, Luigi."

I trudged toward the subway, horrified by this new revelation. If only I'd had my wits about me, I might have checked the time. It was almost three o'clock.

# Chapter 30

"Honey," Luke said softly, the one word holding all the empathy I'd called looking for. I stood outside our offices on Twenty-second Street, trying not to cry from stress. Pedestrians sped past me, taking little notice of the quaking woman outside the door to the Chelsea Sunshine Suites.

"Honey," he repeated. "Calm down. Everything is going to be okay."

"Is it? I've got to sign with GPG now, or I'll miss the chance to recoup my investment. And I'm working with a . . . mobster. That's what Marta had always called him, Pastucci the Mobster."

"Forget about him for a minute," Luke said. "The GPG offer—it isn't a decision *for life*. I don't think you realize that."

"It's three years." At the end of three years Jasper would be eight. And he wouldn't recognize me, because I'd be too busy racking up the frequent-flier miles.

"But, sweetie, it's not. If you sign with GPG, you'll get your debts repaid immediately. And in six months, you'll vest the first third of the sale price. So what if you just gave it six months? If you hate it, you can quit."

"But then I won't get paid . . ."

"So what? You'll lose the other two-thirds of the money. But it's a free country. That's your choice. One step at a time, okay? You don't have to plan your life today. Only the very next part."

I gulped, trying to believe him.

"Julia?"

"Yes?" My voice was a squeak.

"Remember the free-range chickens, Julia?"

"What chickens?"

"You told me about them yourself. The ones that live on the big farms."

I'd once burdened Luke with the myth of the free-range chicken. At the grocery store labels promise us "cage-free" broilers. They're drawn on green grass, by a red barn, under a yellow sun. But it's usually a terrible lie. In truth, they begin life sequestered in a crowded metal shed. Animals living nose to tail feathers with thousands of their relatives were highly susceptible to disease, so the birds aren't allowed outside until they reached five weeks of age.

Then a tiny little door is opened by the farm workers, giving the chickens access to a rectangular little prison yard outside their shed. But do those chickens rush outside to glory in the newfound sunshine? Sadly, no. Those poor scared birds, knowing only life indoors, are too afraid to go outside, even to scratch around under the big blue sky. Just two weeks later they are slaughtered, never having seen the sun.

"Luke, why are you bringing this up?"

"Don't be that chicken, Julia," Luke warned. "Go out in the yard!"

For the first time all day, I laughed. How had I ever landed this kind, funny, smart man? That was all the luck I really needed. All the rest was icing.

My phone gave a beep. I held it out to read the display. Four missed calls.

"Honey, I'd better go. Thanks so much for cheering me up."

"Baby, it's going to be fine. Will you have dinner with me tonight? Out, in a restaurant, like grown-ups?"

"We can do that?" It had been so long since we went out on a date.

"We can bribe Bonnie with . . . concert tickets. Or expensive cosmetics. You choose the place."

"Deal!" I shouted.

When I hung up with Luke, I felt buoyed. Perhaps I could finally look Marta in the eye and move forward.

As I reached for the door of our office building, it flew open. My arm was knocked backward. I lost my grip on both my purse and my phone. Everything fell to the sidewalk.

"Sorry!" Yona tumbled out of the doorway. "Shit. I finally have a new client, and now I'm so late to meet him." We both knelt down to gather up my things. Yona grabbed my fallen phone from the sidewalk and handed it to me. But the wind had picked up, and the other spilled contents of my messy purse began to blow around.

We both dove for scraps of paper that took flight. I captured a gum wrapper, but a yellow Post-it note escaped Yona's grasp. Whatever had been written on it—a shopping list or maybe a reminder that Jasper needed to bring a certain size jar to school for a project—was lost.

I spread my arms over the rest of the embarrassing rubble that was the contents of my life. "Go ahead, Yona. Don't worry. Go meet your client." As quickly as I could, I scooped the rest of the spilled goods back into my purse. Another gust of wind made off with a couple of scraps of paper. But mostly I'd reclaimed my scattered belongings.

"I'm so sorry," Yona gasped. But then she took my advice and ran for the subway. I watched her blue hair bounce along after her, and then I slung my bag back onto my shoulder and went upstairs.

"Do you *know* what time it is? It's three o'clock!" Marta said when I walked through the door. She stood beside her desk, holding a messenger envelope, which I guessed was the latest version of our deal documents.

My eyes darted to the clock. We both imagined that Melissa of Melissa's Munchers might be about to walk into Smith's office in midtown.

"I know it is." I tried to hold tight to Luke's assurances that I wasn't about to make a life-altering decision. Because it sure felt like one.

"Julia, there's something I need to tell you." Marta's lips formed a solemn line. She sank slowly onto her chair.

"What is it?"

Her voice was flat. "I think I might need GPG's health insurance."

Marta had asked about the insurance before. But now as I looked into her haggard face, something clicked—something I'd been too self-centered to pick up on until now. "God, Marta. What's wrong?"

"I have . . ." She swallowed. "I found a lump."

"Oh!" Just before I'd met Marta, her mother had died. From breast cancer. "But . . . it still could be nothing, right?"

She nodded almost imperceptibly. "I'm on a waiting list at the clinic for a mammogram. If they see something, I'll need a biopsy."

Blessed as I was with good health, I didn't know much about hospitals. But even I knew there shouldn't be a waiting list for an X-ray.

At that moment, my big decision got a whole lot simpler. If Marta had corporate health insurance, she could have a mammogram by the end of the day. And—God forbid—if she needed more care, she could take her pick of hospitals.

"Marta, I'm so sorry. For your troubles and also for my flaky behavior." I plucked my desk phone from its cradle. The dial tone waited for me. It was so easy, once you'd made a decision. Like rolling off a log.

"Lord, I didn't want it to be about this," Marta said. She grabbed a tissue out of the box on her desk and blew her nose.

I shook my head. "I'd already decided. I talked to Luke about it just ten minutes ago." I took a deep breath. "We're going to call GPG now, and everything will be fine."

Relief washed over Marta like a rain shower.

I looked around on my desk for Smith's business card. But it wasn't there. With a sick feeling, I set my phone back down and dumped my hastily repacked purse back out on my desk. I saw a lot of pennies, a lip balm without its cap, and one Playmobil man dressed for European law enforcement. But no business card.

"They called, you know. Right after you left. I gave them your cell phone number."

I set down my purse. "Really? I didn't get the call."

Marta was silent for a moment. I looked up to find her face red, her lips pressed together. She was trying so hard not to say it—of course I didn't get the call.

My heart pounding, I opened my finicky cell phone to look at the numbers of the missed calls, but the screen was oddly dimmed. I pressed the "menu" button, but nothing happened. I pressed it again. Then I pressed all the other buttons.

"It's . . . frozen. I can't tell who called." My phone had hit the sidewalk, and it must have broken upon impact.

"I called you twice," Marta said.

"That leaves two more." Frantic, I dug once again through the pile on my desk.

"What are you doing?"

"Looking for Smith's business card. I need his phone number." I sifted through old grocery store receipts, my ANKST attendee pass, pens, credit cards, a MetroCard.

But no white business card.

Marta stood there, her face changing from crimson back to pale. "You can't find it?"

"No, but . . ." I threw the purse down. "We'll just have to get the number some other way." I shook my computer mouse to bring the machine to life. Then I pulled up the GPG website, for contact information.

There was only an 800 number, which I dialed immediately. It brought me to the global switchboard. "GPG, how may I direct your call?"

"Smith!" I said. And then my heart sank. Because I knew what question the cheery operator was about to ask me.

"And what is the first name?"

"It's . . . uh . . . J. P." If only J.P. Smith could have used his real name. I glanced at the clock and was not surprised to see the big hand had inched passed the twelve. It was officially after three.

"There is no J. P. listed," the operator said.

"John?" I guessed. "James? Mr. Smith is in the New York office, if that helps." I was flailing.

"There are . . . four John Smiths and three James Smiths in the New York office," the operator replied. "If you have the department . . ."

Get me the corporate raider department. Stat! "Um, Food Brands?" I guessed. "Or acquisitions?" How long would it be before the operator ditched me?

Across the room, Marta was hammering on her computer keyboard. "Got it!"

"Really?"

"Last month's phone bill."

I hung up on the operator. "Go!"

"Two-one-two," Marta said, with the calm presence of a radio announcer. "Four-nine-six—"

Then our phone began to ring. Marta snatched it. "Julia's Child, this is Marta." Her eyes grew wide. "One moment please, Mr. Smith."

I exhaled with relief. Marta put the call on hold, with a piercing stare in my direction that clearly said no more funny business, Hoolia.

I picked up the line and nodded at Marta. She might as well listen in. "This is Julia," I said as coolly as possible.

"There you are. Look, I don't want to walk into this other meeting without talking to you one more time, okay? I thought the two messages we left you would clear up our feelings on the situation."

I opened my mouth to apologize, but Smith's chuckle cut me off.

"I must say, Julia. I'm surprised. I was sure that after I asked Ralph DaSilva to personally beg you to help him change GPG for the better, you would have responded. But then, after I left you that counteroffer and you *still* didn't call! Let's just say that you're one cool customer. I'd rather have you on my team than play against you. You know what I'm saying?"

Marta's eyes were as round as saucers.

"Hmm." I choked. My mind whirled with possible ways to get off this call until I could figure out what message he'd left on my ailing phone. But short of faking an office fire, I couldn't think of a way to extract myself from the uncomfortable moment.

"Look," Smith said. "It would take Smythe and me some time to try to figure out what other company would fill the same spot at GPG as Julia's Child. And time is money. So let's not fool around. If you'll sign today, I can get the board to authorize a purchase price of $350,000. But really, that's the best we could hope for."

"Um, *errrrf*. . . ." I was having trouble speaking.

"Are you okay?" Smith asked.

I took a deep breath and tried to recover. "Yes. That helps, J. P.

That really does. I, uh, I think three fifty is a number I can live with. But there's one more thing I need to ask you. And I should have asked this earlier."

"Shoot."

"How much travel do you see for us, going forward? How many nights per month away from home?" I tried not to look at Marta, who must be apoplectic by now. But it would matter—to both of us—and I should have realized when Smith called me on Thanksgiving Day that GPG looked at the workweek a little differently than I did.

"I dunno? Six?" Smith began to sound a little wary.

"I think a number like two is more realistic for me," I said.

Silence. "We could meet in the middle, Julia. Four?"

Everything is negotiable. Everything. I was finally catching on. "Let's put down three, J. P. And I'll fly to the meeting in Monterey, but I can't be in D.C. on Friday. But I'll get you those papers before cocktail hour. Signed."

He only hesitated for a moment. "Done. I look forward to signing them too."

After we hung up, I put my head in my hands for a minute, to compose myself. When I looked up, Marta was gone.

I rose from my chair, my legs shaking as if I'd just run a marathon. I peered out our office door, but she was nowhere. I wanted to hug her and tell her everything would be all right. It had been a rough day, for both of us. No, not just a rough day. The last couple of months had really hurt. I just hoped she could find a way to forgive me.

I had the worst kind of adrenaline rush. The big moment was over, but I was jumpy with a bad case of fight-or-flight. I sat down in my desk chair and forced myself to think about dinner reservations. Where should Luke and I dine? Should I pick a celebratory setting—or just somewhere quiet enough for me to tell him every sorry detail of the last twenty-four hours?

I was scanning *Zagat* restaurant reviews when Marta walked back into the office fifteen minutes later. She had composed herself all the way up to a shy little smile that played across her lips. She held a gift bag in one hand. Tissue paper was sticking out from the top.

I held up one hand for a high five, and Marta came over and slapped it. I grabbed her and gave her a squeeze. "I'm so sorry," I said again.

But Marta didn't want my pity. She pretended not to hear me. "Three fifty," she said instead. "I can hardly believe it."

"Me either! Actually, I don't know what to think. Maybe the higher price really did push them to the limit. Or maybe they're jumping around their office right now, laughing about how cheap they just bought our company."

Marta dragged her chair around to the little space between our two desks. "I don't even care," she told me. "I'm just so glad it's over."

"Me too. And again—I'm sorry. I'm so sorry I freaked out at the end."

She held up a hand. "Don't . . . It's okay. Here. I got you something." She put the gift bag on my desk.

"Marta! You shouldn't have." I reached into the bag and pulled out something small, wrapped in tissue. When I unwrapped it, I thought the same thing again. She shouldn't have. Because it was a BlackBerry—a beautiful pink one. And I was still wary about coltan and the cell phone industry.

"It's *refurbished,*" Marta said before I could argue. "This is a *recycled* phone. Instead of becoming landfill, you will give it a new life. No new . . . stuff was used to make it."

"Really? You can do that?" I'd never heard of a refurbished phone. But of course, I'd never shopped for a phone, so how would I?

"Yes!" she said proudly. "Some trendsetter gave up this Black-

Berry Pearl—last year's model—to get the one all the kiddies want now. The brand-new . . . Squeal or Burp or something. And here." She handed me a small padded envelope. "You send your old phone in here, and they'll recycle the parts, okay? This is not a travesty."

I picked up my poor old frozen phone, cradling it in my palm. "Marta," I said. "I don't know if I can give this one up."

"Julia—*why?*" Her exasperation was complete.

I grinned. "This phone is lucky, Marta! It just made us $65,000!"

Then we laughed so hard that tears rolled down our faces.

"You really had me going there," she said, wiping her eyes carefully with a tissue, avoiding her mascara.

I held the old phone up to the bare office wall. "We'll frame it, I think. If we're going corporate, we're going to need decor."

*The Post* (Early Edition), Filed Friday, December 22
By Christine Flannigan

**Queens Mom Trades in Food Stamps for Stock Certificates**

Area single mother Marta Rodríguez used to do her grocery shopping while her son Carlos was at school. "I didn't want him to feel bad like I did. Handing over the food stamps in the checkout aisle was never easy for me."

Always handy in the kitchen, Rodríguez jumped at the chance to attend federally financed job training at La Cucina in Brooklyn. "I thought that just maybe the certificate would help me get a job with decent hours, so I could drop my son at school and pick him up again."

Something even more magical happened to Rodríguez. Working after class in the Cucina kitchen, she met Julia Bailey of Julia's Child. The company was a tiny start-up, but Bailey hired Rodríguez full time. "Starting a business is rough," Rodríguez said. "We worked in the office during the daytime and cooked the food at Cucina by night." Neighbors pitched in to watch Carlos in the evenings, when Rodríguez was needed in the kitchen. "But it's so exciting, starting a business! And it felt so good to be part of something big," says Rodríguez. Working hard, she worked her way up to an ownership stake. "I cried when Julia told me about my own share," Rodríguez notes. "And we weren't even chopping onions."

Fortune smiled on the women entrepreneurs. They recently sold the company to food giant GPG for an undisclosed sum. Both women are staying on to manage the brand for the conglomerate.

"My life is still frantic," says Rodríguez. "The big corporations have a lot more meetings. It's different. We used to just shout everything across the room to each other. Now sometimes Julia and I call each other from twenty feet away. But they do so much for us there. I don't have to shop at Staples for all our office supplies anymore. I have health insurance. And I can see the Empire State Building from my desk."

Now that the company has corporate backing, Rodríguez is happy to report that new recipe development—a task she and Bailey both love—is back on the docket. Rodríguez shares a wonderful whole grain Julia's Child recipe with us below:

## Peas on Earth Bulgur Wheat Risotto

*"Bulgur wheat is a whole grain, so it's healthier than white rice," Rodríguez reports. "There's a lot more protein and fiber. It also cooks up faster than a traditional risotto, and you don't have to stir constantly. So you keep more of the vitamins!"*

### *Ingredients*

**1 medium onion, chopped**
**2 tablespoons olive oil**
**1 cup coarse (No. 3) bulgur**
**2 cups chicken broth**
**1½ cups water**
**¼ pound sliced bacon, chopped**
**2 cups frozen peas**
**⅓ cup freshly grated Parmesan**
**salt and pepper to taste**

### *Instructions*

In a 2-quart heavy saucepan cook onion in oil over moderate heat, stirring, until softened.

Add bulgur, broth, and water and bring to a boil. Reduce heat and simmer, covered, until bulgur is tender and creamy like risotto (about 20 minutes). Stir occasionally.

While bulgur is simmering, cook bacon in a skillet over moderate heat, stirring, until crisp, then drain on paper towels.

Stir peas into bulgur, then stir in Parmesan, half of the bacon, and salt and pepper to taste.

Serve sprinkled with the remaining bacon.

# Three Months Later

# Chapter 31

The park bench was cool to the touch, but the sun warmed my face. It was one of those early spring days that promised New York wouldn't forever remain a howling wind tunnel. I parked myself in front of the sandbox.

It was early in the playground season, so I hadn't thought to bring along our unruly collection of sand toys. Now Wylie and another little boy were having a cold war standoff, both vying for the same bit of wood. Wylie had found it buried in the sand, this pointed shivlike stick that was apparently essential for digging.

In order to scoop sand from the hole he'd made, Wylie put down the coveted stick for just a split second. But that was all it took. The other toddler made his move.

"Miiiiiine!" screamed Wylie, diving after it.

The other boy, blond ringlets hanging into his eyes, dropped it immediately and crumpled onto the sand, sobbing. He was obviously a first child. First children are wimps. Second children know how to go for the throat.

More than once I had wished for a T-shirt I could wear to the park that read, "My *other* child is sweet and well mannered."

But there were no recriminations forthcoming from the mother of the sobbing towhead. She was arguing loudly on her cell phone.

"If the track light is stainless steel," she protested, "why on earth would you order a white track? That won't match." She scooped her sobbing child onto her lap, flashing Wylie and me a generic scowl. "And those pendant lights, my God! The Venetian glass has been done to death. Get them off the elevations."

My irritation began to grow. Who was this stranger forcing me to listen to her ceiling decor woes on a fine spring day?

The little boy sobbed into his mother's lap. She patted him absently on the head, continuing her tirade. "And I don't want to hear the words 'restocking fee' from you again. How do I know if I'll like them until they're actually hanging in the room?"

My blood pressure surged in sympathy with the person on the other end of the call. The playground always brought out my inner sociopath. We came here because Wylie liked it. But I preferred the open spaces of Central Park, with fewer people and less drama.

But, as they say, it takes a village. So I scanned the concrete around my bench, my gaze landing on another stick. Perhaps it would be just as useful in the sandbox. I picked it up and offered it to the fair-haired toddler, who was watching me. "Here you go, honey. Try this one."

He slid off his mother's lap and came over for it, taking it carefully out of my hand, as if it might be some kind of trick. Then he retreated to the spot next to Wylie. The two of them dug side by side, occasionally flashing mistrustful glances at each other.

The other mom finally snapped her phone shut, the plastic clacking together with indignation. She regarded her child, and then her face filled with revulsion. "Eew! Georgie! Don't touch the stick! That's *dirty*." She leapt up, rummaged through the diaper bag on the back of her stroller, and reemerged with a portable box of baby wipes. She extracted one and attacked her child's pale fingers with it. The stick I'd given him went flying from his grasp, and Wylie snatched it up without even breaking the rhythm of his digging.

Georgie began to whimper, while my uncharitable thoughts multiplied. That's it, lady. Teach your child that the natural world is icky. Did this woman understand that her food *grew* in the dirt?

I checked my watch. It was going on eleven thirty. I'd taken the morning off from work to hang out with Wylie. We'd made four-grain pancakes together, and I'd even let him spoon batter onto the griddle. We'd had a blast. In spite of my major cleanup afterward, I could still detect a tinge of maple scent from somewhere on my person.

But now it was time for Bonnie to meet us; I was due at work. Now that Marta had recovered from her lumpectomy last month, I was expected to travel again. Today I'd roll my little suitcase toward the office, in preparation for a dinner tonight in Pittsburgh with a grocery chain executive. And that wasn't as bad as it sounded. I'd been managing to keep the travel below a reasonable limit. And I'd figured out how to steal back the time during the workweek by taking the odd morning or afternoon off. The change in routine was an unexpected pleasure.

At GPG, I wasn't a courageous entrepreneur anymore. But I was certainly less stressed out. I didn't wake up in the night worrying about money. And now—just three months after the acquisition went through—muffets were stocked in six hundred grocery stores. GPG's marketing prowess had proven as impressive as they'd promised. Next year we were aiming for a breathtaking six thousand stores.

Sure, there were new tensions. Sometimes I had to claw back some essential but expensive product feature from the bottom-line-driven culture. But things in corporate land weren't as bad as I'd feared. Though I wouldn't say it out loud, I was actually relieved not to make every single decision anymore.

It was getting late. "Wylie? If we get that sand off of you, I'll let you call daddy with my phone."

He looked up quickly. I think he'd forgotten I was even here. "Otay," he said. He staggered toward me like a drunk at the beach, grains of sand pouring from the shoelace holes on his sneakers. I would have to practically shake him upside down to get it all off.

I pulled him onto my lap and turned down the cuffs of his jeans. I slapped at them to get the sand out.

"Call Daddy now?"

"Just a second, honey." I strained to reach to the ends of his suddenly long legs, pulling off his sneakers and clapping them together. I'd forgotten how much sand the kids were capable of dragging into the apartment in nice weather. It was like living at the beach, but without the view.

"Okay," I said finally. I extracted my pink phone, pressed Luke's speed-dial code, and handed it to Wylie.

"Hi, Daddy! Sing the sheep song again?"

This week Wylie was on a "Baa, Baa, Black Sheep" bender. Luke must have complied with his request, because Wylie's face became serene as he listened. Eventually he said, "Mama? Yes her here. Bye." Wylie handed me the phone.

"That was nice of you," I said, taking it.

"Oh, him so nice," Luke imitated our toddler. "And it's not like anybody can hear me in here."

I knew just what he meant. Luke had taken over my old office at the Chelsea Sunshine Suites last month, right after he finally got a pink slip from the bank.

"Hey, I forgot to tell you. Yona's hair is purple now."

I could easily picture that. "Tell her I say hello."

"She said exactly the same thing."

"Sweetie, I called just to remind you that I'm in Pittsburgh overnight."

"How glamorous."

"Make fun if you want to, but if anyone's diaper leaks in the night, it's all yours."

"We'll miss you, babe. Take care of yourself."

"I promise."

"Take a moment to look for the closest exit, bearing in mind that the nearest one may be behind you."

"Love you too, sweetie. Bye."

My mother always told me that 99 percent of the things I worried about wouldn't happen. She should have told me that sometimes even when they do happen it isn't the end of the world. Luke's pink slip had been a huge worry, but the reality wasn't so bad.

"I've got skills," Luke had said the evening after it had happened. We were lying, naked, in our bed. We had needed to prove that life was not just about the office.

"I *know* you have skills," I'd whispered teasingly.

He rolled his eyes at me. "Baby, I've also got dweeb skills. I can organize peer-to-peer database access like nobody's business."

Apparently the investment bank—Luke's former employer—thought so too. They quickly assigned him a pile of consulting work. There was no security in it, but the pay was pretty good. We didn't know when or if he'd decide to look for a regular job.

The happy beneficiaries of the change were Wylie and Jasper. They were a little confused to occasionally find Daddy lounging around the apartment, but they didn't seem worried, probably because their mommy wasn't freakishly uptight anymore.

I'd learned so much over the past year and a half that I blushed to think back on my entrepreneurial naïveté. But instead of beating myself up over it, I'd learned to appreciate just how well things had actually gone.

For example, Luke had calculated in his spare time that I—Julia Bailey—had actually outperformed Warren Buffett last year. While the rest of the nation was losing buckets of money in a tanking stock market, I withdrew ours to start Julia's Child. Sure, I'd stayed awake nights worrying about my big "investment." But then GPG repaid the money I borrowed from our retirement with the tiniest bit of interest. So even though our money earned nothing last year, most other 401(k)'s plunged in value. Go figure.

Then there were my real estate dealings. There's a saying that goes, "Even a blind squirrel finds a nut once in a while." After the fertilizer debacle, my farmland could not be certified as organic for three years. So I talked to a realtor about selling it. Because the hilltop views were so terrific, she was able to find a buyer who would put only one house on the twenty acres. I sold it—deeded as non-subdividable—to a solar panel factory owner from Connecticut.

Our new neighbor showed us the blueprints. He'd specced out the greenest house I could ever imagine—bamboo floors, photovoltaic electricity, off the grid, with solar hot water. It would be a showplace of politically correct building, down to the zero-VOC interior wall paint.

We broke even on the transaction—without completely ruining the neighborhood.

Kate still isn't speaking to me, but I'm sure she'll get over it eventually. And I still have high hopes for her farming future. She switched her ambitions from vegetable farming to goats' milk cheese. The goats graze on her remaining farmland and on our land too. Her mother told me that she's entering a cheese-making contest in the fall. Maybe some day I can use it in muffets. Chèvre goes well with many flavors.

The only fly in the ointment was the truck that showed up to work on the new house across the road. I couldn't believe what I read on the freshly painted van: "Biden Green Builders." That slick developer had rebranded himself as an eco-home specialist. And business was booming. The man was like a cockroach—he wouldn't die. Our hilltop would line his pockets, and there was nothing I could do about it. Still, I did manage to stop the Lincoln Lodge Condos. That was something.

I realized too late that, as I sat daydreaming about the past year's challenges, Wylie had climbed back into the sandbox. Bonnie was now twenty minutes late, and I would have to go through the entire sand removal routine again and then drag Wylie home against his will.

I stood up to look hopefully, past the iron playground gates, toward the street. And there was Bonnie, walking toward us, unhurried.

I sat down on the bench again to enjoy my last two minutes of sunshine. Feeling very Zen, at least for me, I tried to imagine a scenario that explained Bonnie's tardiness. Perhaps the little old lady who lived just off the lobby had staggered out, choking on a chicken bone, just at the moment Bonnie had left the elevator to meet us. Bonnie would have had to administer the hug of life and then maybe wait for the ambulance to arrive.

I was still grinning at this improbable idea when she strolled up to my bench and took a seat next to me. "Sorry," she sighed. "The lift was out of service. I waited for *hours*."

My first impulse was to ask why a fit young thing like her couldn't run down a few flights of stairs. But I bit it back. "Is it broken again?" I asked charitably.

"No, it was movers," she explained. "They used the key to hold the cab on the first floor while unloading."

"Someone's moving out? Do you know who it is?" Bonnie was more plugged into the building gossip than I ever hoped to be.

"You didn't know?" She eyed me sideways. "People have been talking about it for weeks."

"Who, Bonnie?"

"Why, apartment 510, that's who!"

It took me a second to think through the building's layout.

Then it hit me. That was Emily's apartment! "Really?" I gasped. "I didn't know it was for sale." I had a moment of typical New Yorker angst. Had I missed an opportunity? Did that apartment get better light than ours?"

"Oh, it wasn't for sale," Bonnie said knowingly.

"What do you mean?"

"Emily isn't moving out. Her husband is."

"Oh!" I tried to take that in.

"Apparently, we're not the only ones who thought she was a shrew."

For a second I almost smiled. But then I thought of her two children—two *little* children.

A cloud passed over my carefree day. "My God, what a shame." I looked at Wylie, digging busily in the sandbox, and tried to imagine what on earth my toddler would think if Daddy moved away.

"I don't know, Julia," Bonnie paused. "The thing is—she's happier now."

"Emily? Really?"

"Yep." A few Americanisms had crept into Bonnie's speech lately. "She even offered me a piece of coffee cake."

"Well, that's nice."

"In the playroom."

I sat up straight on the park bench. "You're kidding! Did you slap her? Because I might have."

Bonnie shook her head. "She's nicer now. Seriously. She smiles at me."

"Wow." I was suddenly reminded of a bit of advice I'd just read in one of the parenting magazines that littered my office. When encountering another parent who is behaving badly, you are supposed to stop and remind yourself that that person might be experiencing real hardship—like a medical trauma or job loss. Or a bad marriage.

I tapped my toe on the sunny pavement. I'd gotten better at living in the moment, but perhaps I still had a ways to go toward appreciating my good fortune. Surely it was easier to be a good neighbor when your husband still loved you and your business had been yanked from the jaws of death.

I glanced toward the grumpy mom on the other side of the sandbox, still frowning into her phone. I squinted at her hairdo. Maybe that thinness on top was due to a recent round of chemotherapy and not too many trips to an overzealous colorist at the salon.

"So I guess you probably haven't heard Emily's other news, then."

I whirled around toward Bonnie. "There's more?"

"There is." Bonnie clearly enjoyed having the upper hand in building gossip. "She got a job at the Tudor school."

"A job? What kind of job?"

"Teaching high school chemistry and physics. Also, Bryan can go to kindergarten there next year—at half fees."

My mouth dropped open in surprise. "Tudor is the best school in the city." Little Bryan could fill out his Harvard application within its ivy-coated brick walls.

A recently divorced Manhattan mom would sleep pretty soundly at night given that arrangement.

My brain, enfeebled by the sunshine and pancake syrup, scrambled to adjust to the new information. My neighbor's news swam in a sea of fruit punch, chemistry, and flash cards—and also courage.

I leaned back against the wooden bench and stared at the blue sky. How had I missed, in Emily's voice, the evidence of all the drama playing out right down the hall? The picture looked so much different now. Here sat Bonnie and I, two able-bodied adults looking after one two-year-old. But somewhere nearby Emily bravely soldiered through her day with the knowledge that her husband wasn't coming home. Tonight or ever again.

At that moment, something became crystal clear. When Emily watched me blithely pass the childcare baton over to Bonnie, she probably heard exactly the same little "pop" sound that I heard whenever I saw another mother break the seal on a fruit punch drink box. The truth is that every one of us takes shortcuts. It is the only way to survive. I might have a little more fun in my life if I could just learn to accept it. My eyes fell on Wylie's progress in the sandbox. Somewhere between the ages of two and thirty-five, I'd forgotten how to just live in the moment.

Slowly, I got up off the bench. "Bonnie, I've got to run. You know I'm—"

"Away tonight. I remember."

"Thank you." I turned to look her in the eye. But she was scrolling through text messages on her phone, without a care in the world. "I'll see you tomorrow, Bonnie." I turned toward the sandbox but then turned back. "Wylie is coated with sand," I warned her.

"Okay, Julia."

I put the odds at about fifty-fifty that Bonnie would actually remember this vital bit of information before those little sneakers made it onto my rug. I knelt on the edge of the sandbox. "Bye, sweetie. Mommy has to . . ." I stopped. "I have to go to work now. Can I have a kiss?"

Wylie looked up and frowned, measuring the distance between his digging and the edge of the sandbox. Then, deciding that the risk of theft was just too great, he gathered up the two sticks and a plastic cup he'd found somewhere, pressed them safely to his belly, and wiggled over to the edge where I waited. "Bye, Mama."

In spite of my rewarding job, where I cheerfully waged war against chicken fingers and refined sugar, this part never got